SKULL DUGGERY

AARON ELKINS

BERKLEY PRIME CRIME, NEW YORK

THE BERKLEY PUBLISHING GROUP
Published by the Penguin Group
Penguin Group (USA) Inc.
375 Hudson Street, New York, New York 10014, USA
Penguin Group (Canada), 90 Eglinton Avenue East, Suite 700, Toronto, Ontario M4P 2Y3, Canada
(a division of Pearson Penguin Canada Inc.)
Penguin Books Ltd., 80 Strand, London WC2R 0RL, England
Penguin Group Ireland, 25 St. Stephen's Green, Dublin 2, Ireland (a division of Penguin Books Ltd.)
Penguin Group (Australia), 250 Camberwell Road, Camberwell, Victoria 3124, Australia
(a division of Pearson Australia Group Pty. Ltd.)
Penguin Books India Pvt. Ltd., 11 Community Centre, Panchsheel Park, New Delhi—110 017, India
Penguin Group (NZ), 67 Apollo Drive, Rosedale, North Shore 0632, New Zealand
(a division of Pearson New Zealand Ltd.)
Penguin Books (South Africa) (Pty.) Ltd., 24 Sturdee Avenue, Rosebank, Johannesburg 2196,
South Africa

Penguin Books Ltd., Registered Offices: 80 Strand, London WC2R 0RL, England

This is a work of fiction. Names, characters, places, and incidents either are the product of the author's imagination or are used fictitiously, and any resemblance to actual persons, living or dead, business establishments, events, or locales is entirely coincidental. The publisher does not have any control over and does not assume any responsibility for author or third-party websites or their content.

SKULL DUGGERY

A Berkley Prime Crime Book / published by arrangement with the author

PRINTING HISTORY
Berkley Prime Crime hardcover edition / September 2009
Berkley Prime Crime mass-market edition / August 2010

ISBN: 978-0-425-23602-4

BERKLEY® PRIME CRIME
Berkley Prime Crime Books are published by The Berkley Publishing Group,
a division of Penguin Group (USA) Inc.,
375 Hudson Street, New York, New York 10014.
BERKLEY® PRIME CRIME and the PRIME CRIME logo are trademarks of Penguin Group (USA) Inc.

PRINTED IN THE UNITED STATES OF AMERICA

10 9 8 7 6 5 4 3 2 1

Acknowledgments

My thanks to Professor Allison Galloway of the University of California-Santa Cruz, who was generous with her time and expertise on mummification and mummies.

Some of Gideon Oliver's forensic deductions couldn't have been made without two unusual and provocative scientific papers. Providing the titles of the papers would give away more information about *Skull Duggery* than I'm willing to reveal, but I would certainly like to thank the authors and to give the citations for those curious enough to pursue the matter:

Journal of Forensic Sciences, vol. 52, no. 6, November 2007. Paper by Alexandra M. Croft and Roxana Ferlini. Ms. Croft was also helpful with additional information and kindly reviewed a section of the manuscript.

Forensic Science, Medicine, and Pathology, September 2007. Paper by Paranirubasingam Paranitharan, Jacqueline L. Parai, and Michael S. Pollanen.

ONE

NOT for nothing had Flaviano Sandoval been the village police chief for almost six months now. For one thing, he had learned to recognize trouble when he saw it. And this man sitting across the desk from him, oh, he was trouble, all right. Definitely not a local—Sandoval knew everybody who lived in Teotitlán (*everybody* knew everybody who lived in Teotitlán)—and for sure not a *turista* come to shop for weavings or to stay at the Hacienda Encantada up the hill. So what else could he be? Only trouble.

And trouble was something Flaviano Sandoval was averse to, by disposition and by constitution. If ever there was a man *not* cut out to be a police chief, it was Flaviano Sandoval. Small, soft-bodied, and sharp-featured (some might say rodent-faced), he had little ability and no great desire to project a command presence. He was fretful, easily intimidated, and prone to nervous stomach upsets. It had never been his aim to be a police chief. It had never been his desire to be a police chief. His desire was to one day be mayor of Teotitlán. But traditions were traditions, and before one could be considered for that esteemed post, one had to prove one's civic merits in a long-established progression of service positions. For two years he had served as chairman of the school board, for a year before that, as the administrator of the municipal marketplace. In six more months, God willing, he would have finished this grueling, nerve-racking tenure as chief of police with mind and body whole, and would move on to become the executive officer of the village council. And one year after that—again, God willing—he would be elected as *alcalde*, from which the step to mayor was virtually assured.

But for now he was still the *jefe de policía*, and trouble was the last thing he wanted. The man had been spotted an hour earlier, at about five P.M., slogging up the steep, cobbled street toward the resort, and his looks had set off alarm bells: a jail bird's face, heavy-jawed and sleepy-eyed, with a drooping Emiliano Zapata mustache and a dirty, graying ponytail hanging down in back from under a tattered *campesino*'s hat, and with leathery, pockmarked skin as creased and pouched as an old valise that's sat out on top of the bus too many times. Blue-green tattoos— lizards? snakes?—twisted up the sides of his neck from the grimy collar of his denim jacket. Pompeo, the senior of Sandoval's two policemen, had stopped him to talk to him. When he found that the man had no identification, had a total of six pesos on him, and had a story that didn't add up, he'd brought him in to see the *jefe*.

That had spoiled the *jefe*'s day right there. Pompeo was a good sergeant. Unlike Sandoval, he'd been born to be a cop. He loved the work and he was big and fierce-looking enough to be intimidating in a way that Sandoval never could. (If truth be told, Sandoval was a little afraid of him himself.) Pompeo had been there for a decade, so he knew the ropes and he'd been the main reason that Sandoval had thought he could cope with the chief's position at all. If Pompeo took care of the street situations—the traffic run-ins, the occasional quarrelsome drunk—Sandoval, who had taken a month-long correspondence course in public administration, after all, could surely handle the administrative matters. Also, Sandoval had given himself a reasonable command of English, of great use to a local police chief on summer weekends, when the place was lousy with tourists.

The one fly in the ointment was that Pompeo sometimes—now, for instance—took his job too seriously. Why had he stopped the man in the first place? Had he been hurting anyone, threatening anyone? No, he was just walking peaceably up the hill, and what was the law against that? Probably he was heading up past the Hacienda Encantada and out of town entirely. The dirt road wound through the dry hills all the way to San Lucas Tepitipac. That was probably where he was going. If Pompeo had just let him continue on his way, he would not be a problem. Or at least he'd be somebody else's problem, which was just as good.

But here the man was, sitting right in front of him. Pompeo, as conscientious as ever, had made his official report of the detention, and unless the chief wanted to tear it up and erase it from the log, he was stuck with it. But this Sandoval would not do. Despite his many and varied self-acknowledged deficiencies, he was a man who was faithful to the regulations and to his responsibilities, as he understood them to be.

Besides, what if Pompeo found out?

So far the stranger had told Sandoval that his name was Manuel Garcia (a likely story; if there was a more common, less traceable name in Mexico, Sandoval would have liked to know what it was), that he was from the village of Santiago Matatlán, and that he was on his way to Oaxaca to look for work, but the second-class bus that he'd thought would take him to the city didn't go there after all, and had dropped him off in Teotitlán to catch a bus that did.

Pompeo was right. None of it added up. Sandoval didn't like the man's story, and he certainly didn't like the man. It wasn't that this Garcia was belligerent exactly, but he wasn't what you'd call cooperative either, and there was an indefinable air of sleepy menace about him. Sandoval was ill at ease being in the same room with him. Ask a question and Garcia would answer, but at his leisure, with a weary, downward curl on his lips, and sometimes even a sigh, as if he'd been through this a hundred times before, and his patience was being sorely tried, and would you mind getting on with it so he could go on his way, since you were just going through the motions, and there was nothing you could do to him. Surly, that's what he was. Contemptuous. He'd dealt with the police before, Sandoval had no doubt about that. Probably he'd been in prison—that face, those tattoos—maybe even in the United States.

"Ever been north of the border?" Sandoval asked.

"No." That was the way most of his answers had been. One or two words, or three at most.

"Ever been in prison?"

"No, not me." He yawned and gestured with his chin at the coffeepot on the burner. "How about a cup of that coffee, Chief?"

"Help yourself," said Sandoval. "The cups are on the sink." He watched Garcia get up to pour himself a cupful. He wasn't a particularly big man, but he was bull-necked and thick-chested, and he carried his arms a little away from himself in that showy way that serious weight lifters have. More evidence of US jail time, Sandoval thought.

That was one of the truly crazy things about the *Yanqui* prisons: weight lifting rooms. Why in the world would you want to give your bad guys bigger muscles?

Garcia sat down with his coffee, which had been on the burner for eight hours now. (Coffee-making was the responsibility of the junior officer, Pepe, who could not be dissuaded from the notion, taught to him by his mother, that the longer coffee sat, the more tasty and restorative the brew. It had been all Sandoval could do to get him not to boil it for five minutes.) Garcia took a sip of the tarry stuff and made a face, but had another swallow anyway. Two were enough, however, even for a tough guy like him. He set the cup on the desk and leaned back with another sigh, an audible, resigned sigh, to see what Sandoval's next pointless question would be. He scratched listlessly at his chin. It had been four or five days since he'd shaved, and stiff, silvery bristles glistened on his jaw.

It was clear that the man thought he wasn't dealing with a real cop here. Well, that was true enough. Sandoval knew only too well that he wasn't a real cop. All the same, he wasn't without resources. The village had sent him to Mexico City for a week-long training program. And as part of that program, he had undergone a full day's instruction, complete with role playing, on techniques of interrogation. He had learned a few things there. He had learned that one doesn't lay all one's cards on the table up front, oh no. One baits a trap and then gently, subtly, helps the interrogee fall into it.

He steepled his fingers at his chin and smiled in a friendly, relaxed manner, although his heart was thumping away. "I understand," he said casually, "that the bus driver let you off here and told you you could catch a bus to Oaxaca in the morning? Is that correct?"

"That's right."

"Well, that's very interesting. It's true there is a bus

from here to Oaxaca, but if I remember correctly, the bus from Santiago Matatlán also continues right up 190 to Oaxaca. Why then would he let you off here?"

"I'm just telling you what he told me. Maybe he wanted me off the bus. I don't think he liked me."

That part certainly held water, Sandoval thought. So much for that trap, but he had more than that to work with. "I see. But you know, now that I think of it, unless I'm mistaken, it no longer makes a stop in Teotitlán at all. So how—"

"I didn't say it stopped *in* Teotitlán," Garcia said without even a momentary pause. "He dropped me off at the junction, where the road heads into the village. I walked in from there." Sandoval had to hand it to him. Very cool, very sure of himself.

"I see," he said yet again, scowling. "To get the morning bus to Oaxaca, the one that leaves from the market square."

"That's right, unless there's another bus stop."

"No, it's the only one. So then exactly what were you doing on the road up to the Hacienda Encantada?"

"I don't know nothing about no Hacienda Encantada. I was going up in the hills, find someplace to sleep where no one would bother me."

Sandoval was thoroughly discomposed by now. He was no good at this sort of thing; why did he even try it? He didn't believe a word of Garcia's story, but he didn't see what he could do about it. The man was too experienced for him; he knew a fraud when he saw one. One thing Sandoval did know: the sooner Garcia was out of Teotitlán the better, but nothing could be done about that until morning. All he could do for now was to see that he made no trouble tonight.

"Well, my friend," he said, "we'll give you a nice place to sleep. And I don't think anyone will bother you."

"You're putting me in jail?"

"Just for the night," Sandoval said, first darting a glance into the outer office to make sure Pompeo was there, in case Garcia was going to make things difficult. But Garcia merely shrugged.

"Do I get a meal out of it?"

"Unless you have an objection to goat meat tacos."

Another shrug. "Okay. And what happens in the morning?"

"We'll see in the morning."

He signaled through the doorway to Pompeo, who marched Garcia off to the women's cell. (There were two cells in the municipal building, one for men and one for women, but the men's was currently occupied by the Herrera brothers, who were sleeping off too many glasses of mezcal at their sister's wedding, which left only the women's cell.) Garcia went without a word, contracting the burly muscles of his shoulders; a bodybuilder showing his stuff.

Sandoval hoped with all his heart that *nothing* would happen in the morning, that he'd simply send Garcia on his way and be done with it, but there were of course obligations that went with his job. For all he knew, Garcia was a dangerous fugitive. If it came about later that Sandoval had done no checking on him, it might well bring the unwelcome attentions of the attorney general's office and the state police, the *policía ministerial*. Talk about trouble.

He downloaded onto his computer the photo that Pepe had taken of Garcia as a matter of routine. This he attached to an e-mail query to the *policía municipal* of Santiago Matatlán, asking what they could tell him about the man. He did it with a little smile of satisfaction. Garcia would no doubt have been surprised to learn that even here, in this out-of-the-way little village, the police had certain high-tech methods at their disposal. Santiago Matatlán, about twenty kilometers to the south, was a mezcal-producing village even smaller than Teotitlán; perhaps six hundred souls. The police would know everything that went on there. And they had a computer too.

He sighed and raised his eyes to the ceiling. "Just let it not require that I have any dealings with the state police," he prayed silently. Nothing good ever came of dealing with the *policía ministerial*, as he had learned through hard experience.

When he'd first become chief, there were only a few village ancients who had any recollection of the last time someone had been murdered in Teotitlán, and they didn't remember it themselves, recalling only their parents talking about it when they'd been children: a woman had bashed her straying husband's head in with a stone *mano*. That had happened more than fifty years ago, before Teotitlán even had a police chief. None of Sandoval's predecessors had ever been confronted with a homicide.

And what had happened? With only two measly weeks on the job under his belt, he had been confronted with one. It had been a terrible experience, the worst experience he'd ever had. No doubt it had taken years off his life, and it was a marvel that he hadn't developed ulcers.

A group of Canadians who had been staying in a bed-and-breakfast in Teotitlán had been hiking in the dry hills near the village. One of them, in falling down the shaft of a long-abandoned silver mine, had discovered the body—the skeleton, really—of a young girl. He had reported it to Sandoval, who had brought in old Dr. Bustamente, the district's *médico legista* (or *médico forense*, as he had taken to calling himself since *CSI* had started appearing on Mexican television), who had declared that she'd been murdered: a savage series of blows to the head, a finding that was soon confirmed by the state *médico legista* in Oaxaca.

So in had come the swaggering *policía ministerial*, thuggish and intimidating, to take charge, issuing commands, making threats and accusations, frightening old men and women, interrogating respectable people with terrible sexual questions, things people in Teotitlán never even thought of before. The worst of it was that for a whole month the *policía ministerial* worked on it, terrorizing the whole village, and in the end they never did solve it. And so the poor child's bones now lay in a box in some grisly police storeroom somewhere in Oaxaca, instead of in a Christian grave in the Teotitlán cemetery, where Sandoval and the elders wanted to inter it.

And so the mere thought of the *possibility* of having to deal once more with those arrogant, overbearing bullies in their sinister black uniforms straight out of some old Gestapo movie (and very fitting that was) had his stomach churning now.

But, happily, it appeared that this was not to be. The reply from the police chief of Santiago Matatlán was waiting for him when he came in the next morning:

> This man, Manuel Garcia, is not a resident of Santiago Matatlán. He appeared here two days ago, unable to give a satisfactory reason for his arrival. He has committed no crime of which I am aware, but his appearance and manner are not wholesome. I sent him on his way, and I suggest you do the same.

Nothing could have suited Sandoval more. At 8:10 A.M. he stood with Garcia in the parking area between the church and the covered market, having first fed him a jail breakfast of buttered tortillas, refried beans, and cocoa. At 8:15 the Oaxaca-bound bus rattled in its predictable fifteen minutes late. Sandoval handed Garcia a fifty-peso note he'd signed out from the treasury—the fare was ten pesos—and told him to keep the change.

"Thanks."

He watched as Garcia mounted the steps into the bus.

"Better if you don't come back here," he called after him, not unkindly.

Garcia turned and laughed. "Back here? Not a chance. You won't see me again, not in this lifetime."

"God willing," Sandoval mouthed to himself, watching with relief as the bus got on its dusty, noisy way.

TWO

"FOLKS, if you look out the windows, you'll see a pod of orcas only a hundred yards off the port side, at about eleven o'clock."

At the announcement, most of the starboard passengers arose en masse to make for the windows on the other side. Ordinarily, Julie Oliver would have been among the first, but this time she simply sat there, her eyes glued to the laptop on the table in front of her. She and Gideon were returning from one of their periodic weekend "city fixes"—a concert or opera at the Royal Theatre, a walk in the gardens, a good restaurant or two—in Victoria, British Columbia, closer by forty miles to their home in Port Angeles, Washington, than Seattle was. Like the cyber-enlightened twenty-first-century couple they were, their noses had been buried in their laptops since the MV *Coho* had left Victoria's Inner Harbor, the Empress

Hotel—that grand, old, ivy-covered dowager—had disappeared behind the headland, and the ferry had slipped into the pale, thready winter fog of the Strait of Juan de Fuca.

"Julie," Gideon said, "did you hear? There are orcas on the other side."

"Can I ask you a question?" she said instead of answering and then didn't wait for his reply. "Can you tell me what in the world made me think this Hacienda thing next week was a good idea?"

"Sure. You said it would be nice to go somewhere warm and sunny for a week. You said it would be a snap, a free vacation; you said there would be good food, interesting surroundings, and exotic ruins. You said it involved next to no work for you and none at all for me."

"Did I?" she said grimly, still staring at an e-mail. "It appears I may have misspoken."

The "it" they were talking about was the result of a telephone call from Julie's cousin Annie, who managed the Hacienda Encantada, a small, rustic/luxury dude ranch and resort, mostly patronized by Americans and Canadians, located in the hills above the peaceful little weaver's village of Teotitlán del Valle in Oaxaca, Mexico. Annie, it seemed, had to go back to Winston-Salem in mid-December to clean up the final details of a messy divorce, and could Julie fill in for her for a week or so? It was the slow time of year, so there really wouldn't be much to manage. Julie would live right there at the Hacienda—best room in the place—so lodging and food would be taken care of. And Gideon was more than welcome to come along if he wanted to. The food alone, Julie assured him, was worth coming for. They had a wonderful Oaxacan chef that he would love. Dorotea's cooking was famous. Her recipes had been featured in *Sunset* and *Gourmet*.

It meant that Julie would have to take vacation time

off from her supervising park ranger post at Olympic National Park, but December was a slow time of year in the Olympics—not many wayward hikers to rescue—so it had suited her fine. As icing on the cake, the Hacienda would pick up the round-trip airfare—for both of them.

It hadn't been hard for Julie to convince Gideon to join her. Not only did it sound terrific, but mid-December would be during his winter break from the University of Washington-Port Angeles, and so Julie had called Annie back the next day to tell her the deal was on.

It wasn't as outlandish a proposition as it seemed on the surface. The Hacienda Encantada was owned by a man named Tony Gallagher, Annie's uncle, a long-time expatriate American, who ran the place pretty much as a family affair, with the managerial staff made up of fellow expatriate Gallaghers, and one or two in-laws. One of the in-laws was Julie's favorite uncle, Carl Tendler—Annie's father—who had lived and worked there as head wrangler and stockman for well over thirty years, since its preresort existence as a working ranch. He had first come as a twenty-two-year-old in 1972 for a summer job, had fallen in love with and married Tony Gallagher's sister in 1975, and had settled down. Annie had come along a few years later and had lived her early life there, attending an American boarding school in Oaxaca City. But in 1997, at nineteen, she'd fallen for a sharper named Billy Nicholson, a flashy, good-looking yoga instructor from North Carolina who was conducting a workshop at the Hacienda, and had followed him back to North Carolina and married him, against her father's warnings. When they broke up five years later, she returned to the resort, remorseful and contrite, to gratefully take on the job of resident manager.

As for Julie, she had spent her high school vacations helping out at the Hacienda and had found the life so exotic, so glamorous—to say nothing of having a schoolgirl crush on her handsome, taciturn, Gary-Cooper-like Uncle Carl—that, against the advice of her parents, she had entered a community college to study hotel management with the aim of eventually working full-time at the resort. Although a year in the program and a bit more maturity made her conclude that the hospitality industry might not be her cup of tea, she had at least a basic grounding in the field.

Thus, taking over for a week—or so she said at the time of the phone call—was a no-brainer. True, she hadn't been there since she was nineteen, but all she'd have to do was coordinate meals and meal times for the guests, arrange transportation from the airport for them, plan recreational outings, handle intake if any new guests came along, and one or two bits of administrivia that might or might not require her input . . . in other words, a piece of cake. There'd be plenty of time to do things with Gideon. She expected that her afternoons and evenings would be virtually free.

And then had come this new e-mail from Annie. Tony's brother, Jamie Gallagher, who was their accountant/bookkeeper, would be leaving for Minnesota in a couple of days, a long-awaited opening for arthroscopic knee surgery at the Mayo Clinic having popped up. Would Julie mind keeping an eye on his part of the business too?

"So now," she said, "I'll have to post expenses to the ledger, record income, make sure the peso–dollar conversions balance, pretty much all-around handle the revenue and expense streams, really. I hope the Hacienda survives."

"I'll help out," Gideon said gamely, although he didn't see how.

She responded with a gentle smile. "Thanks, honey, but I don't see how. You have many wonderful strengths, but keeping expense accounts isn't one of them."

She was putting it nicely. He was hopeless with money. Before Julie came into his life, he had stopped even trying to balance his checkbook. Whatever the bank told him his account contained at the end of the month (and it often came as a great surprise), that's what he compliantly posted.

"I could be your enforcer," he offered. "You know, the strong-arm guy if they don't want to pay up?"

"I'll certainly keep that in mind," she said with a smile. "Oh, heck, it won't be that bad. The place is going to be practically empty. Only a few rooms booked. Frankly, I'm more worried about you."

"About me? What's to worry?"

"Well, if I have less time available, what are you going to *do*? You can't spend all your time visiting the archaeological sites."

"I'm not going to do anything. I'm going to vegetate. That's the point."

"So you say, but I've yet to see you do it. You're not taking along any work at all?"

"Nope. My prep for next quarter is done, the paper on Neanderthal locomotor biomechanics has already gone off to *Evolutionary Biology*, and I have no outstanding forensic cases. Nothing."

She closed the laptop's lid. "Well, I don't know why I should be worried. Some old skeleton will turn up for you; it always does."

"No way, not this time. I'm not bringing any tools with me; no calipers, no nothing. Nobody will even know how to find me, so what could happen?"

"Something will happen," she declared. "Come on, let's see if we can still see the orcas."

He got up to go with her. "What could happen?" he repeated in all sincerity.

THREE

EVEN at the best of times, Dr. Bustamente, with his bald, bony head, scrawny neck, and narrow, hunched shoulders, bore a remarkable (and frequently remarked-upon) resemblance to a vulture. But never so much as at this moment, thought Flaviano Sandoval. The old buzzard had been leaning over the leathery carcass for twenty minutes, probing, prodding, scrutinizing, his beaky proboscis almost buried in the dried-out cavity that had once held a full complement of internal organs.

Not that the thing on the table would have held interest for any but the most starving of vultures; not anymore. It had been out in the sun a long—a very long—time, and had been found the day before by old Nacho López while he was out in the hills gathering firewood a couple of kilometers from the village. Findings had been scarce, so with his burro, he had strayed from the usual paths, paths that had been in use for a thousand years and more, since the days of the Old Ones. He had seen the thing from a distance, lying in an arroyo that ran along the base of a line of low cliffs, and he had thought he'd struck gold: a gnarled madrona trunk, he'd thought, something that had washed down from the wooded areas higher up during the last rainy season. Madrona was the best of all firewood, rarely found and hard to chop, but how it burned! Not only that, but this was a big trunk, thick as a man. It would save him an additional four-kilometer, mostly uphill trek to where the trees started, and his legs weren't what they once were. He hurried to it, hauling along the braying, increasingly stubborn burro. But Nacho's eyes weren't what they'd once been either, and he was almost on it before he grasped its real nature. So shocked was he that his eyes had rolled up in his head and he had fallen down on the spot in a dead faint.

It wasn't as if the old man had never seen a mummy before. Anyone who spent any time in these parched hills and valleys had come across them: shriveled, sun-blackened mice, rabbits, birds, even the occasional goat that had strayed from its herd and been lost. But a *man*? A withered, grinning mockery of a man still dressed in a few shreds of human clothing? It was the devil's work, enough to make anyone swoon.

When he had come to, he had hurriedly untied the two old canvas feedbags from the burro's back with shaking hands and had ridden the animal home to tell his wife, who had sent him to tell the priest, who had told the *jefe*.

That had been late yesterday afternoon, too late to do anything about it before dark. But this morning, Sandoval, old Nacho, and the burro had gone out into the hills to retrieve the body. They found it where Nacho said it was, in an arroyo at the base of a cliff, not more than a hundred meters from where the little girl's skeleton had been found earlier (a bad omen, Sandoval thought at the time). Pepe, the junior of Sandoval's two policemen, had come along to help with the lifting that would be necessary. But in the end, Sandoval had had to get it up onto the burro by himself. Young Pepe, although he offered to assist, looked so pale and faint-hearted that Sandoval hadn't the heart to ask him. As for Nacho, once he'd pointed the thing out, he had crossed himself and retreated, refusing to come within ten meters of it. Sandoval wasn't feeling at his most stout-hearted himself, but the remains were so light and so rigid that he had had no trouble getting them onto the animal without assistance.

He was much relieved that the smell (almost nonexistent) and the feel (like parchment) of the thing had been nowhere as bad as he'd expected. It was terrible to look at, all right, but then it wasn't necessary for him to look very closely to set it on the burro's back and quickly cover it with a tarpaulin, during which he did a great deal of squinting and eye-averting. Still, by the time he'd gotten the tarpaulin tied down, he could feel his stomach acting up.

As soon as he had assured himself that what Nacho had seen the previous day was truly a body, he had used his cell phone to alert old Bustamente, the district *médico legista*. Bustamente had immediately driven in from Tlacolula and was now waiting impatiently—almost avidly, Sandoval thought unkindly—in the cemetery, at the door of the two-room concrete-block building, one room of which served as municipal tool and equipment storage, and the other as the village mortuary. Once the body was in the windowless mortuary room and on the ancient, enameled-iron embalming table, Bustamente had taken charge of it, a responsibility Sandoval was all too happy to relinquish.

He had planned to remain there with the doctor, having steeled himself to do what he regarded as his duty. And indeed, he managed to last through the cutting away of the tattered clothing and even to assist in a gingerly fashion. But his resolution began to fade when the boots came off to reveal not the hide-like tissue that covered the rest of the body, but horrible, greasy skeleton feet: eaten-away bones held together by rotting ligaments. Still, Sandoval held his ground, despite the noises coming from his stomach.

Not for long, however. When the leathery skin proved too tough for Bustamente's scalpels, the doctor had gone grumbling into the storage room and emerged with a pair of heavy-duty pruning shears. "Ha, these should do the job," he said, clacking them together and advancing on the corpse. That had been too much for Sandoval, who fled.

He took the opportunity to walk the few blocks to his office in the municipal building to swallow a couple of spoonfuls of Pepto-Bismol and sit quietly with the shades down for twenty minutes to settle his stomach. It didn't help much. Beyond even the revolting physical aspects that were bothering him, he just didn't have a good feeling about this business. Maybe the corpse itself didn't have a bad smell, but everything about it did.

He remained in the office as long as he could, long enough to swallow another dose of the Pepto-Bismol. The second one did calm some of the roiling that was going on inside him, but it did little for his frame of mind. He returned with sinking heart and dragging step to the mortuary as Bustamente was just straightening up from the body, from which the entire front wall had been removed, so that it was wide open, like a picture in a medical book. On Bustamente's face was a look of pinched satisfaction that struck terror into Sandoval's heart. God help him, he'd *known* this was going to be trouble.

"Well?" he said gruffly.

"This man has been murdered," Bustamente pronounced, relishing every word and speaking as if he were on the stand, somberly addressing the court as an expert witness. It was something the old fellow couldn't have had the opportunity to say very often in his long tenure.

"Murdered," Sandoval repeated hollowly from the depths of his chest. It was exactly what he'd been praying not to hear. What had he done to deserve this? How could this be happening to him *again*? It was incredible: only two murders in the last half-century, and both of them during the one-year tenure of Flaviano Sandoval, whose stomach fluttered at the idea of looking at a corpse. It was unbelievable, unfair, not to be borne.

However, once more he steeled himself to face the matter head-on, as the responsibilities of his position demanded. "What makes you think he was murdered?" He could hardly get the words out.

Bustamente bridled. "I don't *think*, I *know*." He crooked a bony finger at the police chief. "Come over here," he commanded and led him to the sink. "Look at this." When Sandoval realized he was looking at a man's chest just sitting there in the sink like a slab of rawhide, his insides started gurgling again.

Wordlessly, Bustamente stuck his finger into a dark hole not far from the middle of the slab. "You see?"

"From a bullet?" Sandoval asked. If he squeezed his eyelids together, leaving just a slit, he could see it without really seeing it.

"Without question." He removed his finger. "You see how the borders of the perforation appear to have been eroded or eaten away? So that the hole is 'cratered,' as we might say?"

"Yes," said Sandoval queasily, although all he could make out through his squint was a roundish hole with blackened edges. There was no denying, though, that it was the right size for a bullet hole. He had shot enough rabbits to know as much.

"This eroded area is what we refer to as an 'abrasion collar,'" Bustamente continued, in the manner of a teacher talking to a not-too-bright pupil. "It is the result of scraping from the rotating motion of the bullet as it penetrates the skin. Being unique to gunshot wounds, it leaves no doubt as to the source of the penetration. Judging from the size of the hole, I would guess the bullet was .32 caliber, but I leave that to the experts."

"I see. And it would have killed him?"

Bustamente uttered a croaking, incredulous laugh. "Certainly, it would have killed him. Imagine if it had happened to you." To illustrate, he jabbed a bony forefinger into Sandoval's chest at about the same spot. "It would have exploded your heart, devastated it."

"Ah," said Sandoval, whose heart was, in fact, feeling more than a little devastated. Murder. Tumult. Inconvenience. The State *Procuraduría de Justicia* taking over his office, taking over the whole municipal building, all four rooms of it. The *policía ministerial* giving him orders, making clear their contempt for him, swaggering and bullying their way through the village. Detectives . . . judges . . .

It was only what he'd expected, he thought with a resigned sigh. *Expect the worst,* his stern, cheerless father had counseled him on many an occasion, *and you will get what you expect. Only it will be worse.* Sandoval had quoted it to one or two people and they had laughed. But his father hadn't meant it as a joke, and the message had sunk in.

"And if by a miracle that were not enough," continued Bustamente, "the fall would have finished the job."

"He had a fall too?"

"A long one. There are many broken ribs. Was he perhaps found at the foot of a cliff or mountain, a height of some kind?"

"Yes."

Bustamente was pleased. "You see?"

Sandoval heaved a forlorn sigh. "This means I will have to report the matter to the *policía ministerial*, doesn't it?" he said glumly, already knowing the answer.

"The sooner the better, I would say. I would not waste any time. They don't like delays."

"And what happens to the body? Do you take it away with you?"

"Not me!" exclaimed Bustamente. "I submit my own report. That's the end of my responsibility."

"So what do I do with him? We can't just leave him here."

"I suggest that is precisely what you do. Lock the place up securely and await the attentions of the *policía*, who will not be long in coming, I promise you."

Sandoval nodded soberly. *If only old Nacho had stayed on the regular paths like anyone else. Or if he had to stray sometime, couldn't he have waited a few measly weeks longer?* Sandoval would no longer have been the *jefe* by then; he would have been safely, agreeably, delightfully engaged in the administration of the village council's affairs, with no responsibility for corpses or murders or—

"You have a problem on your hands, Chief Sandoval," Bustamente observed.

"You're telling me."

"No, I mean an additional problem. I found no bullet. I searched the thoracic cavity thoroughly. It's not there."

Sandoval frowned. "But why should you expect to find the bullet? It might be anywhere. Do you expect to find the bullet when you shoot a rabbit or a deer? Bullets continue on their way—"

Bustamente shook his head. The problem was, he said, that there was no exit wound. The mummified skin on the back and sides of the body was intact. *Ergo*, the bullet had never exited. But he had searched the thoracic cavity thoroughly and it was nowhere to be found.

"I don't understand. How can that be?"

Bustamente twisted his skinny neck, working out the kinks. "Shall we go outside now? I want some fresh air."

They went to a stone memorial bench in the cemetery, where they sat awkwardly side by side. Sandoval himself felt a little better there; the air was fresh and he was among family. It seemed sometimes that half the population of Teotitlán was either a Sandoval or related by marriage to a Sandoval. Bustamente offered him a cigarillo, was turned down, and lit one for himself.

"So then where is it, this bullet?" Sandoval asked. "If not inside the body, then where?"

"There is only one possible answer." Bustamente got his cigarillo going, shook out his match, and emitted twin streams of blue smoke from his nostrils. "It could only have fallen back out through the perforation by which it entered."

That didn't sound right to Sandoval. "But can a bullet do that? Come out through its own wound?"

"I don't see why not. It's not usual, that's so, but—"

"And you said it was a problem for *me*. Why is it a problem for me if you found no bullet?"

Bustamente dropped the barely smoked cigarillo onto the concrete pad that supported the bench and ground it out under his sole. He arched his scant eyebrows. "Do you want to turn in a report to the *Procuraduría de Justicia* in which you tell them you were not capable of finding a bullet that probably lies within a meter of where the corpse was discovered? Would you prefer the *policía ministerial* to find it for you?"

"I would not," Sandoval said softly, but with feeling.

Bustamente uttered a short laugh. "I should think not. You had better return to where he was found and locate it. And if you do not find it there, you must search every millimeter of earth on the way back. That is my considered advice. It may well have come out while the body was on the burro."

Sandoval blew out his cheeks and exhaled. What a job this was going to be. "I'd better get started now." They both stood up. "Is there anything else you need to tell me?"

"Nothing that would interest you," Bustamente said curtly. "I will have my own report for the police next week. And now if you'll excuse me—"

Flaviano Sandoval was by nature a mild, even a timid, man, given to diffidence and conciliation, as opposed to temper outbursts, but at this he bristled. "I *am* the police," he said forcefully. "If you have additional information, I wish to know it."

But Dr. Bustamente was not a man to be intimidated, least of all by Flaviano Sandoval. "I meant the real police," he said drily, but it was beyond him to resist demonstrating his expertise. "If you must know, however, I can tell you that it is my judgment that to become desiccated to this extent, he had to have been lying out in the open for at least eight months, more likely ten."

"And I would say no more than six months," Sandoval said, still bristling.

Bustamente stared at him. "Chief Sandoval, I have twenty-two years of experience in these matters. I have certificates in forensic medicine, in clinical pathology, in maxillofacial pathology . . ."

Sandoval let him rattle on. It was Bustamente's fault he was in this mess—well, in a way it was—and he owed the officious, self-important old man a comeuppance.

"Six months," Sandoval repeated when Bustamente paused for breath. "No more."

Bustamente smiled a lipless smile. "Oh yes? And perhaps you would care to tell me on what premise you base this learned conclusion?"

"On the fact that I know who this man is, and he was most certainly alive six months ago."

That very satisfactorily took the wind out of Bustamente's sails. "You know . . . you saw . . . well, who is it—was it?"

"He claimed his name was Manuel Garcia. A vagrant. I had him in the jail for a night in May. Then I sent him on his way. I myself put him on the bus to Oaxaca. I watched the bus leave."

Bustamente leaned back, narrow-eyed, reassessing him. "And why did you not bother to tell me this earlier?"

"Because you didn't bother to ask me," Sandoval said spitefully, but a moment later he felt a stab of guilt—well, a prick of guilt—partly because he knew he was being petty, but mostly because he knew it wasn't the truth.

Why then had he kept it to himself? Because he'd been hoping that Bustamente would conclude that there was nothing sinister about the man's death, that it had been the result of exposure, or a simple fall, or a heart attack, or best of all that the cause had been impossible to determine. Then Sandoval would have had Garcia quietly buried in a nameless grave at the far corner of the cemetery, an anonymous, unmourned death with no follow-up required. To have supplied his name would only have complicated things, and to no useful end. That far he'd been willing to go to preserve his and the village's tranquility. But homicide? Murder? No, duty required otherwise, and for Sandoval duty was paramount.

Besides, Pompeo was sure to find out.

"And what else do you know about him that you neglected to tell me?" Bustamente asked coldly.

"Nothing at all."

Nothing beyond what he knew within ten seconds of setting eyes on him: Manuel Garcia was going to be trouble.

* * *

ALL the rest of that day, Sandoval, Pepe, and Pompeo searched diligently, twice walking the two kilometers that the burro had carried the body, and then back; four times altogether. The chief's back locked up with an audible click after two hours of bending and stooping, so that he was reduced to prodding at objects on the road with a stick. Young Pepe began complaining of neck and knee pains not long after that, and even the granite face of the indestructible Pompeo wore a look of suffering by the time they were done. In all, they retrieved sixty-five pesos in small coins, five shotgun pellets (collected, just in case), and a Belgian five-cent Euro coin. But of anything even vaguely resembling a .32-caliber bullet? Not a sign, not a hint.

TWO or three times a week—the number was left to his discretion—Sandoval had his dinner up at the Hacienda, a familial perk that went along with his being the brother of their award-winning cook Dorotea; a delightful arrangement as far as he was concerned. He had eaten there the previous evening, and being conscientious about presuming upon the Gallaghers' courtesy, he would ordinarily have avoided dining there twice in a row. But after the day he'd had, he was in sore need of the restorative powers of Dorotea's cooking. An exception was in order.

He parked his car in the lodge's lot and made his way, somewhat more stiffly than usual, to the buffet table in the dining room. Sometimes he would eat with the guests to keep up his English skills—necessary because on summer weekends the village overflowed with American tourists—and because it pleased Mr. Gallagher to show off his relationship with the *jefe de policía*. But Tonio Gallagher wasn't in residence this week and Sandoval was in no mood to sharpen his English. Instead, he carried his food to a separate nook at the back of the dining room that was kept for the various Gallaghers. He sat himself slowly and carefully down, with something between a groan and a sigh. As always, the smell of Dorotea's thick, smooth mole sauce went a long way toward reviving his spirits.

After a while he was joined by old Josefa Gallegos, who supervised the housekeeping staff, and Annie Tendler, the receptionist. Josefa was Mexican and Annie was American, but both, he knew, were somehow related to Mr. Gallagher, as was everybody else in a management position at the Hacienda. From the beginning it had been a family affair.

As usual, Josefa had little to say. Elderly and increasingly deaf, she gave him a grunted *buenas tardes* and immediately set to attacking her *enchiladas de pollo con mole poblano*. Annie, also as usual, was more talkative.

"You don't look your usual cheerful self, Chief," she said in her perfect, idiomatic Spanish.

Sandoval had always found Annie easy to talk to—always a smile at the corners of her mouth, that one; never grumpy or taciturn, a good talker and a good listener both—and before they'd gotten to their coffee and flan he'd told her the whole story.

"We looked and we looked. It's nowhere to be found, Anita. You don't know how I hate to turn in my report without having found it. The *policía ministerial* will find it, I know they will—they have so many resources at their disposal—and we will look like bumbling incompetents. *I* will look like a bumbling incompetent."

"You're positive it's not still in the body somewhere?"

"Yes. Well, not positive, no, but that is what Dr. Bustamente says. And I'm afraid to poke around in that thing
myself. I wouldn't know how to do it. I don't *want* to do
it." He shuddered. "And then on top of that, there is the
report I am required to file with the *policía ministerial*.
How do I do that, what do I write? I know nothing of such
things. The last time this happened, everything I did was
wrong, but did they tell me how to do it right? They did
not."

"Couldn't Dr. Bustamente help you with that?"

"Bustamente," he said scornfully and drew himself
up. "I refuse to give him the satisfaction."

"Chief Sandoval," Annie said slowly, "I have an
idea."

He looked at her with a modest upsurge of hope. An
idea was one idea more than he had. "Yes?"

"You know I'm going to the United States in a couple
of days. Well, my cousin Julie is arriving tomorrow to
take my place, and her husband is coming with her on
vacation. I've never met him, but he's a forensic scientist
who works on such things all the time. He might be able
to help you, to examine the body, maybe find the bullet,
or at least give you some advice. Maybe he could help
you with your report. I'm sure he would know about these
things."

Sandoval considered. "But would he be willing to do
that? A prominent man, on vacation, after all . . ."

"From what Julie tells me about him, he'd like nothing
better."

"He hasn't seen that thing," Sandoval muttered.

"What have you got to lose by asking him?"

"Indeed, nothing," Sandoval said thoughtfully.

"He's supposed to be very famous, you know. They
call him the Skeleton Detective."

"Skeleton detective." Sandoval uttered a short laugh
as he dug into the flan, then uttered what was for him a

rarity: a joke. "I suppose you wouldn't happen to know any mummy detectives?"

"Not enough chiles in the flan," Josefa muttered in her thickly accented English, possibly to them, possibly to the flan itself. "She's supposed to be such a wonderful cook, how is it she don't know to put enough chiles in the flan?"

FOUR

IT was a view of the ancient city that the builders them-selves had never had, and had never imagined that any-one, not even the great birds of the air, could ever have.

Julie had nudged him from an in-and-out doze to look at it.

"We there? Already?" Gideon murmured, eyes not yet altogether open.

"No. Almost. But look down there. I'm not sure if it's Aztec, or Mayan, or what, but I knew you wouldn't want to—"

"If it's near Oaxaca," he said, yawning, "then it'd be Mixtec or Zapotec. Where exactly—" His eyes popped all the way open and then some. "Wow, that's Monte Albán! I didn't know we'd see it from the air. What a sight."

At twelve thousand feet the Mexicana jet had dipped its wings to afford the passengers a better view, and he hungrily drank it in. He'd been to Monte Albán before, but he'd never seen it from above, and from here, looming over a countryside of small, rectangular farms from its table-topped mountain setting, it was truly stunning, the second-grandest city in all of ancient Mesoamerica (only Teotihuacan, on the outskirts of Mexico City, was larger). Its creation was an accomplishment of unimaginable effort. The mountain had not always been table-topped. In one of the great feats of antiquity, the Zapatecos had leveled it in about 500 BC and had then begun building their monumental terraces and plazas and step-pyramids and tombs. It had been a thousand-year project.

"There, that's the Grand Plaza," he whispered, "and that's the ball court, of course, and that's the Observatory, although nobody knows if that's really what it was used for. And—"

"It's gigantic," Julie said. "How many people lived there? There must have been thousands."

"There were. From 600 to 800 AD, something like 35,000 people lived there. Then, by 900 AD, it was deserted, abandoned, and Zapotec hegemony over the whole area was replaced by dozens of competing little—"

"Why was it abandoned? A war?"

"Nobody knows for sure. Apparently, though, it wasn't a war. The current theory is that it had to do with the collapse of Teotihuacan, its biggest trading partner. But the theory that I buy, and this is really fascinating . . ."

As it is with many people, Gideon's strengths were also his failings. An animated, witty lecturer, always among the university's most popular professors, he did sometimes overdo it. Among his most endearing, most annoying traits—derived from the optimistic premise that everyone must surely be as fascinated, as mesmerized, by archaeology and anthropology as he himself was—was to treat the world as his classroom. "Launching into lecture mode," Julie would whisper warningly to him when he got carried away among friends, or even simply "lecture mode." In fact, just a murmured side-of-the mouth "launching" was usually enough to do the trick by now. The moment he realized he was at it he ceased, usually with some embarrassment. He knew enough droning old pedants to live in dread of turning into one. But when it was just the two of them, good sport that she was, Julie was disinclined to stem the flow.

He was still at it twenty minutes later, bubbling with enthusiasm, after the plane had landed at Xoxocotlán International Airport (usually referred to, for obvious reasons, as Oaxaca Airport), a small, single-terminal affair with a couple of runways carved out of a landscape of dry brown fields.

"But think about how *hard* it was to build. Shaving off the top of a mountain was just the start," he said as he pulled their bags from the luggage rack. "All those huge stones they used to build it had to be dragged all the way up from the valley floor almost fifteen hundred feet below—a hundred and fifty stories. Think about that. These were small people; the men were only five feet tall or so. How did they do it? They hadn't figured out the use of the wheel for transportation yet. And what about shaping the stone? They had no metal tools. How did they do *that*? *Why* did they do it?"

"Carl," she said.

"And how did they—what?"

"The man coming toward us—the cowboy. That's my Uncle Carl. He's here to pick us up." She shook her head, smiling. "God, he never ages. He looks the same as he looked fifteen years ago. *More* than fifteen years ago."

Julie gave her uncle a happy hug, then made the introductions. Gideon liked him right away. A lanky, loose-limbed man, perhaps an inch shorter than Gideon's six-two, he was in denims and scuffed boots and carried a hat in his hand; not the ubiquitous straw *campesino*'s sombrero that was on just about every male head in rural Mexico, but a genuine cowboy's ten-gallon Stetson (although Gideon had read somewhere that a ten-gallon hat would hold only three gallons of water), convincingly sweat-stained and curled.

Gideon saw right away why he reminded Julie of Gary Cooper. He was appealing in the same lean, rawboned way, graceful and awkward at the same time, with a weathered, wise, kind/stern face and a reserve that somehow managed to convey both shyness and a serene self-assurance. He even had a lazy Western twang to go along with all this; Montana, Gideon thought, or the Dakotas. The only off-note was the sharply delineated fish-belly-white expanse of skin from just above his eyebrows to his thinning widow's peak. Clearly, the hat he was holding in his hand was rarely off his head in the outdoors.

His daughter Annie, for whom Julie would be filling in, was waiting at the curb outside, beside a dusty red Ford Explorer SUV with the Hacienda logo, a photographic blowup of a man and a woman on horseback on the side. Annie, like Julie in her mid-thirties, was plump and pretty (in a squirrel-faced kind of way) and as voluble and feisty as her father was strong and silent. Her welcoming hug of Julie involved emphatic, bilateral cheek-to-cheek air kisses, during which her steady stream of chatter never missed a word.

"Dorotea's making a late breakfast snack for you," she was chirping as they got into the van. "*Quesadillas de queso*; she makes them with epazote and green chiles . . . yum! I wasn't going to join you—I've already had breakfast, but I'm making myself hungry. Maybe I'll have just one. . . ."

Gideon sat in front with Carl, so that Julie and Annie could catch up more easily, and the two women gabbed happily away about people he'd never met, with names either unknown to him or only hazily familiar. He had grown a little sleepy again—it was just after eight o'clock in the morning; they had taken a red-eye from Mexico

City rather than staying the night at an airport hotel—so he was content to sit quietly and watch the scrub-dotted countryside slide by, so starkly different from the green, cool ambience of the Olympic Peninsula. And Carl was the sort of man who was just as happy, or probably more so, to be sitting in companionable silence as he would be to making conversation.

The airport was on the south side of the city, on the way to Teotitlán, so in no more than ten minutes they were free of the bustle of city traffic and the scrawled political graffiti, and out in a wide, flat valley checkered with the same small, rectangular farms he had seen from the air. Most were communally owned, he'd read, a result of the sweeping nineteenth-century reforms of Benito Juárez. Here in Oaxaca, Juárez's home, virtually all of the old haciendas and large ranchos had been broken up. There were alfalfa plots, corn, garbanzos, maguey (for making mezcal), cereal crops for animal feeds . . . not that he could tell one from the other, of course, but so he'd read and so he believed.

There were small communities on the flanks of the distant dun-colored hills on either side, but buildings in the center of the valley, along the highway, were scarce. There was an occasional isolated roadside tourist shop— weavings, mezcal, crafts—but no businesses geared to the locals. And those few scattered dwellings that existed near the highway were in small family compounds enclosed within high whitewashed walls, although every now and then one in brilliant tangerine orange, or canary yellow, or chartreuse green would bring him suddenly awake.

When, after a while, he was awake enough to tune in to the conversation behind him, Annie was bringing Julie up to date on things at the Hacienda. Her uncle Jamie, the resort bookkeeper, had indeed left for Minnesota a few days ago to have his knee operated on. Annie would be staying through today so she could orient Julie on things, but she would head for Winston-Salem the next morning to wrap up the last of her divorce. Tony Gallagher was back home in Mexico City at the moment—

"Oh, I'm sorry," Julie said. "I'd love to have seen Uncle Tony." Tony, being Carl's brother-in-law, wasn't actually Julie's uncle, but she had come to refer to him that way when she was working at the Hacienda. She had felt strange calling him "mister," she had once explained to Gideon, and she'd been too shy to call him "Tony," so "Uncle Tony" it had been. For whatever reason—perhaps that he was younger—Tony's brother Jamie, who had exactly the same relationship to her that Tony did, was just plain Jamie. Interestingly enough, Annie, who was niece to both of them, called neither of them "uncle."

"You *will* see Tony," Annie said. "He's planning on coming down in a couple of days."

"You mean Tony doesn't live here?" Gideon asked. "He lives in Mexico City?"

"On the outskirts," Annie said. "In Coyoacán. In this fabulous gated community surrounded by other rich *Yanquis*, assorted strung-out rock stars, and the occasional Colombian drug lord. He only comes down here once a month or so for a few days."

"So who runs the Hacienda? I mean, who's in charge?"

"Nobody's in charge," Julie said. "It's a family affair. No boss, really. Right, Uncle Carl?"

"Well, yeah, I guess that's true," Carl said. "We just kinda get along, muddle through, you know? Jamie makes sure we get the bills paid, and Annie kinda keeps an eye on things around the place, keeps us all in line. Not that much to it, really."

"Says you!" Annie said, then loyally added: "And you do plenty too, Pop. The place wouldn't even exist without you."

"Aw, hell, I just look after the horses," Carl said softly.

"But Tony does own it?" Gideon asked.

"Oh, Tony owns it, all right," Carl said with a nod. "You got that right."

"Okay, fill me in a little, would you, folks? Tony Gallagher is an American, isn't he? How did he come to own the Hacienda Encantada?"

"Well, yes, he's an American citizen, all right," Annie said, "because he was born there, but he was raised on the Hacienda, although it wasn't the Hacienda back then. See, his father—my grandfather— Julie, didn't you ever tell this husband of yours all this stuff?"

"Of course I did. He just didn't pay attention, although he did put on a pretty good act."

Julie and Gideon both laughed, and she reached forward to give his shoulder an affectionate squeeze with just a little bit of a wicked twist at the end. The thing was, it was exactly the kind of thing he was always accusing her of when she failed to commit to memory some fascinating point he'd made about skeletal morphology or protohominid locomotion.

And the excuse he gave now was just about as lame as hers usually were. "I guess it didn't seem to appertain to anything concrete at the time. Now that I'm here, it's become highly germane."

"*Appertain*," Carl said, appreciatively rolling the word around his mouth, trying it out on his tongue. "*Highly germane*. Whoa. Does he talk like that all the time, sweetie?"

"I warned you," Julie said. "He's a professor."

"Right," said Gideon. "It's what I do. Hey, I even know some better words than that. Wait till you get to know me. But go ahead, tell me about Tony."

"You tell him, Pop," Annie said. "Pop knows the whole story better than anyone."

"Well, okay, sure," Carl drawled. "Guess I better start with the place itself. . . ."

A hundred and fifty years ago, the Hacienda Encantada had been a genuine hacienda, a real working sisal ranch, including a small factory where the sisal was made into rope. But by the 1940s the property, then an eccentric compound of decrepit nineteenth-century buildings surrounded by almost eighty acres of maguey plantings from which the sisal had been made, had stood, unused and moldering, for twenty years. It had been bought in 1947 by Annie's grandfather, Vince Gallagher, a wounded Army veteran who had combined his military payout with his life's savings to live out his dream of ranching in some sunny, warm place as far away from his home in International Falls, Minnesota (officially the coldest city in the continental United States) as possible. Knowing little about either ranching or farming—before the war he had worked as a steamfitter—he hired an "agricultural consultant," on whose advice he tore out the exhausted old magueys, replacing them with tobacco plants and coffee trees, and invested heavily in stock for fighting bulls and fine Arabian riding horses.

Things didn't work out as hoped, however. The consultant turned out to be a crook, bullfighting turned out to be illegal in Oaxaca (who knew?), and the plantings had a hard time of it in the rain-starved hills. Only the horses, against all odds, were a success, but only a modest one. Worst of all, his new Mexican wife, the beautiful, flashing-eyed Beatriz, decided after her first trip to the United States that she liked International Falls better than Teotitlán and began spending more and more time there with the Minnesota Gallaghers, who were glad to take her in, not only having taken a genuine liking to her, but relishing the chance to penalize Vince for having chosen to leave in the first place. And with medical care far superior to what was available in Mexico, she made sure to be in Minnesota for the birth of each of her three children. Eventually she would spend more than half the year there, almost always taking their children with her.

It made for a lonely life for Vince, who, underneath his romantic expatriate veneer, was really a family man at heart. Still, he managed to keep the place going—barely—by raising and selling his horses, and later on by boarding them and working with an Oaxaca tour agency that specialized in back-country treks. In 1975 he brought in Carl, the Montana-ranch-raised son of an Army buddy, to handle that end of the business, and there Carl had remained ever since.

In 1978, Vince, a two-pack-a-day man (three packs a day in his twenties) had died from complications from the emphysema that had plagued him for ten years, and Tony Gallagher, then about twenty-five, a year older than Carl was, had taken over the ranch.

"Tony was the oldest of his children?" Gideon asked.

Annie answered for Carl. "That's right. Tony was the oldest, then my mother—Blaze was her name—and then Jamie. In fact my grandmother died giving birth to him, do I have that right, Pop?"

"Well, not long after. Anyway, to go back to after Vince died and Tony took over . . . Whew, talk about a new broom. . . ."

Carl paused to give his full attention to making a left turn from the highway. As with everything else, he was a focused, deliberate, unhurried driver—he took his time, patiently waiting a good twenty seconds for a rattletrap pickup coming from the other way to approach and get safely by. ("*Go*, already," Annie mouthed silently, rolling her eyes.) Finally, when the highway was clear for as far as the eye could see, he turned onto a narrow, potholed, shoulderless, utterly deserted, but more or less paved road. The rusted green sign read, 2 KM TEOTITLÁN. In front of them the road crested a low rise, then disappeared into dry, gently undulating brushland dotted with small farms, with the stark brown hills in the distance. Carl took up the story again as they started down.

Tony Gallagher, young as he was, had a good head for business and was a natural salesman besides. There were a couple of Mexico City mining outfits that had been angling for mineral rights to the land—gold and silver concessions—but Vince had been turning them down in hopes of getting them to up their offers. Tony took a different, tougher tack: They wanted the mineral rights? Fine, but the only way they were going to get them was to buy the land itself. He maneuvered them into a bidding war and eventually sold off almost all of the original rancho, seventy-five of the eighty acres, for almost $500,000—this was in 1980 money—keeping only the hacienda complex itself.

The mining operations failed, but Tony had made out like a bandit. He used the money to restore the hacienda buildings and convert them to a high-end dude ranch/retreat/resort, and within three years the Hacienda Encantada was in the black. After that he'd made a lot of money in the markets. He'd made his primary home in Coyoacán since 1995, living there now with his fourth wife, the Miss Chihuahua 1992 second runner-up. But every now and then he liked to spend a few days at the Hacienda to see how things were going, make some simple repairs—he loved working with his hands—

"Ha!" Annie cried. "Working with his hands is right! He comes up here to get away from his nutball wife Conchita and make himself a sweet little love nest with whoever his current local sweet patootie is. The repair work's his cover with Conchita."

"Annie," Carl said, "that's not the kind of thing I like to hear coming out of your mouth."

"I thought I was being generous," Annie said. "You guys will meet her, don't worry; he loves to show them off. Who is it now, Pop? Is it still Preciosa the Pretentious? It must be a year now. Isn't he about ready for a new one?"

"Come on, now, Annie," Carl said, "that's no way to talk about your uncle."

"Hey, am I knocking it? More power to him, I say. I just wish he had better taste."

"Annie—"

"You two will love Preciosa, She of the Swanlike Neck," Annie said. "I guess she's some kind of international hotel management consultant. Tony met her at a conference in Mexico City where she was a speaker. Every time she shows up here, she's got some new harebrained scheme that he makes us try."

"Annie," said Carl, "don't you think you're being a little hard on her?"

"What, Swimming with the Fishes wasn't harebrained?"

"Well," Carl said, "it wasn't a bad idea to begin with. It just didn't work out."

Annie emitted a honk of a laugh. "I'll say! See," she said to Julie and Gideon, "she was all worked up about the idea of putting in a kind of Swimming with the Dolphins attraction?—like they have in Hawaii?—in a mostly dried-up pond we have out back, so we lined the whole thing with concrete—it cost a mint—but of course, dolphins can't make it here, so she went to work to find a local fish that could, and that wouldn't mind a bunch of humans floundering around with it. Unfortunately, the one she came up with, *carpa cabezona*, had an English name that seemed to turn off the Americans for some reason. Don't ask me why, but Swimming with the Bighead Carp just never caught on."

Even Carl joined in on the laughter with a soft, throaty chuckle.

"But you know," Annie said, "we'd put a lot of money into it—"

"*Tony* had put in a lot of money," Carl corrected.

"—on water flow control, and drainage technology, and so on, so the *next* year, Preciosa has an even better idea of how to recoup. 'I know, let's turn the pond into a therapeutic mud bath!' So we did. Well, the problem there was that the people who put it in were pool people. They didn't really know how to drain a mud bath properly or keep it clean, so within a couple of months, you didn't want to be within two hundred yards of it." She made a face. "Ooh, that was nasty."

Carl had to agree. "That was pretty nasty, all right."

"On the other hand," Annie said, "Preciosa's a hell of an improvement over the one before. Rosie was *really*—"

"All right, that's enough now," Carl said sharply. "Tony's affairs are—" He corrected himself. "Tony's personal life is not your affair. Not mine either."

"Yes, Pop," Annie said meekly.

Gideon thought a slight shift of subject was in order. He turned toward the back. "And your mother, Annie, did she—"

"We lost her," Carl said curtly, closing down the conversation the way a slamming iron door closes down a corridor.

Now what did I step into? Gideon wondered.

FIVE

IT was a while before he found out. The rest of the drive was completed without further talk, other than work-related dialogue between Julie and Annie, and when they reached the Hacienda there were some difficulties to contend with. For one thing, there was a minor kerfuffle over their room. It seemed that Josefa, who supervised the housekeeping staff, had gotten things mixed up. ("I'm shocked. Shocked," Gideon heard Annie mutter.) Josefa had followed instructions to have their room spruced up, but she had mistakenly thought that they wouldn't be arriving until the next day. Thus, the room was presently in mid-sprucing, its floor strewn with cleaning supplies, touch-up paint, and bedding and linens fresh and not so fresh. It would be a while before it was usable.

In addition, two American women, in for a workshop to be conducted at the Hacienda, had been waiting there for twenty minutes, drinking coffee, impatient and angry, for somebody who spoke decent English to show up to register them and give them keys to their room.

"Oh, we don't use keys here," Annie said pleasantly, "unless you really want them. I'm so sorry you were kept waiting, ladies. If you'll come with me to the office, I'll get you set right up. I hope you'll let me offer you a bottle of wine at dinner tonight to make up for the inconvenience?"

And off she went with the considerably mollified couple to register them. A twitch of the head brought Julie along too, presumably for some hands-on training. "We'll see you in a few minutes," Annie called back to Gideon. "Ask Dorotea to make me a quesadilla too, will you?"

Carl, still withdrawn and focused inside himself, mumbled something about tending to the horses and withdrew to the corral and stable, which were down the hill a little from the resort buildings via a dusty track. Gideon was left to himself at a table on the broad flagstone terrace of the main building, the *Casa Principal*. That was fine with him. The morning air was dry and fresh and agreeably warm—in the sixties—and the terrace, overlooking the village, was an altogether pleasant place for a still-sleepy man to be. He slouched happily in a comfortable wicker armchair, legs outstretched, face turned up to the December sun. Dorotea had wordlessly plunked down a steaming mug beside him, and the wonderfully aromatic cinnamon-and-chocolate-scented Mexican coffee slid down his gullet like honey.

The Hacienda Encantada, sitting as it did atop its own hill, dominated Teotitlán del Valle almost like a baronial castle in France dominated its feudal lands; almost like (this took a little more imagination) the far grander Monte Albán dominated its low-lying surroundings. Seen from where Gideon sat, the tranquil little village was laid out like a scene on an old picture postcard: two main streets,

a covered market, and in the center a domed, turreted
eighteenth-century church with two ornate bell towers.
Red-tiled roofs. Stuccoed walls. Except for a parked yellow school bus and a few taxis in the square in front of
the market—the drivers lolled nearby, smoking and chatting in the shade of a tree—there was nothing to remind
one it was 2008 rather than 1908, and not much to remind
one that it wasn't 1808.

The community was close enough that the sounds of
village life drifted up to where he was sitting. Apparently,
a morning market was in progress; he could hear the
sounds of women's voices and children's laughter, along
with the occasional dog bark and the cackling of poultry.
There were radios playing somewhere too—Mexican pop
music—and what sounded like a brass band practicing.
And weaving in and out of the narrow streets a truck with
a loudspeaker mounted on the cab traveled slowly along,
braying its message, too far away for him to make out.
Julie had told him that, in the absence of a local newspa-
per, this was the way the town got its community news. In
the parched brown hills behind the Hacienda goats were
doing some braying of their own. Interesting, he thought
drowsily, so many different sounds floating on the air,
and yet such an overall sense of quiet, of remoteness. He
could understand why Julie liked the place so much.

All the same, he could sense the first intimations of
restlessness already nibbling away at his contentment.
What was he going to *do* for the next few days? Sitting out
here, bathing in warm sunshine in the middle of December, was terrific . . . for an hour or so. And a horseback
ride or two into the hills was inviting. And he did want to
visit a couple of the nearby Zapotec ruins. Put all those
things together and they would account for what, eight
hours? Twelve, maybe, if he took his time? Then what?
As usual, Julie had been right: he should have brought

along some work. What had he been thinking? Why hadn't he at least—

"Nice, isn't it?" Julie said, slipping into a chair beside him and setting a manila folder on the table.

"I can see why you like it." He pulled himself up in his chair, smiling. "You look pretty. Did you get the annoyed ladies squared away?"

"Oh, I think so. They're part of a group of ten. Comrades-in-arms of yours; fellow professors, here for a workshop."

His interest perked up. Maybe things weren't going to be so bad. "Really? What field?"

"Various, I guess. The workshop is called . . ." She consulted an index card from the folder. ". . . Surmounting Gender Politics and Phallocentric Norms on Campus: Building a Feminist Agenda to Challenge Heteronormativity in the Academic Workplace."

He slunk back down in his chair. "Whoa, I think I better keep a low profile."

"I told them you were the chairman of your department and that I knew you'd be glad to join them for a session or two, if they liked."

"It's a good thing I know you're kidding. . . . Uh, you *are* kidding?"

"I'm kidding. Your secret is safe with me. What's . . ." She consulted the card. ". . . heteronormativity, anyway?"

"As far as I understand it, it's a feminist term for the 'mistaken' belief that there are two—and *only* two— sexes, male and female, which results in the marginalization and persecution of—"

"Never mind. I don't think I want to go there."

You and me both, Gideon thought.

She looked up, smiling, and jumped out of her chair. "Dorotea, it's so good to see you!" she cried in Spanish. Julie's Spanish was better than Gideon's adequate but limited command. She had learned it during her teenage summers at the Hacienda and had taken two years of it in high school and another in college in the days when she had planned to work there. Dorotea, who had brought out another mug of coffee for her, seemed more annoyed than pleased to see her.

"They didn't tell me you was coming until this morning," she griped in English. "And they sure didn't tell me you was bringing *him*." She wiped her red hands disgustedly on her apron. "If he wants any dinner, I got to send Felix down for another chicken."

"I suspect he will want some dinner," Julie said pleasantly.

"I figured," Dorotea said, stomping back to the kitchen.

"Is it something about me?" Gideon asked, looking after her, "or is she always like that?"

"Pretty much always," Julie said.

"I seem to remember you telling me I'd like her."

"I said you'd like her *cooking.* Those are two different things."

"I'll say. All the same, if you don't mind, I think I'll have you taste my food before I try it."

"Oh, you'll get used to her. That's just the way she is." She sank back into her chair and inhaled the steam from the mug, "Mm, isn't this coffee wonderful? I forgot how good it was. Dorotea told me how she does it, but of course it doesn't taste the same at home." She smiled to herself and took a couple of long swallows, eyes closed. "Did you notice that Carl got a little upset there in the car?"

"It was hard not to notice. What did I say wrong, do you know?"

"You didn't say anything wrong. It's my fault for not telling you that Annie's mother is a touchy subject."

"Are you just being charitable here? It's not just another case of insufficient attention?"

"I'm just being charitable," Julie agreed.

Gideon smiled. "So, tell me again and I promise to pay attention. Was she 'lost' as in 'died' or 'lost' as in 'divorced'?"

"Neither. 'Lost' as in 'ran away and never came back.'"

"From her husband and her little baby? Ouch."

"Ouch is right. She ran off with one of the hands, abandoning poor little Annie and leaving Carl to take care of her. Annie's not even sure she has any real memories of her."

"Probably doesn't," Gideon said. "She probably just remembers stories she heard." He shook his head. "That's tough."

"Well, from what I can tell, she handles it just fine. But apparently Carl's never gotten over it, gotten over Blaze. It's been almost thirty years, but Annie thinks he's still in love with her. Oh, what's more, they left with a heck of a nest egg; her boyfriend Manolo robbed the ranch payroll and they took off with it."

"Robbed the ranch payroll?" He laughed, but Julie didn't crack a smile. "You're serious? This is starting to sound like Butch Cassidy and the Sundance Kid."

"Well, you have to remember, this was before the place was a resort. It was an honest-to-God horse ranch, and the hands were paid in cash. And Jamie would drive to the bank in Tlacolula every month—there wasn't one here in Teotitlán back then—to get the payroll and bring it back. And—well, Manolo robbed him. On the road. At gunpoint. Sixteen thousand dollars. A lot of money in 1979, especially down here."

"You ain't just whistling Dixie, kiddo," Annie put in, having rejoined them, also armed with a mug of coffee. She sat herself down comfortably. "Filling Gideon in on the family skeletons, eh?"

Julie was embarrassed. "I was just explaining to Gideon why your father suddenly clammed up in the car."

"Yeah, no problem. It's sad, isn't it? Almost thirty years and I think he's still in love with her."

She gazed down at the village, the mug held in front of her face in both hands. "I was really little, so I don't really remember it. Besides, they wouldn't talk about it in front of me; I mean, Blaze was my mother, right?—but I knew something that wasn't kosher had happened, and later I learned all about it. Jamie was only a kid himself, fifteen years old, so losing all that money that he was responsible for practically killed him. You know what Jamie's like, anyway—well, you do, Julie—so you can imagine." And to Gideon, by way of explanation: "Jamie's kind of . . . earnest, you know? He takes things to heart."

"Jamie's the worrier in the family," Julie said, smiling.

"A good thing too. This family could use a worrier."

Annie paused to try her coffee, found it too hot, and blew on it. It had been a while since Gideon had seen an adult do that, but somehow it seemed fitting for Annie. "Anyway, on account of that and some other things, I guess the ranch was on the edge of going bust until Tony conned the mineral people into buying most of it, and turned what was left into . . ." She spread her arms and gestured, palms up, at the complex of buildings, patios, and terrace around them. "Ta-daaa. And the rest is history." She sighed, settled back, blew some more on her coffee, and sipped thoughtfully at it.

"Well, I can understand why your dad doesn't like to talk about it," Gideon said. "Sorry I opened a can of worms."

"Don't worry about it," Annie said. "It's just something we don't mention in front of him. I'm not even sure Pop knows I know the story. What they told me at the time was that my mother had to go to the hospital, and then they just dropped the subject. Pop himself just could never bring it up again, and I knew better than to ask questions. He even put away his pictures of her. I found them when I was about ten, in a crate near where he keeps the horse feed. She was *so* beautiful. I kept a photo of her standing with Pop, with me in her arms, and put the others back. I don't think he's opened that crate even once."

"It's too bad he never remarried," Julie said.

"Remarried? Hell, he never even had a girlfriend. Well, a couple of times a year he travels for a week or so on horse business, so who knows, maybe there's some old flame out there, but I can tell you he never brought one back home. Or made out with any of the guests, either. And you should see the way some of the female guests come on to him. They don't know I'm his daughter, of course, so they talk about him in front of me." She grimaced. "It's disgusting."

She leaned forward. "Let me tell you something about my father. He is the most loyal, honest, decent man you will ever meet. What he seems like is exactly what he *is* like. After Mom took off, he figured his job was to raise me, and that's just what he did." She paused for a wry smile. "But I inherited my mother's genes, I guess—in everything but looks, dammit—because at nineteen I ran off with that miserable shmuck Billy Nicholson, idiot that I was. Why? Because he looked like Robert Redford. And then when I came crawling back here with my tail between my legs? Pop took me in without a word of reproof and got me set up in this job, for which I am eternally grateful. That was eight years ago, and there's still never been a word of reproof, not a single *word*. Never even an *I told you so*, which he had every right to say. That man is something else, let me tell you. My hero."

The somewhat awkward silence that followed this soul-baring was broken by Dorotea, who called loudly from the doorway in Spanish that their breakfast was on the buffet table, and in they filed.

"If this is a 'late breakfast *snack*,'" Gideon said, "I can hardly wait to see what an actual breakfast looks like."

On the table in front of them were the promised quesadillas—seven of them, not the expected three— freshly made tortillas covered with cheese and chiles, folded into half moons, and arranged in a semicircle. But there was also cubed melon and papaya, a bowl of yogurt, biscuits, jam, a pitcher of pink, frothy juice that, on inquiry, turned out to be ginger-spiked hibiscus juice— and, of course, more of the wonderful coffee. The three of them loaded up ("Well, since there are extra quesadillas, I guess I'll have a couple, after all," Annie said. "Wouldn't want them to go to waste.") and took their food back out to the terrace. The sun had climbed higher by now, and although it wasn't unpleasantly hot, Gideon put up the umbrella to give them some protection from the glare.

Gideon and Julie, who hadn't eaten anything since dinner the night before, were ravenous and the food was marvelous, and for a few minutes their only conversation had to do with how wonderful it was, much of it expressed in appreciative grunts and murmurs of one syllable. Annie took a proprietary pride in Dorotea's skills, explaining that what made the tortillas so exceptional was not only that they had been made that morning with fresh *masa*— hand-ground corn flour—but that real, old-fashioned lard had gone into it "by the handful." This did nothing to take the edge off their appetites, and all of the quesadillas were efficiently demolished, three by Gideon.

When they were back to drinking coffee and picking at the biscuits and jam, Annie suddenly clapped her hands together. "Damn, I almost forgot! Hey, Gideon, are you interested in helping out our police chief and looking at this skeleton they found?"

"A skeleton?" Gideon's world was suddenly flooded with light.

"I mean, a mummy. I mean, this dead guy they found, a murdered guy, they couldn't find the bullet—"

It took a minute or two, but eventually she got the story

out, and a beaming Gideon said he'd be pleased to help if he could. Or even if he couldn't.

"Okay, let me give Chief Sandoval a call right now." She got up to go to the office, which was in a separate building. "The body's in this little room at the cemetery. When do you think you could look at it?"

"How about now?"

"Now?" Julie exclaimed. "Gideon, you were on a plane all night. When I came out here fifteen minutes ago you were falling asleep."

"Well, I'm wide awake now." He beat a tattoo on the table to prove it.

Julie shook her head. "I knew skeletons could do that to him," she said to Annie. "Now I know mummies can too."

"Oh, your room's ready," said Annie, who had caught a signal from Josefa in the courtyard behind them. "Why don't you go get yourself unpacked up there while I call?"

The Hacienda Encantada consisted of five nicely restored nineteenth-century buildings around a cool, tree-shaded brick courtyard with hammocks and rocking chairs in various pleasant niches. Sombreros and binoculars hung from the walls for the guests to use. Other than the Casa Principal with its dining room, kitchen, and terrace, there was the old sisal factory storehouse, the largest structure, with fourteen guest rooms; the old chapel, now cut up into the lodge office and the meeting room; the old factory building itself, the Casa de Máquinas, converted into five upscale guest rooms, one of which was Gideon and Julie's (the best, according to Julie); and the Casa del Mayordomo, a beautiful old house with a pillared portico, once the estate manager's home, now divided into five suites for the Gallaghers and their relations: one for Jamie, one for Annie, one for Carl, the smallest one for Josefa, and the largest one kept available for Tony.

"Like it?" Julie asked as Gideon pulled open the heavy, studded oak door of their room. "It's been fifteen years, and as far as I can tell, the whole place looks better than ever."

He would have said he loved it in any case because Julie was obviously anxious for him to be pleased, but in fact he liked it a lot. As promised, there was no television set, no telephone, no alarm clock.

It was a single large space with an eighteen-foot beamed ceiling and smoothed, red-painted concrete flooring. Through a door was a tiled bathroom. The furniture—king-sized bed, nightstands, lamps, round table and chairs, wardrobe, bureau—was all hand-carved in a rustic, squarish, pleasingly simple mission style. All very uncrowded and open. Geometric weavings, finely done and probably local, were on the floor on either side of the bed and in front of the wardrobe. A hammock hung in one corner.

"This is great. The whole place is great."

There was a double tap on the door. "Okay," Annie said, letting herself in. "Chief Sandoval's on his way. It's only a two-minute drive up from the village. He'll tell you all about it on the way back down. You'll find his English is pretty good—well, passable."

"That's good. I don't think my Spanish is quite up to 'passable.'"

Julie was chuckling. "I *told* him something like this would turn up," she said to Annie. "It never fails."

Gideon hunched his shoulders. "What can I say? Remember what that psychic in Hawaii said? She said it was my aura. Skeletons are very attracted to me."

"And vice versa," said Julie.

SIX

AS mummified remains went, they weren't that bad.

The body had been out there long enough, and in an environment that was hot enough and dry enough, so that there was nothing anyone would call a stench—just an earthy, musty smell, like decaying bark on the forest floor. And it had dried out enough that the skin—the *hide* was more like it, at this point—no longer glistened with exuded fat or other nasty effluvia. It had become a stiff, brown parchment-like object whose appearance had more in common with the mummy of Ramses II than with anybody who'd been walking around on two legs six months earlier.

All of this came as a welcome relief to Gideon. Like any forensic anthropologist, he took satisfaction and pleasure in working with skeletons, in reconstructing, at least in part, the living human being—sex, age, habits, appearance, occupation, the whole history of a life, and often the nature of its death—from a pile of bones. But fresh, or rather not-quite-fresh, corpses were another thing. Unlike most of his forensic colleagues, he had never inured himself to the nasty phases that bodies went through on their journey from flesh and blood to bare bones—"decomps," as they were called in the trade. In what he considered the immortal words of the Munchkin Coroner of Oz, he preferred his corpses "not only really dead, but really most sincerely dead," the older the better. A decade was usually a safe bet, a millennium better still. He was, in a word, squeamish.

But then he'd never meant to become a forensic anthropologist, had he? A quiet, scholarly career as a professor of physical anthropology was more what he'd had in mind. His doctoral dissertation had been on early Pleistocene hominid locomotion, and he had assumed his subsequent teaching and research would keep him immersed in the femurs, pelves, and tibias of that period, a comfortable million or so years back. Indeed, his academic life had done just that. But physical anthropology professors were necessarily expert "bone readers," and like others in the field, he had been called on to put this expertise to more contemporary uses. And in truth, it had proven fascinating, if sometimes stomach-churning, this scientific detective work. Nowadays, to his own surprise, he felt himself a little at loose ends if he wasn't involved in some forensic case or another.

And, as Julie suggested, it was never very long before one came and found him. Even in Teotitlán del Valle, Oaxaca, Mexico.

Sandoval, a small, soft, nervous, harried sort of man who reminded Gideon strongly of someone—he couldn't put his finger on whom—had filled him in on the finding of the body and on Dr. Bustamante's conclusions concerning it. Now, gloved hands behind his back—a pair of disposable gloves had been provided for him—Gideon stood looking at it from three or four feet away, the chief fidgeting away at his side. The earthly remains of Manuel Garcia, if that was really his name, were lying mostly on their right side on the chipped, enameled tabletop—a type of embalming table that had been up-to-the-minute a hundred years ago. One knee was drawn up, the other extended. The left arm, twisted so that the palm faced up, was stiffly stretched along the left side and down toward the drawn-up knee, the right arm hidden beneath the body.

Below the waist, the left side—the uppermost side— had rotted away here and there, allowing glimpses of the skeletal underpinnings—the sharp rim of the innominate, the knobby, yellow, lateral condyles of the femur and tibia. A couple of inches above the knee, the bone had once suffered a break, possibly when he'd been a child. It had healed a long time ago, but it had been badly set, or more likely not set at all, so that there was a kink in the bone, an angle that didn't belong there.

"Healed transverse fracture, distal third of the right femoral shaft," he murmured automatically, making mental notes for his report. "Fully remodeled but poorly set, with medial and cranialward displacement of the distal segment."

"What?" Sandoval said, alarmed.

"It's nothing to do with his death," Gideon said. "I was just thinking out loud."

The right side appeared to be intact. The face too was intact but much shriveled, so that the mustache looked outlandishly big—a Mario Brothers mustache, a Groucho Marx mustache—and the strong, crooked, brown teeth were bared in what looked like a snarl. The eye sockets, of course, were empty. Stiff whitish hairs bristled around the mouth. The feet were nothing but bones and ligaments, with no skin on them at all.

He moved a little closer, hands still behind his back (he had learned that he did better when he approached this kind of thing gradually). The musty smell became more noticeable, mostly, he thought, because the interior of the thorax was open to the air. Dr. Bustamente had not used the Y-incision typical of autopsies, in which the arms of the Y begin at the lateral ends of the collar bones and come together at the sternum, and the tail runs from there down the center of the abdomen, all the way to the pubis, usually with a neat little jig to spare the navel. The resulting flaps can then be peeled back to expose the insides. Instead, Bustamente had simply hacked a rough oval all the way around the perimeter of the chest and the upper part of the abdomen, and pulled off the entire front wall of the body. He had used a pair of shears, a still-shaken Sandoval had told him. *Shears!* As if he were cutting up a hunk of cowhide for a saddle!

But with mummified remains, Gideon knew, such a procedure wasn't unusual. On a body like Garcia's, the hide was thick and hard enough to take the edge off a scalpel after one swipe, and the flaps were almost impossible to bend and peel back away from the sternum. Using a sturdy pair of shears to remove the entire chest wall in one piece was the simplest route, and Bustamente had taken it.

He took the final step necessary to reach the table and leaned over the remains. There were no identifiable internal organs to be seen; no heart, no lungs, no liver, no adrenals, no kidneys, only some dry, blackened, anonymous lumps of tissue sticking to the ribs and inner wall of the hide here and there. It was a picture-book stage C4 of the Galloway categorization of mummified remains: "Mummification of tissues with internal organs lost through autolysis or insect activity."

The rib cage seemed to be complete, although it had suffered many fractures. Most of the ribs had snapped, some at multiple points. It took an enormous amount of force to do this much damage, Gideon knew. The rib cage was the most flexible bony assemblage in the body (if it weren't, breathing would be a bit tricky). With much of it made of highly elastic cartilage, it gave before it bent, and it bent before it cracked, and it cracked before it snapped.

"The cliff he was found at the base of; how high was it?"

Sandoval shrugged. "Not so very high, perhaps fifteen meters."

Fifteen meters. Five stories, more or less. That was more than enough to do this kind of damage. Bustamente had probably been correct about his having fallen from the top, or at any rate from some considerable height. Either that, or, like the unlucky guy in the Saturday morning cartoons, he'd been walking under that upper-story window just when the safe fell out of it.

"He was found on his left side, I take it?" Gideon said.

The question startled the jittery, preoccupied Sandoval, made him jump. "Let me think . . . yes, on his left side. How did you know?"

"Well, because that side didn't get as mummified; it's more eaten away. That's because the bugs that do the work were more protected from the sun's dehydration."

"I see. Yes."

Gideon still hadn't moved. "What was he wearing, Chief?"

"Wearing?" Sandoval was impatient. It was help he wanted from Gideon, not more questions. "I don't know . . . *clothes*. . . . What difference does it make?"

"It'd be nice to see if there are any bullet holes in them, even blood, perhaps. The *policía ministerial* will want them too. Do you still have them?"

Sandoval's stricken look was answer enough. "Dr. Bustamente, he didn't say . . . so I just . . . I just . . . Really, there wasn't much left, only a few shreds. . . ."

"What was he wearing on his feet, do you remember?"

"On his feet? I don't know, sandals, like anybody else. It was warm."

"Are you sure? Not shoes? Boots, maybe?"

"No, I'm not sure," Sandoval said querulously. "What difference does that make? Who cares . . ." His brow furrowed, then smoothed. "Yeah, you're right. Boots—leather boots, up to his ankles. I helped Dr. Bustamente take them off. But how do you know *that*?"

"Same reasoning, nothing mysterious. The feet are almost completely skeletonized. See, the heavy leather acts as a kind of umbrella against the sun. The tissues stay moist, and the maggots and beetles can work away on them at leisure. Bodies that are heavily clothed don't mummify. On the other hand, of course, you're pretty unlikely to find heavily clothed bodies in environments that are conducive to mummification in the first place, so—"

But he had lost Sandoval, who was getting squirmier by the moment and making the kinds of faces that go along with a growing stomachache. Clearly the chief was anxious for him to stop talking and get on with it.

Taking pity on him, Gideon switched gears. His more general examination could wait till later. *"Bueno, vamos a ver sobre esa bala, sí?"* he said to make Sandoval a little more comfortable, and perhaps to show off his Spanish a little. *Well, let's see about that bullet, shall we?*

Apparently he got it right, because Sandoval responded with a vigorous nod. *"Sí, señor, por favor."*

"Bien, dónde está la cómoda?" he asked. *Okay, where's the chest?* He wanted to start by looking at the entry wound that the doctor had found.

"La cómoda?" Sandoval echoed blankly, obviously not comprehending. *"Dónde está la cómoda . . . ?"*

Gideon sighed. This was the kind of reaction he often

got when he showed off his Spanish a little too much. Or his German. Or French. Or Italian. As if they went out of their way not to understand their own language. He decided, as usual, that things would go better if he stuck with English. "His chest," he said, patting his own to clarify.

"Ah, his *chest*," said Sandoval. "Aha-ha, yes, sure, I see. Well, it's over there." He pointed to a sink along the back wall: cast iron, coated with white enamel, of about the same antique vintage as the embalming table. In it the thing lay, outer side up. Gideon had known what to expect, of course, and yet he was unexpectedly affected—embarrassed, really—to find himself looking down at something so . . . so personal, so intimate, so oddly *naked*; a chest, a human chest, lying there in the chipped, discolored, enamel bottom of an old sink, ten feet away from the body to which, in all decency, it still should have been attached. A pair of nipples, a few sparse, graying chest hairs, a navel, an old appendicitis scar—

He swallowed and made himself concentrate on the wound, a comma-shaped hole a couple of inches to the left of center, just below the left nipple. It was half an inch wide at its greatest width and surrounded by an irregular ring of dark, abraded flesh. The hole was big enough for him to insert his gloved pinky, but not big enough for his ring finger. Entry-wound sizes could be wildly variable, but this was about right for a .32-caliber slug, as Busta- mente had suggested, or perhaps a 9 mm one. Between the two of them, bullets of these sizes accounted for the majority of firearm homicides in the United States, and probably in Mexico as well.

And a bullet penetrating there—right *there*; he pressed a thumb to the same spot on his own chest to feel what lay beneath—would most likely enter the fifth intercostal space about an inch to the left of the edge of the sternum, possibly clipping one of the two bordering ribs, the fifth or the sixth. Whichever, it would then necessarily plow into either the left ventricle of the heart, or that part of the right ventricle that extended to the left of the sternum. Either way, it wouldn't have been good news for the heart. Or for Garcia. Death within a few seconds.

But there was something about the wound, about the ribs, something that had him wondering . . . wondering. . . .

"Let's go back to the table," he murmured, returning there with Sandoval trailing behind. A quick survey of the body's exterior confirmed Bustamente's observation that there was no exit wound in the back wall of the thorax or along the sides. As Bustamente had said, if a bullet had entered Garcia's body, it had never exited.

If.

Sandoval read something in Gideon's face: doubt, uncertainty . . . His own worried expression lightened a little. "What? What is it? Is there something—"

Gideon quieted him with a motion of his hand. "Give me just a second. I need to . . ."

The words trailed away as his attention focused hard on the shattered rib cage, in particular on the broken, splintery fifth and sixth ribs. Then he straightened up and returned to the sink, where, for a long few moments, he stood looking down at the dry, brown chunk of hide; at that comma-shaped hole.

Sandoval followed him. "What is it?" he pressed. "What have you found? What are you thinking?"

"What I'm thinking," Gideon said slowly, after a silence that practically had Sandoval ready to explode, "is that Dr. Bustamente may have been wrong."

Sandoval blinked. A tremor of hope ran over his face. "Wrong? You mean . . . he didn't get murdered?"

"No, I'm not ready to go that far yet, but you see, the thing is, bullets don't come out of the holes they go in by."

"But Dr. Bustamente, he said—"

"No, they just don't. They can't, not unless they haven't

quite penetrated the skin in the first place. But this hole goes clean through, you see?"

The reason they couldn't come out was that, while an entry wound itself might remain open, the track that a bullet made through the underlying soft tissue closed up after the slug's passage. Of course it was hypothetically possible, Gideon supposed, that in a case like this, where the internal organs had all pretty much disappeared so that the bullet might have been rattling around an empty torso, that it had found its way back out through the entry hole while the body was bouncing along on the burro. But he had never heard of such a thing happening, and the possibility seemed too remote to consider seriously.

Besides, he had a better hypothesis.

It was too much for Sandoval to handle. "So . . . so . . . what does it mean? Where is the bullet? If it entered through this hole here and there is no other hole by which it came out, and it did not come out through the same hole, then . . . then . . . ?"

"Then we need another explanation, and mine is that this isn't an entry wound at all; it's an exit wound."

"But the, the abrasion collar . . ." He pointed at the abraded area around the hole. "Dr Bustamente, he said an abrasion collar—"

"And he was right. An abrasion collar usually does denote an entry wound. The bullet's rotation—"

"Yes, yes, I know," Sandoval said, hurrying things along with a rapid, rotating motion of his hand. "Dr. Bustamente explained very thoroughly. *Very* thoroughly."

"Okay, good, but, you see, there *is* a situation in which an exit wound can show an abrasion ring very similar to the one around an entrance wound, and that's when the skin is pressed against something—a floor, a wall, the back of a chair, even clothing, something like a belt—when the bullet exits. The pressure keeps the wound from tearing wide open the way a typical exit wound would, and the abrasion comes, not from the bullet itself, but from the skin's being scraped raw by whatever it's impacting against."

"And that's what this is?"

"I think so." A *shored exit wound*, it was called, "shored" in the sense that whatever the skin is pressed against shores up and supports the edges of the opening.

"And if that's the case," he went on, "we have to ask—"

But Sandoval's despondency had gotten the better of him. "Entrance wound, exit wound, what difference does it make which way the bullet was going? Murdered is murdered." He made a hopeless, harassed gesture with both hands and Gideon suddenly realized whom he reminded him of. With his round but pointy-chinned, mobile face and gleaming, bulgy eyes, he was like a Mexican Peter Lorre; Peter Lorre in *Casablanca*, at his squirrelly, angst-ridden best.

"Oh, but it makes a big difference," Gideon said. "Just bear with me now, Chief. Think about it for a minute. If this is an exit wound, then where's the entrance wound?"

Sandoval frowned. "If . . . what?"

"There's no other hole of any size anywhere on the torso or abdomen. This is the only one. How can that be? Obviously, you can have an entrance wound with no exit wound, but how can there be an exit wound with no entrance wound?"

Sandoval jerked his head in frustration. "Please, *pro-fesor*, have mercy . . . can't you just . . . ?"

"Chief Sandoval," Gideon said quietly, glad to be able to tell the chief something he so desperately wanted to hear. "I don't think this is a bullet wound at all."

Once again, Sandoval's eyes lit up, but warily this time. He'd already had his hopes raised once, only to have them promptly dashed. "But what then would it be? You said yourself, there is no entrance wound. How can an object exit from a body if it has never entered it?"

"It can do it if it's been inside all along."

"If it's—" Sandoval did a classic double take. "If . . ."

"Come on," Gideon said, "I want to try something."

He bent to pick up the slab of all-too-human hide, hesitated as a brief shiver of distaste ran up his spine, then grasped it resolutely by its edges and returned with it to the embalming table, the utterly perplexed Sandoval tagging along a couple of feet behind him. Once there, Gideon held it to the front of the body in about its natural place, although the warping and twisting that went along with mummification made it impossible to do this precisely. Then, grasping the rear portion of the broken sixth rib with his other hand, he tugged it a quarter of an inch upward, which put its front end directly in line with the hole in the chest. A little gentle pressure on the chest, a slight rotation, and the rib's jagged, broken end pushed through the hole with a fit so tight, so near perfect, that when he let go of both chest and rib, they remained locked together, unmoving.

Sandoval stared, openmouthed. "A rib?" His plump face crinkled with happiness. He began to laugh. "A *rib* made this hole? His own rib? From inside?"

Gideon laughed along with him, pleased for Sandoval's sake. It had been the form of the wound that had gotten the gears of his mind going: somewhere between round and oval, but with a little tail hooking out of it. "Comma shaped" was the way he had described it to himself, and the term had rung a bell with him. "Comma shaped" was also the shorthand term he used in describing to his students the shape of the thoracic ribs in cross-section. *Comma-shaped hole, comma-shaped shaft of bone . . . Could it be . . . ?* he had wondered.

It could, and it was.

"He must have hit on his left side," he said now. "So that when the broken rib punched through, that side was flush up against a rock, or against the ground, which would have resulted in the abrasion ring."

"Then there is no reason to believe he was murdered?" Sandoval said joyously. He had the result he'd wanted but had hardly dared hope for. "A simple fall, no more!" Then, deciding the situation required more decorum, he gravely added: "A terrible, unfortunate, fatal fall, the poor man."

"Oh, it would have been fatal, all right, enough to kill him twice over." He had pulled the chest slab off the rib and laid it aside while they'd been talking, and was again peering into the chest cavity, with the body still on its side.

"What are you looking for now?" Sandoval asked a little nervously.

"Nothing in particular," Gideon said truthfully. "But I've hardly looked at him. As long as I'm here, I ought to see what else I might be able to come up with. You never know."

"Oh, I don't think there's anything else that's necessary, do you? Perhaps you would permit me to buy you a cup of coffee now? We have an excellent coffeehouse here, yes, right here in Teotitlán, the American tourists kept asking for it, you see, and now I myself have developed a taste for cappuccinos, ha-ha . . . ." On he nattered, arching his body backward, trying to manifest enough psychic force to draw Gideon away from the table. He didn't like the idea of Gideon continuing to poke around and coming up with God knows what.

Sandoval's psychic force had no effect on Gideon whatever. "Well . . ." He was probing gently with his fingers at the cervical vertebrae, or rather at the dried ligaments and intervertebral fibrocartilage that held them together. "Most of the time, people killed in falls—falls from heights—die because they fracture their spines up here in the neck, which tears apart their aortas, so I just wanted to see if . . . ah, indeed, that's what we have here. The first cervical vertebra—the atlas—has been completely separated from the second one, the axis. The ligaments and fibrocartilage are torn clear through. In the absence of anything else, that's a pretty good cause of death right there."

"So, that's that, then," Sandoval said joyously. "A job well done! *Muchísimas gracias, profesor,* I am so grateful—"

"Hold on, now," Gideon murmured, mostly to himself. "What have we here?"

Something had caught his eye, toward the back of the rib cage; he rubbed away a bit of dried, tarry black matter, impossible to identify (*crud* was the technical term usually employed), that was stuck to the interior surface of one of the ribs, and bent to take a closer look. "I'm afraid we might have something worth looking into after all," he said softly.

Sandoval's shoulders sagged. The faintest, saddest of sighs escaped his lips. He'd known it was too good to be true. "What?" he asked in a grim monotone, a voice of doom.

"Well, I'm not really sure," Gideon said. "It looks like . . . it almost looks like . . ."

What it almost looked like—what it very *much* looked like—was a bullet hole. In the ventral surface—the inside surface—of the seventh rib on the right side. Like many of the other ribs, this one had snapped about halfway back, the front piece still connected via the costal cartilages to the sternum, the rearward piece still attached by ligaments to the vertebral column. The hole was in the rearward segment, about three inches from the vertebral column, so that it faced diagonally forward. Much smaller than the wound in Garcia's chest, almost perfectly round even when seen from a few inches away, and penetrating only partway through the body of the rib, it might have served as a textbook illustration of the not-uncommon situation in which a bullet, having expended almost the last of its energy in getting most of the way through the body, had just enough oomph left to penetrate the surface of the rib but not enough to make it all the way through.

Now it was Gideon who was perplexed. If this was a bullet hole, then where was the original entrance wound? There was only one possibility: the chest wound that Gideon had so confidently, so magisterially, declared to be an exit wound and not even a ballistic exit wound at that. Could a bullet have entered there, under the left nipple, on a trajectory that took it diagonally through the thorax, transpiercing the left lung, the heart, and the right lung before plowing into the ventral surface of the seventh rib on the other side?

Short answer: yes, it could. Had he been wrong, then, about the broken rib breaking through the chest wall to leave the comma-shaped wound? Given the fit of rib to wound, that seemed virtually impossible. Well, highly— *extremely* highly—improbable. But if he was right about that, about there not being an entrance wound, then where had this bullet hole in the seventh rib come from? How had the bullet entered the body?

Again, *if.*

"It almost looks like what?" Sandoval pressed. "Tell me."

"Look, I may have already jumped the gun once today. If it's okay with you, let me look him over a little more thoroughly before I do it again."

What he wanted now was a good, clear look at that seventh rib, but the room was ill lit for a skeletal examination; windowless and with only a pair of discolored fluorescent tubes on the ceiling that threw a flat, undiscriminating light on the body. He needed a slanting light, something that would throw into sharp relief the bumps and crevices and indentations that were the essence of his work.

"Chief, could you possibly get me a flashlight of some kind?"

"But I want to know—"

"Please."

Sandoval, having little choice, gave up ungracefully. "They got some work lamps in the other room," he said grudgingly.

"No, I want something small, something I can move around inside the torso. The smaller the better. And if you can find a magnifying glass, that'd be helpful too."

"Okay, okay," he snapped. He turned on his heel, stomped into the equipment room next door, and returned in a few seconds. "Is this small enough?"

"Perfect," said Gideon. It was a tiny but piercingly bright single-cell Maglite flashlight, the kind that was made to carry on a key ring. "Couldn't have picked a better one myself." Sandoval had brought a magnifying glass as well, an old-fashioned round one with a metal frame and a wooden handle.

He flicked the light on, rotated the knurled head to focus the output into a narrow beam, picked up the magnifying glass, and went to work.

"Ah," he murmured. "Mm. Sonofagun."

"What? What is it?" pleaded Sandoval.

But Gideon in the midst of a skeletal examination was not easy to reach. "Oho," he said. "So." And looked up at the ceiling, cogitating.

At which point Chief Sandoval came to the end of his tether. "What is it?" he cried in a strangled voice. "What have you found? *Was he murdered or was he not?*"

"Let me just see if—"

"*Por favor, señor—sí o no?*"

Gideon sighed. From Sandoval's point of view, that was

of course the critical question. It was naturally enough a question that he got asked a lot by cops, and it was one that he couldn't, in all truth, answer definitively; then, or now, or ever. He was a physical anthropologist. What he knew was bones. Sure, he was often able to say with confidence that a skeletal wound was made (or wasn't made) by bullet, knife, or club, but the absence of such wounds on the skeleton was hardly evidence of *non*murder. The rib cage is made more of air than of bone. There is plenty of room between the ribs for blades or bullets to find their way to the vital organs.

On the other side of the coin, no skeletal wound that he *did* find was unconditional proof of murder. In themselves, broken bones don't kill people. Sure, a bullet-shattered skull was a pretty good clue that you had a homicide on your hands, but even then it wasn't the damage to the skull, but to the brain, that was the immediate cause of death—or, as forensic pathologists had it in one of their more charming locutions, was "incompatible with life." Broken bones, even if you break all two hundred and six of them, are not a good thing to have, but they are not "incompatible with life." Not strictly.

But there was no point in going into all this with Sandoval. He answered as truthfully and simply as he could: "I think so. Yes."

The air went out of Sandoval. "I see," he said wretchedly. Then, as an apathetic afterthought: "How then was he killed?"

"I need to do a little more work on the body," Gideon said instead of answering. "Do you think you could find me a screwdriver next door?"

Sandoval stared at him. "A *what*?"

"A . . ." Gideon groped for the Spanish word. *"Un . . . un desarmador,"* he said, amazing himself by plucking it out of whatever dim neural recess it had been hiding in, patiently waiting to be summoned, probably for the first time since he'd learned it decades ago. *A wonderful thing, the human mind.*

"*Un DESARMADOR?*" Sandoval bleated, no less bewildered.

After a couple of frustrated seconds, Gideon realized that this time it wasn't a question of Sandoval's not understanding, it was a question of not believing what he was hearing. *First a pair of shears, now a screwdriver; what next, a hammer and nails?*

Gideon couldn't help smiling. "Right, can you get me one? Not the flat-bladed kind, the Phillips head. *Feeyeeps*," he amended, giving the spelling his best Spanish pronunciation.

"*Feeyeeps,*" Sandoval echoed robotically. "*Sí. Un desarmador de cruz.*" He turned toward the door.

"And a piece of wood."

"And a piece of wood," Sandoval said, beyond astonishment now. "Sure. What kind of wood? How big?"

"It doesn't matter. Any old piece of scrap lumber. A board."

His actions, when Sandoval came back and handed the items to him, proved that Sandoval was not beyond astonishment after all. The screwdriver and the board, a foot-long piece of whatever the metric equivalent of a two-by-four was, were taken to the sink, where the board was placed on the sturdy counter beside the basin. Gideon picked up the screwdriver, raised it over his head, and drove it hard into the board. A second time. A third. Sandoval watched, openmouthed.

Gideon held the board up to examine it. "Mm," he said inscrutably. "Let's go back to the body now."

He stood gazing down once more at Manuel Garcia. He had already satisfied himself that there were no other visible perforations in the hide; just the wound in the chest. But the left arm, extending rigidly down and slightly forward along the left side, partially blocked his view of the axilla—the armpit—and the area just below it, and this was a region Gideon particularly wanted to see now. Placing one hand on Garcia's left shoulder joint to steady the body, he used the other to grasp the left arm just above the elbow and began to pull gingerly.

Nothing happened. Barely any give at all. Cowhide—stiffened cowhide—was in fact very much what the body felt like. He took his stance again, set his feet, grasped the arm more firmly—

Sandoval flinched and paled. "I think I need to go to the police station for a few minutes now," he murmured, hurrying the words. "There are things that must be attended to. Would that be all right?" He was already making for the door. "I'll only be a couple minutes," he yelled over his shoulder and was gone.

"Take your time," Gideon said, envying him. He wouldn't have minded leaving for this part too. The bones in mummified remains had been known to snap when you tried to move the limbs, and he was all set to flinch himself—he was already flinching mentally—if that were to happen. He took in a breath, held it, and pulled harder, steadily and slowly bearing down on the shoulder joint. Something—not bone, thank God—gave, and the arm moved an inch, two inches. Enough. It remained in the position to which he'd pulled it. The humerus hadn't broken or popped out of its socket.

He let out his breath, wiped off the sheen of sweat that had beaded on his forehead, and bent to see under the arm. The skin there had folded over itself in the process of loosening and mummifying, and it took him a good ten minutes to pry the fold apart with his fingers so that he could see what might be hidden within. He was just straightening up when he heard Sandoval's car pull up outside the building. The chief, who'd been gone about twenty minutes, came in, preceded by a wintergreen gust of Pepto-Bismol. He had brought two cardboard cups of still-steaming cappuccino, one of which he handed to Gideon, who gratefully gulped half of it down. *The Sacred Bean Café* was the logo on the side.

"Pretty good, huh?" Sandoval said with a reasonable semblance of cheer.

"It sure is. Thanks."

"See, didn't I tell you?" The break and the Pepto-Bismol had done him good. While hardly happy with the way things were going, he did seem reconciled to his fate.

For a while they stood beside the table, companionably drinking their coffees.

"So, *profesor*, he was murdered? That's it?"

Again, Gideon gave him the short answer. "I believe so. Someone did their best, that's for sure. But not with a gun."

"But how? If not by bullet, then by what? Show me."

Gideon guessed that there was little genuine interest behind the request, that Sandoval was merely playing the role that he thought was expected of him as police chief. But then Gideon wasn't a man who needed a lot of coaxing when it came to providing skeletal edification. To ask was to receive.

"Sure, I'll show you. Take a look at this." He grasped the rear segment of the seventh rib and pulled it slightly forward. "What do you see?"

Sandoval studied it. "A hole," he replied sensibly.

"But not all the way through."

"No, not all the way through."

"But *almost* through." Gideon turned on the Maglite and held it behind the rib. "See? Look *into* the hole. You can see that some light comes through."

"Ye-es," Sandoval said slowly, peering hard. Perhaps, thought Gideon, he really has gotten interested, or at any rate curious. "I can see a little point of light, where the bone is just barely broken all the way through."

"It's not just a pinpoint, Chief. Use the magnifying

glass." Gideon kept the flashlight steady behind the rib. "What's it shaped like?"

Sandoval peered through the glass. His eyes widened. "Ah, I see. It's . . . I don't know . . . it's like a, like a tiny star . . . no, like a little *equis*."

Equis. The Spanish word for the letter *X*.

"Yes, that's one way to describe it," Gideon said. "Or you could call it a cross?"

"I suppose so, yes."

"And when I asked you for a Phillips-head screwdriver a little while ago, you called it *un desarmador de . . .* ?"

"De cruz." Sandoval's eyes widened. He straightened up. "Cross! A cross-shaped screwdriver!" He bent to stare through the lens again. "Then a screwdriver made this hole?"

For an answer Gideon held up the board for him to see the indentations the screwdriver had made. Each thrust had left a neat little *X*-shaped dent in the wood, all identical to one another and almost exactly like the one in the rib. The conclusion was inescapable. Garcia had been stabbed, at least once, with a Phillips-head screwdriver, which had penetrated the front of the rib, its tip breaking through the back just enough to leave its *X*-shaped perforation. The initial *X*-shaped perforation in front had, of course, been obliterated by the round shaft as the thrust continued.

Sandoval straightened up, his forehead wrinkling. "Stabbed to death by a screwdriver . . ." He scowled. "But wait—there is no wound in the skin, no entrance wound. How can—?"

"Ah, but there is an entrance wound," Gideon said. "Three of them, in fact."

He showed Sandoval what he had found under the arm: a cluster of three tiny black holes in the armpit.

"They're so small," Sandoval said.

"They were small enough to start with, so they were able to contract and close up a little afterward," said Gideon. Whichever one made the hole in the rib would probably have gone through the lungs and the heart and thus killed him. Even if it hadn't, he could very well have bled to death.

Sandoval still looked puzzled. "But to be stabbed in the, the . . ." He sought the English word and failed. *"En el sobaco."* He indicated his own armpit. *"Three* times! Why would . . . how would . . ."

"It's not that uncommon," Gideon said. "Someone tries to stab you, you throw up your arm to protect yourself—" He demonstrated. "And, ouch, that's where you wind up getting it."

"I see. Yes, it's all very interesting." He thought for a moment. *"Profesor—"*

"Please, call me Gideon."

Sandoval responded with a cautious smile. "Flaviano." Self-consciously, very formally, they shook hands. "You know . . . Gideon . . . I must file a report on this. What you told me—the ribs, entry wounds, exit wounds—I don't know if I can explain—"

"Oh, don't worry about that. I'll write it all up for you to include with your report. It'll have to be in English, though. My Spanish isn't good enough for material like this."

"Thank you. When do you think you could do this?"

"I can do it right now, if you like."

"Ah, good. The *policía ministerial*, they won't be happy if I wait too long." He sighed softly.

Mention of the *policía ministerial* put an end to his relative good humor, which had been ebbing anyway over the last few minutes.

"Well, look at the bright side," Gideon said, taking a page from Julie's playbook.

"Yes? What is the bright side?"

"You have the satisfaction of knowing Dr. Busta-mente's findings are dead wrong."

That earned a twinkle of the eye and a furtive little grin. "Well," Sandoval said, cheered at least a little, "let's go back to the police station now. You can use the computer there. But first, lunch."

SEVEN

THERE were only two restaurants in the village, both on the main street, Avenida Juárez, and Sandoval took Gideon to the Restaurante el Descanso, the smaller and simpler of the two, a clean, plain place—in the United States, it might have been called a deli-bakery—where Sandoval had a hamburger and Gideon got a bowl of creamy Oaxacan-style gazpacho, made with eggs and sour cream, and garnished with jicama and cumin-coated tortilla chips. When asked, he said, truthfully enough, that it was delicious. Sandoval made a show of insisting on picking up the tab, but if any money changed hands, Gideon never saw it.

From there, they walked the two blocks to the Palacio del Gobierno, a stuccoed one-story building where police headquarters, consisting of two currently empty jail cells, a hallway with two desks jammed side-to-side against the wall, and the chief's "private" office (doorless), were housed. One of the hallway desks had a fairly new Dell computer on it, and Gideon was seated there to write up his report. A baby-faced police officer offered him a cup of coffee from the countertop coffeemaker, but Sandoval, standing behind him, made head-shaking, throat-cutting motions warning him otherwise, and he politely declined and got to work.

AN hour later, Gideon was done. Most of the time had been wasted in trying to put together something close to his usual forensic report, covering all the typical bases: age, sex, condition of the body, old broken leg, and so on, but all of this wound up being deleted. In the first place, he hadn't been asked to do, and hadn't done, anything approaching a thorough examination. In the second, the state police, the *policía ministerial*, were sure to pursue this more thoroughly on their own, with their own experts. Third, and most important, they hadn't asked for his help and weren't anticipating it. Gideon, sensitive from long experience to issues of turf, decided it would be less than tactful to unexpectedly dump a formal, jargon-loaded case report, written by a prying, meddlesome *Yanqui*, into their laps. Sandoval would surely take the heat for it, and Sandoval was worried enough already.

With reason, Gideon thought. From what he'd heard and read about them, the Oaxacan state police were, or were alleged to be, a belligerent, thuggish bunch with a reputation for being easy to irritate and quick to anger. In the end, he boiled it down to a single unvarnished paragraph with a minimum of inferences:

On December 14, 2008, I was requested by Flaviano Sandoval, chief of police, Teotitlán del Valle, to examine a mummified body found in the nearby countryside. This brief examination was made after an earlier partial autopsy by Dr. Ignacio Bustamente, *médico legista*,

Tlacolula District. It is my opinion that the deceased was stabbed at least three times with a Phillips-head screwdriver (*un desarmador de cruz*), the entry wounds clustered in the left axilla. One of these thrusts left a diagnostic, X-shaped perforation in the vertebral portion of the left seventh rib. The deceased also suffered massive trauma to the thorax in the form of severe compression of the rib cage, resulting in numerous injuries, one of which was a compound fracture that punctured the chest wall below and medial to the left nipple.

> Respectfully submitted,
> Gideon Oliver, Professor
> Department of Anthropology
> University of Washington

If I can be of further assistance, please feel free to contact me through Chief Sandoval. I will be staying at Teotitlán for the next several days.

He leaned back in his chair, read it over, considered deleting those last two sentences—if they wanted his help they could find him, so why push it?—but finally decided to let them stand, and hit the print button.

ANNIE threw back her head and laughed. "You asked him where the guy's *cómoda* was and he didn't know what you were talking about?"

"That's right," a still-puzzled Gideon said. "Doesn't it mean 'chest'?"

"Yeah, it means "chest"—only like in 'chest of drawers.' You know, *cómoda* . . . commode?"

"Is that right?" Gideon said, also laughing. "So what's my kind of chest? I mean—"

"*Pecho*," Carl supplied with a smile.

"Ah, *pecho*," said Gideon with his usual ineffective snap of the fingers. "Of course. Like 'pectoral.'"

With Julie, they were having predinner drinks in the dining room, at the table in the rear that was kept for the Gallagher clan, separated from the others by a waist-level bookcase. It was a beautiful late afternoon and Gideon had initially wanted to have drinks out on the terrace, but two of the four close-together terrace tables were occupied by the feminist professors' group, which was in the midst of extremely heated discourse, from which Gideon thought it wise to keep a safe distance. He was brave about many things, but he was not brave about this, and he had thought it was a good idea to take the prudent course and go inside. Carl had seconded the motion after hearing some of what they were saying. "Sounds like fightin' words to me," he'd said.

Over tongue-stinging but wonderfully refreshing *micheladas*—bottles of Tecate beer spiced with lime and chile sauce—Gideon had been telling them about the day's events and they had been listening with interest.

Annie had just begun to ask a question when her telephone played the opening bars of "*La Cucaracha*." She took it from her bag, flipped it open. "Hello?" She broke into a smile. "Are you, really? . . . Both of you? . . . Well, that's great, everybody'll be pleased. . . . Yes, they got here yesterday . . . No, I won't be here, but I should be back in a few days. . . . Sure, you too." She flipped the phone closed.

"Guess what? Tony's driving down early. He'll be here tomorrow."

"Hallelujah," said Carl with absolutely no expression. *Not exactly a shout of joy,* Gideon thought. *Wonder what that's about.*

Julie was considerably more animated. "Really?" she said, grinning. "Oh, it'll be great to see him. I was afraid we might miss him."

"And I have better news for you than that," Annie told her. "Jamie's coming down with him. The knee's doing better than expected, so he's flying down to Mexico City in the morning and he'll drive down with Tony. He's raring to get back to work."

At this news Julie really lit up. "Jamie'll be here tomorrow? I can leave the bookkeeping to him? I don't have to do that horrible stack of accounts payable, and bank reconciliations, and God knows what else? I've been scared to death to touch them, I don't know anything about QuickBooks or—"

"Fear no longer," said Annie. "You're off the hook. Leave all that stuff for the man. Jamie thrives on it. Hey, look who's here. Greetings, *jefe*."

Chief Sandoval, who had just entered, was approaching them somewhat tentatively. After a round of greetings and an introduction to Julie, he stood there looking undecided.

"Have a seat," Carl said, pulling out a chair for him. "Gideon was just telling us about your mummy."

Sandoval remained standing, shifting nervously from one foot to the other. "Well, that's what I came about. I e-mailed my report—also your report, Gideon—to the police in Oaxaca, and they want me to come in to speak with them." A despairing sigh. "I have to go tomorrow morning to the offices of the—I don't know how to say it in English—the *Procuraduría de Justicia*—"

"It's like the state attorney general," Annie contributed, and to Gideon: "The police here report to them."

"Yes, attorney general," said Sandoval. "I am to meet with Sergeant Nava. I remember him from before, from the little girl. Not such an easy man to get along with." He turned a pleading, apologetic look on Gideon. "I was wondering if . . . I was wondering . . ." He paused encouragingly, as if wanting Gideon to finish the sentence for him. "Wondering if . . ."

"Yes?" Gideon was at a total loss. "Wondering if?"

"Wondering if . . ."

"Oh, for God's sake," Annie burst out, "he's wondering if you would go with him."

"To talk to the police?"

"Yes." Sandoval launched into an excited flood of words: "I'm afraid if he asks me things, how will I answer? I know about traffic accidents, about people who drink too much mezcal and get in fights. What do I know of bones, of wounds? What if they want to know more? What if they want to know how—"

"Sure," Gideon said, "I'll go with you."

"*Thank* you!" Sandoval, practically going limp with relief, sagged into the chair that Carl had pulled out for him.

"Have yourself a *michelada*, Chief," Annie said. "You look like you could use one. Stay for dinner, why don't you?"

"But already I come here three times this week. I don't like—"

"Oh, break a rule for once, it'll do you good. Come on, we'd like to have you."

Sandoval grinned and relaxed a little more. "Well, okay, maybe this one time." After a swallow, he looked curiously at Julie and wagged his finger at her. "Hey, wait a minute, I know you. Didn't I used to see you . . ."

Julie smiled. "You have a good memory, Chief. You used to see me right here. I was Julie Tendler then, Carl's niece, just a teenager helping out for the summer."

"Oh, yeah, I remember." He smiled fondly at her. "And I was Memo Sandoval, Dorotea's dumb big brother, still thinking I had to be a weaver, only I stunk at it."

"Well, I'm sure you're a good police chief."

"From what I've seen, he is," said Gideon gallantly.

Sandoval responded with a modest shrug and changed the subject. On his way in, he had passed the women's group on the terrace. "You know, maybe it would be better for me to join your guests outside?"

"Well, now, I don't know that I'd—" began Carl.

But Sandoval was already heading for the terrace. "Tonio, he likes that I do this. The ladies especially, always they are impressed to know the chief of police. To meet me," he said complacently, "makes them feel protected. I answer the questions."

"You wouldn't think so to look at him," Annie said, watching him go, "but our timid little chief has quite an eye for the ladies. He does seem to get along with them too."

"I don't know about these particular ladies, though," Julie said, seeing the women turn as one toward the lone, innocently approaching male. "Hm, I wonder why the phrase 'lamb to the lions' leaps to mind."

Gideon concurred. "They'll eat him alive."

Twenty minutes later, as they were starting on their dinners, the chief was back, shell-shocked and staring.

"Madre de Dios," he mumbled as he sat down with his tray. "Those ladies."

Mercifully, the others refrained from pursuing the subject.

EIGHT

THE offices of the *Procuraduría General de Justicia* were located well south of downtown Oaxaca, out near the airport, in a once-palatial nineteenth-century building that had gone sadly to seed. There were still touches of elegance to be seen on the outside—ornate grillwork on the upper-story windows, the remnants of fine stuccowork here and there, panels of veined marble, a pair of fountains flanking the grand stone entrance stairway, a row of elaborately wrought metal benches—but all was run-down and tatty. The stucco was flaking, the rusted fountains no longer flowed, and the benches had been painted so many times, and were so in need of yet another coat, that they were a mottled black and white, impossible to tell whether the black had chipped away to reveal the white or vice-versa. In some places—the arms, or the ornamental rosette that topped their backs, the successive layers of paint were worn all the way down to bare, gray metal. On one rosette Gideon was able to make out a single brave word in bold relief: *Libertad.*

The building itself, coated in two equally repellent shades of green, was also seriously in need of a new paint job (in different colors, one would hope). Only the neat line of flowering shrubs along the foundation showed signs of loving, or at least painstaking, care.

All this Gideon had to take in on the fly as he and the heavily perspiring Sandoval walked rapidly—trotted, in the smaller Sandoval's case—over the brick-paved front plaza and up the two flights of wide, curving stone steps to the entrance. From Sandoval's point of view, the day had gotten off to a disastrous start. He had allowed what he thought was more than ample time for the drive from Teotitlán, but he'd taken a wrong turn somewhere and had had a terrible time finding the place. Thus, instead of being fifteen minutes early for his two o'clock appointment, they were ten minutes late. They would have been only five minutes late had matters not been made worse when, having no convincing credentials to produce, he had been denied entrance to the official-business parking lot and had had to park on a side street two blocks away. As a result, Chief Sandoval, who had been a nervous wreck to begin with, was practically a moving puddle by the time they got there.

Once through the entrance they found themselves in a plain lobby that smelled of disinfectant, unadorned except for much-thumbed sheaves of official-looking documents hanging on cords from the walls. People moved in and out of corridors radiating from the lobby, the bureaucrats and civil servants (confident, decisive, focused) easily distinguishable from the ordinary citizens (apprehensive, uncertain, demoralized).

On one wall was a building directory, from which Gideon read aloud: "*'Director de la Policía Ministerial, planta sótano.'* Basement."

"Dungeon," Sandoval amended in a strained voice.

At the bottom of the stairwell they were blocked by a hulking giant with an imposing black mustache. He was at least a couple of inches taller than Gideon's six-two, and a whole lot wider, dressed in black military fatigues and combat boots, with the blunt, squarish black handle of what appeared to be a 9-mm Beretta sticking out of his belt.

He looked them offensively up and down. "You're in the wrong place," he said dismissively in Spanish. "This is police headquarters." With a jerk of his chin he gestured for them to get the hell back upstairs.

Sandoval instantly began babbling away with a stammering, apologetic explanation for their presence that got nowhere until Gideon interrupted.

"We have an appointment with Sergeant Nava," he said in Spanish.

Until now, the cop had fixed his attention mostly on Sandoval. Now he turned it on Gideon and came a step closer; two steps. Whatever he'd had for breakfast, it had been heavily doused with cumin and garlic. "You're not Mexican."

"No. American."

"American." Disdainful, skeptical. "What's your business here in Oaxaca?"

Gideon was quickly learning why the Oaxaca police, and to a lesser extent the police of Mexico, had the reputation they did. And it wasn't simply the man's size and attitude that intimidated, it was that gun stuffed so thuggishly into his belt. Was that meant to *be* intimidating (which it was)? What, could they not afford holsters?

"I've already told you why we're here," he said sharply, answering discourtesy with discourtesy. "Now where can we find Sergeant Nava, please?"

The cop narrowed his eyes, glared at him and opened his mouth to speak, at which point Sandoval started in again, grinning and wheedling and talking twice as fast as before. "Officer . . . sir . . . I'm the, the chief of police, you see—from, from Teotitlán del Valle? I have . . . there was . . . Sergeant Nava, he said to . . . he knows me, he told me—"

He was cut off by a weary bellow from down the hall. "Donardo, for Christ's sake, will you put an end to that goddamn racket and bring them back here?" Gideon's Spanish wasn't up to getting every word, but following the gist was easy enough.

"Yes, Sergeant," Donardo muttered with a roll of his eyes. Giving them a silent look that made it clear they had made no friend of him and would be wise not to cross his path again, he turned and led them down a linoleum-floored corridor bordered by a string of ramshackle office cubicles constructed from shoulder-high, building-grade plywood partitions that had been nailed together and covered over in watered-down white paint, the many knot-holes, patches, and joints still plainly visible.

Sergeant Nava's cubicle was no different from the ones they had glimpsed on their way: a cramped enclosure with an old metal desk and chair, a computer, a file cabinet, two unmatched metal chairs for visitors, and papers and files scattered over every available surface. There was nothing in it that wasn't utilitarian in the extreme; not a photograph, not a coffee cup, not an ashtray. The sergeant himself was cut in the Donardo mode, thickly built, blackly mustached, wearing black fatigues with the gun tucked into his belt. He was, however, marginally more polite than his subordinate—not polite enough to smile or say hello or get out of his chair, but enough to indicate with a wave of his fingers that they should take chairs as well, into which they squeezed, Gideon with some difficulty. With the back of the chair shoved right up against the wall to make some space, his knees were still pressed against the desk.

Wordlessly, Nava watched them sandwich themselves in. Then, with a tired sigh, he leaned back—he had more room than they did—and addressed Sandoval.

"So. You again. This time a mummy."

Sandoval giggled. "Yes, Sergeant, I'm afraid it's me again. I'm sorry to bother you with this, but I knew that the proper action, in a matter such as this, was to inform you at once, so after Dr. Bustamente kindly—"

"This happy little village of yours—it's getting to be quite a dangerous place, isn't it? As bad as Mexico City."

"Well, this didn't happen *in* the village, Sergeant. Neither did the other one, the little girl. They were both found—"

Nava silenced him with a brusque motion of his hand. "All right, just tell me about it. And speak more slowly, for God's sake. I already have a headache." He jerked up the cuff of his shirt, grasped the face of his watch between thumb and forefinger, and studied it, sending a clear message: *I am a busy man. My time is extremely valuable. I will allot a little of it to you, but be quick about it.*

Still, he listened to what Sandoval had to say, or at least he allowed Sandoval to talk without interrupting him, other than the occasional finger-waving "Yes, yes," to hurry him along—for almost five minutes. But he made it no secret that his mind was elsewhere. He asked no questions and jotted down only a couple of brief notes. Obviously, he wasn't much interested in the case, for which Gideon couldn't blame him: a drifter, his body subjected to the depredations of the desert for half a year before anybody found it, with no apparent clues as to who had killed him or why—there wasn't much the *policía* were going to be able to do about it, or, frankly, much impetus for them to try. Nava was doing pretty much what an American police sergeant would do in his place: going through the motions for the record. But most American sergeants, or so Gideon hoped, would have done it a little more courteously.

Sandoval too was quick to spot the lack of interest, and it cheered him up perceptibly. His thoughts flowed across his mobile face as clearly as if he'd spoken them: maybe this wasn't going to be as bad as he'd feared, maybe they'd just tell him to go ahead and bury the body and they'd get around to it when they could sometime, maybe—

Nava had been thumbing abstractedly through the thin folder that Sandoval had supplied, and his first question, interrupting Sandoval in mid-sentence, was directed at Gideon. He held up the report on Garcia's body.

"You're Professor Oliver? You wrote this?"

"Yes."

"It's in English."

"Yes."

"But obviously you speak Spanish."

"Speak, yes—a little. But I don't write it well enough for a police report. I assumed you'd have somebody here who could translate. I'll be glad to help."

"Mm." Nava's lips, barely visible under his mustache, were pursed. Sandoval held his tongue, only too happy to have the sergeant's attention directed at Gideon and not at him. However, when Nava spoke again it was to Sandoval. With a jerk of his head at Gideon, he said, "If you think we are paying for his report, you're mistaken. It was authorized without my permission. God knows we spent enough on your last case. Unless you have a budget for it, he will have to go without his fee."

"There's no charge for my services," Gideon said, more curtly than he'd intended, but the continuing rudeness from Nava and from the guard had riled him. In most matters he didn't have a particularly short fuse, but some things could quickly get under his skin, and gratuitous rudeness from people in positions of power was one of them. Especially when they were gun-toting guys with necks that were thicker than their heads. Bullying was what it was, plain and simple. Still, he understood all too well that he was in a culture not his own, with mores he wasn't accustomed to. His readiness to take offense at this sort of treatment in similar situations had gotten him into difficulties more than once before. He resolved to do better at holding his temper, if for no other reason than to keep from getting Sandoval into trouble.

Fortunately, Nava hadn't even noticed his sharpness. He was thinking, his fingers drumming on the desk. He lifted his head and called: "Cruz! Who knows English around here?"

The reply came over the partition from the next cubicle. "The colonel speaks very good English, Sergeant."

"Maybe, but I'm not bothering him with this. The less he knows about what's going on, the happier I am. Is there no one else?"

A moment of thoughtful silence. "I'm pretty sure his adjutant knows some too. Corporal Vela."

"That will be better. All right, I have something for you to take to him for translation."

"Now?"

"No, next month. Of course, now."

Another mustached, slab-like face loomed up over the shoulder-high partition, although on Cruz it came only up to the middle of his chest. *Where do they get these monsters?* the physical anthropologist in Gideon wondered. In Mexico, especially this far south, you wouldn't expect to run into too many men over five-seven or five-eight. But he'd yet to see a member of the *policía ministerial* who wasn't a good six-two, and built like a UPS truck to boot.

With the cubicles as compact as they were, Cruz didn't have to come around for the report, simply reaching a brawny, black-clad arm down for it.

"Now make sure you ask the colonel first if it's all right with him if we borrow Vela for a few minutes," Sandoval cautioned, handing it up to him. "We don't want to get into trouble with him." Gideon thought he saw Nava's right hand make an incipient sign of the cross, a warding off of calamity. "You know what he can be like."

"I know, I know."

Nava began to wrap up their interview, but Cruz was back before a minute had gone by. "The colonel wants to see him," he told Nava.

"He *does*?"

Sandoval paled. "Mother of God," he said in English, "I don't want to see no colonel." He looked futilely around him for help.

"Not you. Him." Cruz pointed at Gideon. Sandoval closed his eyes and sagged with relief.

"*Him?*" Nava was puzzled. He looked at Gideon, looked at Sandoval, and looked again at the folder, reassessing. Was there more to this than he'd realized, some import he hadn't grasped, something on which he'd better make sure he was up to snuff?

"All right, Cruz, if the professor wouldn't mind . . ." An inquiring pause, a newly polite manner, to which Gideon responded with a nod to show that no, he didn't mind. ". . . take him there, please." Then he turned to Sandoval with freshened interest and a deferential gesture. "Perhaps, Chief Sandoval, if you would be kind enough to go over this in a little more detail. . . ."

Trailing behind Cruz, Gideon, wondering himself why a colonel—a very high level in the Mexican police system—would take an interest in something like this, walked down the corridor past another half dozen cubicles, where the hallway widened out to create a sort of anteroom in front of a wooden door, a real door that opened and closed, the first he'd seen here. Beside it was a desk at which yet another six-foot-plus cop in black sat at a computer. Corporal Vela, Gideon assumed, and was proved correct when he picked up a telephone, hit a button, and said: "He's here, Colonel. Yes, sir."

He got up, went to the door, opened it, and politely motioned for Gideon to enter. "Please," he said in English.

Gideon sucked in a breath, stood up straight, promised himself not to lose his temper, and walked into a room that was like the important offices in the building must have been in the glory days before the place was chopped up into cubicles: a shining slate floor (instead of tired old linoleum); a high plaster ceiling (instead of a low-hung one of acoustic tiles) edged with ornate floral cornices; tall, mullioned, Gothic-arched windows on two sides; heavy, black, old furniture in a sort of Hispanic-Victorian style, oiled and gleaming. All very imposing and forbidding, as if designed to make a petitioner or a miscreant feel inconsequential, vulnerable, and small. Add a few age-darkened fifteenth-century Spanish paintings of crucifixions and martyrdoms, Gideon thought, and it would have made a fine office for a deputy grand inquisitor. There were age-darkened paintings on the walls, all right, but they were portraits of high-collared nineteenth-century officials and bureaucrats.

In the exact center of this room, under a rudely hammered iron chandelier that had once held oil lamps but now had electric bulbs in ornamental hurricane-lantern fittings, was a massive, carved desk. At it was the fear-inspiring colonel himself, under the circumstances an astonishing sight. Dwarfed by the huge desk and his thronelike carved chair, looking directly at Gideon, he hardly seemed to be a member of the same species as the gorillas Gideon had been running into until now; closer to a marmoset, and a good-humored, wise old marmoset at that. Nor was he swathed in grim matte black either, but wearing a Yucatecan *guayabera*, the embroidered, open-throated, and distinctly informal white shirt worn outside the trousers. On his lined, clean-shaven, mahogany-skinned, twinkly-eyed face was a perfectly delighted grin.

"Hello, my friend," he said in elegantly accented English. "How are you? And how is your beautiful wife, the charming and gifted Julie?"

Astounded, even speechless for a couple of seconds, Gideon stared at him. ". . . I don't believe it. . . . *Javier*?"

"None other," said Colonel Javier Marmolejo, coming out from around the desk (and not coming up much higher than he'd been when sitting in the big chair). They shook hands warmly and even tried a brief, gingerly *abrazo*, although their size difference made it awkward, and neither of them went in much for such things in any case.

They stepped apart to look each other over. "Well, you've gotten a little older, Gideon. Is that a bit of gray I see in your hair?"

"Yes, a little," Gideon said. "I have to say, you sure look exactly the same." This was a bit of a lie. Seen close up, Marmolejo had grown even more wizened than he'd been before; he was beginning to look less like a monkey than the mummy of a monkey. But there was no mistaking the wit and intelligence that still flashed in his eyes. "Except where's the ever-present cigar?" Gideon asked. "I don't think I've ever seen you without one before."

"Oh, I've given up cigar smoking. At my age, one has to care for one's health."

Gideon couldn't help laughing. "You mean cigar holding," he said. The Marmolejo he remembered had always had a cigar around, all right, but it was strictly a prop cigar. Gideon couldn't remember ever seeing him light it.

Happily chuckling, Marmolejo took him by the arm to a grouping of handsome leather armchairs and a low table in a corner of the room near the windows. "My old friend, I was amazed—thrilled, as you can imagine, but amazed—to see your name on the report. What in the world brings you to Oaxaca?"

"I'm here on vacation, Javier. Julie is filling in for her cousin at a resort in Teotitlán, and I'm along for the ride. But I still don't—"

Marmolejo laughed and held up Gideon's report. "And this is how you spend your vacation? Performing forensic analyses on corpses? Well, I can't say I'm surprised."

"Well . . . this just came along. I mean, I just happened to be . . . Hey, never mind about me. What are *you* doing here? The last time I saw you . . ."

The last time he'd seen him had been in Mérida, on the Yucatán Peninsula, where he had been an inspector in the Yucatecan State Judicial Police. Gideon had met a lot of interesting and unusual policemen in his life, but Javier Alfonso Marmolejo took the cake, a real one of a kind. Half Mayan Indian, born in his Mayan mother's village of Tzakol, a huddle of dilapidated shacks near the Quintana Roo border (Gideon had been there once; what he chiefly remembered were the pigs sunning themselves in the middle of the single, muddy street), Marmolejo had not learned Spanish until he was seven, when his father moved the family to Mérida. At ten, he was one of the army of rascally, going-nowhere kids selling takeaway snacks of sliced coconuts and grapefruit and orange slices from homemade carts around the main market square. Against all odds, he had gotten himself through school and saved enough to buy his way into the then graft-riddled Yucatecan police department. A drastic cleanup a few years later had resulted in throwing out half the police force, but Marmolejo's integrity and abilities had been recognized and he'd been kept on. A few years later he'd graduated from the national police academy in Mexico City—one of the few provincial cops to do so, and probably the first Mayan Indian—and, in his forties, had gone on to a master's degree in public administration from the

Universidad Autónoma de Yucatán. He'd studied English and German, he'd become an educated man, and now, in his mid-fifties, here he was a full-fledged—

". . . full-fledged colonel!" Gideon said. "In Oaxaca, five hundred miles from Mérida. How did that happen?"

"A thousand, actually," Marmolejo said. "And although I am indeed a full-fledged colonel, as you are generous enough to point out, I am not a colonel in the Oaxacan police force but in the PFP, the Federal Preventive Police, to which I applied three years ago and to which I was subsequently admitted. My assignment to Oaxaca is a temporary one." He eyed Gideon, his head cocked. "Why are you smiling?"

Gideon was smiling because he was remembering a comment a mutual friend had once made about the striking incongruity between Marmolejo's furtive, cunning appearance and his often elegant English: "You look at the man and you expect 'I don' got to show you no steenkin' bedge.' Instead, you get Ricardo Montalban." And he was smiling because he was still thinking about the absent cigar, remembering Marmolejo's uncanny ability to have an unlighted one wedged in his mouth on and off throughout the day without making a gummy, oozy mess out of it. Unlike most unlit-cigar fanciers, he didn't chew on the things any more than he actually smoked them. There had been a running joke about it in Yucatán: *Do you think he really has more than one cigar, or is that the same one he brings with him every day?*

"I'm smiling because I'm just so damn glad to see you again," Gideon said, which was also true enough on its own. "But go ahead. If you're with the *federales*, what are you doing behind a desk in Oaxaca?"

His responsibilities with the PFP, Marmolejo explained, involved straightening out local police forces with less than stellar reputations, an assemblage in which the Oaxacan *policía ministerial* was—or at any rate, had been—a prime member. The initial impetus for sending him here had come in 2006, when federal police more or less had to take over the city during a string of violent anti-police protests with which the local police couldn't cope. In the aftermath, the feds had concluded that a general housecleaning was in order and Marmolejo had been one of three experienced federal cops temporarily assigned to high-level line positions in Oaxaca. He functioned as the titular head of homicide investigations, but his primary responsibility was to mount a thorough review of past cases. The Oaxaca police, beset by graft, negligence, and plain old bungling, had a sorry history of dubious case closures and unresolved investigations, and it was Marmolejo's job to dig out the worst of them and rectify what could be rectified. Not only could he reopen old investigations; he'd been given full authority to demote, indict, or summarily boot out dishonest, obstructive, and incompetent cops. He had in fact, done exactly that with his predecessor in this fine office, the notorious, corrupt, and roundly hated Colonel Salvador Archuleta, at that time the second most powerful cop in Oaxaca.

No wonder Sergeant Nava wanted to keep on his good side.

"Interestingly enough," Marmolejo told him, "one of these 'cold cases,' as you call them, and a relatively recent one at that, involves this same village of Teotitlán and this same Chief Sandoval of yours. I was looking at it only this morning."

"Yes, he was telling me about it." Gideon hesitated. "I can't say he was too happy with the way the police ran things then. He's petrified at the idea of going through it again."

Marmolejo nodded. "I've been going over it, and I can't say that I'm too happy with it either. And as you might guess, it is a case that disturbs me deeply."

"It does? Why?"

Marmolejo scowled. The question surprised him. "Why? A young girl, an innocent barely into her teenage years, murdered after God knows what was done to her, her body callously thrown down a mine shaft and left for the worms? An investigation ended after a single month, with the child never identified, with no one charged, no credible suspects named? How can I not be disturbed?"

"I see. I didn't know she was so young."

"Yes, only thirteen or fourteen. Or so the forensic report concluded. The remains had been there for some time, you see. They were skeletonized."

"It was a skeleton?" Again Gideon hesitated, not wanting to give offense. But being Gideon, he was interested. "Um, are you sure it was a girl? I mean, when you're dealing with someone as young as that, determining sex from the skeleton can be tricky."

"Can it?" Marmolejo asked. "I didn't realize."

"More than tricky, really. You see, if the secondary sexual characteristics—the ones on the outside—haven't fully developed yet, the skeletal indicators aren't all that reliable either. In fact, until you get to eighteen or so, you're on pretty thin ice when it comes to sex. I mean, a competent anthropologist might be maybe sixty or seventy percent confident, but that's not good enough to be much use in an investigation, and it's sure not good enough to go into court with."

"You don't think so? If all my leads had a sixty or seventy percent chance of proving accurate, I would be a happy man. And a far more successful policeman."

"Not when it comes to sexing a skeleton. Look at it this way. Sixty percent right means forty percent wrong. But there are only two sexes to begin with, so you can do damn near as well flipping a coin, and it's a whole lot less work."

"Yes, I see your point." Marmolejo considered. "This interests me. Would you be interested in seeing the report for yourself?"

"If you think I might be able to help, sure." Or even if not.

"Good." Marmolejo went to the door. "Alejandro, can you put aside what you're doing and translate something for Professor Oliver, please? The forensic report on the unidentified child from Teotitlán del Valle. And bring me the entire file."

As he returned, Gideon was struck all over again by what a truly tiny man Marmolejo was. Standing no more than five-two in his ridiculously small, well-cared-for oxfords, and dressed in *guayabera* and neatly pressed, light blue trousers, he seemed as improbable a cop as Sandoval. But Gideon knew better. Marmolejo was quick-witted, astute, and thorough, with an enviable intuitive-ness, a kind of outside-the-box sixth sense that Gideon liked to think had something to do with the mystical teachings of his Mayan heritage—or rather that he would have thought, had he not been the thoroughgoing rational empiricist that of course he was.

"The new case you've brought is interesting too," Marmolejo said, sitting down. His toes—but not his heels—touched the floor. "A Phillips-head screwdriver? An unusual weapon, wouldn't you say?"

"First time I've ever run into it myself. But there was a report on something similar in one of the journals not long ago. Otherwise, I'm not sure I would have realized what I was looking at."

"And what do you surmise from it?"

"From the fact that it was a Phillips-head screwdriver? Nothing. Well, no, not quite nothing. I think we can assume that it was unpremeditated, a crime of passion, a spur-of-the-moment thing."

"On the grounds that a killer planning murder would hardly bring along a screwdriver as his weapon of choice?"

"Right. Listen, Javier, do you think there might be a

connection between the two killings? I mean, two dead bodies found in the space of a year near a town that hadn't had a murder in fifty years . . ."

"Oh, no, I shouldn't think so. I understand the man, Garcia, was killed only six months ago. The little girl was found a year ago, and it was estimated that her body had been there for five years."

"Ah, I didn't know that either."

Corporal Vela returned with the translated report and handed it to Gideon. "I'm sorry, this was not easy for me. English to Spanish, I can do this. Spanish to English— not so good. Also, there was some words, scientific words I did not know to translate. I leave them in Spanish."

"I'm sure it'll be okay; a lot better than I could do," Gideon said. It was the syntax of the original, not the technical vocabulary, that would have been likely to give Vela trouble. Scientific terms, inasmuch as they were mostly Latin or derived from Latin, were pretty interchangeable from language to language. While Marmolejo began to go through the case file, he settled back to read. There was only three-quarters of a page, not much more than he had written on Garcia.

Examination of skeleton remains, Case Number 08-Teo dVl, conducted 23 May 2008, by Dr. Gerardo Puente Orihuela, forensic physician, Oaxaca ministerial police. These remains was previously examined by Dr. Bustamente, médico legista, Tlacolula District. Remains are very partial and was too much chewing by animales.

Bones Present:
The cráneo and the mandíbula, the right clavícula, the right pelvis bone, the left leg bones, numerous bones of the hands or feet, and some tooths.

Time Since the Death:
I estimate that these bones are since five years exposed.

Condiciones patológicas:
None

Trauma:
The cráneo is muchly broken into pieces. Frontal bone, zigomático, maxilar bone all are broke. My conclusion is these breakings are from the fuerza despuntada at the time of the death and that they directly caused or contributed to the death.

Gideon looked up. "*Fuerza despuntada*—that would be 'blunt force'?"

"Blunt force," Marmolejo agreed.

Gideon nodded. It was impossible to say without more detail, or without having seen the bones for himself, whether or not the doctor's conclusion was accurate. Conceivably, the damage could have occurred through some kind of accident after death, or could have been due to carnivore foraging. But on the face of it, perimortem blunt force trauma as the cause of death—murder, in other words—certainly seemed like a good bet when you took the context (a body presumably flung down a mine shaft) into consideration. So far, he had no dispute with Dr. Orihuela.

Years:
Was determined from the status of epífisis closings as well as erupción of the tooths. The second muelas was present, but not the third, indicating the age of more than twelve years.

"*Muelas?*" Gideon asked. "Molars?"

"Molar teeth, yes," said Marmolejo.

"Mm." Gideon went back to reading.

Certain epífisis of the bones has begun to connect but not yet completed. Other ones are completed. This condition

indicates the presence of more than twelve years but not
so many as sixteen years. Therefore, I estimate this individual person had thirteen to fifteen years.

Thirteen to fifteen seemed perhaps a little overly
specific coming from someone not trained in physical
anthropology, but it was also evident that the doctor had
some grounding in developmental osteology and dentition, so one could probably assume that he was at least
roughly in the ballpark. But the next entry, the last, gave
him pause.

Género:
The skeleton is a female. This is showed from the shape
of the pelvis and certain other factors.

"Now there I do have a problem," he said aloud.
"Sex."

"Indeed, a problem for us all," Marmolejo murmured
without looking up.

"Sex determination," Gideon amended with a smile.

Now Marmolejo looked up, frowning. "A mistake? It's
not a female?"

Gideon was pleased at the colonel's ready acceptance
of his judgment; back in Yucatán, it had taken a while
to win him over. All the same, a little backing off was
required. "No, I wouldn't go that far. It's just that Dr.
Orihuela didn't give any details. 'Shape of the pelvis and
certain other factors'—well yeah, sure, the pelvis would
be your best bet, but it's full of shapes; there are all kinds
of curves and angles and measurements. Some are reliable, others aren't. Which did he mean? Did he use more
than one? In any case, whatever he did use, it's hard to
see how he could have been that sure of himself; not with
a thirteen- to fifteen-year-old. Now if he said, 'This skeleton would appear to be that of a female,' okay. Or 'in

my opinion, the skeleton is probably that of a female.' Or
'most sexual indicators suggest the sex is female.' But just
a flat-out 'the skeleton is a female'? Sorry, I have to have
my doubts."

Marmolejo stroked the corners of his lips. "So it might
be the skeleton of a boy and not a girl?"

Gideon understood why this was of concern. If the
police had been operating on the assumption that the
remains were those of a female and they were actually
those of a male, they would have been looking in all the
wrong places. The entire investigation would have been
thrown off track.

"I don't like second-guessing your pathologist," he
said, "but . . . well, let me just say I have to wonder about
his being that cut-and-dried about it. Yes, sometimes children's bones do sexually differentiate at an early age—
these are quantitative criteria we're dealing with, after all,
continuous variables ranging from no visible development
at all to completely developed, so some kids are going to
be ahead of other kids, ahead of the crowd, the same as
they are in height, or weight, or mental development. I've
seen kids myself, almost that young, with enough skeletal
sexual differentiation to definitively mark them as boys
or girls . . . but I haven't seen them very often, and that's
what's worrying me. It's possible, of course, that this just
happens to be one of them, but . . ."

He trailed off, thinking. "You know, there's another
possibility, Javier," he said after a moment. "It's probably
more likely, now that I think of it—and that is that it's
the *age* he was mistaken about. Determining age is a lot
harder than figuring out the sex."

"Of course. With sex one has two possible choices.
With age, there are many."

"Yes, that's part of it, but it's also that the criteria are
more complex. You have to know a lot more about skeletal

development to read those epiphyseal unions than you do to evaluate the sex indicators."

"So now you are suggesting that we may be dealing with a female after all, but an adult female?"

"Right. If she were an adult there wouldn't have been much problem in properly determining the sex. Of course, if that's true, then the police would still have gone off entirely in the wrong direction. They would have been investigating the murder of a child, when in reality it had been an adult."

Marmolejo sighed, but he did it with a smile. "Gideon, I already begin to regret bringing you into it. Before, we were faced with trying to identify a female child. Now that you have looked into it, it seems we may be trying to identify a female child *or* a male child *or* a female adult. How is it," he mused, probably thinking about the Yucatán case he had earlier been involved in with Gideon, "that the more information your expertise provides, the less information we seem to have?"

"Interestingly enough," Gideon said, laughing, "you're not the first person to make that observation. Well, look at it this way: at least I've eliminated the one remaining age-sex possibility. Assuming that Orihuela had any idea of what he was doing, which seems likely, you can forget about the category of adult male. You won't have to waste any time exploring that particular avenue."

"No," Marmolejo said dryly. "Merely the other three."

"What can I say?" Gideon said. "I sure wish I could have seen those bones myself."

Marmolejo emitted a mild, interested "Ah?"

It seemed to Gideon that the colonel had something up his sleeve. "There wouldn't be any photos in the file, would there?" he asked hopefully. "I might be able to tell something from them."

"Unfortunately, there are none."

Gideon spread his hands. "Well, then, I don't know what else—"

"No, no photos were taken, alas. All we have are the bones themselves."

Gideon blinked. "You still have them?"

"According to this file, we do." He tapped a page in it. "Until this moment I was unaware of it myself."

"And I could see them?"

Marmolejo smiled. "I suspect I can arrange it. When would you like to do it?"

"How about now? Who knows, I might be able to come up with something else as well." He was three-quarters out of his chair.

"No, my friend, not so fast. They're not here. According to this, they're in a government warehouse in Xochimilco, north of the city. I can have them brought here on tomorrow's morning run, which generally arrives in the early afternoon. Would you be free then? Say two o'clock, to be on the safe side? I have no doubt you will continue to astound and confound me with more of the wonderful osteological rabbits that you pull from your hat with such seeming ease."

"I don't know about the osteological rabbits," Gideon said with a smile, "but yes, tomorrow afternoon is fine. Javier, why was the case closed after only a month? That's pretty short for giving up on a murder investigation, wouldn't you say?"

"I would." He clapped his small, clean hands together soundlessly. "Let's find out, shall we?"

He went to the door and opened it. "Alejandro, will you ask Sergeant Nava and Chief Sandoval if they would be kind enough to join us? Tell them I would like to talk about the young girl's skeleton that was discovered last year near Teotitlán. Oh, and coffee for all, if you please. Espresso, I think." To Gideon he said, "You will forgive me if I speak Spanish. Nava has no English."

"I'm sure I'll be able to follow most of it."

When the two entered a few moments later it was hard to tell who was more scared, Nava or Sandoval. Both seemed surprised when they were motioned to the arm-chair area and not the visitor's chairs at the desk. Nava no longer had a gun stuck in his belt. Sandoval wouldn't sit down until he was specifically asked to, and when the coffee arrived, he couldn't quite make himself believe it was meant for him until Marmolejo personally poured it and slid a demitasse cup and saucer toward him.

"Chief Sandoval," a smiling Marmolejo said, as Sandoval tremblingly lifted the cup to his lips, "I've been looking at the file concerning the case you were involved in last year. Perhaps you can tell us a little more about the circumstances under which the girl's remains were found. You would know more about that than anyone else."

With a visible effort, Sandoval managed to set the cup back on its saucer with only a minimum of clatter. "Well, there's not much to tell, sir. They were discovered when a Canadian tourist fell into an old mine in the hills about three kilometers east of my village."

"And what type of mine was it? Copper? Silver? Gold?"

"It was an old silver mine, Colonel. They say it's a thousand years old." He paused. *"La Mina de los Muertos."*

"The Mine of the Dead?" Marmolejo repeated in Spanish. "And why was it called that, do you happen to know?" Gideon could see that he was trying to set Sandoval at ease, asking questions he thought the man could answer.

"Oh, that's not its real name," said Sandoval, who did indeed seem to be growing more confident with this line of questioning. "I don't think it has a name. People started calling it that maybe ten years ago, when someone found an old skeleton in it, in another passage."

Marmolejo's eyebrows drew together. "Do you mean another *human* skeleton?"

"Oh yes, but one of the Ancients, an Old One, you know? A thousand years old, maybe more."

"Ah," Marmolejo said with a sober little smile. "And now we find ourselves dealing with a New One, eh? A Young One. Well thank you, Chief. Now, Sergeant Nava, please tell me how it was it that you were made aware of these remains?"

The two men gradually relaxed further as Marmolejo asked his innocuous questions, gently and with no intimation of fault-finding or accusation, at least until he came to the crucial question.

"Sergeant Nava, can you enlighten me as to why the case was closed after a single month?"

Even before this, Nava's huge, thick-fingered hand had been having trouble manipulating the tiny cup and saucer; watching him was like watching a trained bear trying to do some delicate trick that was too minuscule for his paw. Now he carefully, clumsily put them, clattering, down on the table. "It wasn't *closed*, colonel," he said, looking nervous again. "It was *suspended*."

"Ah, suspended. I see. And can you tell me why it was suspended after a single month?"

"There was no place to *go* with it, sir. We couldn't find out who the victim was. We looked through the records of three years ago, five years ago, eight years ago, to try to find a girl of that age who was missing. In all of Oaxaca we found no one it could possibly have been. And there were no clues—the murderer, the motive—nothing. And the case, it was so old—" Marmolejo made the smallest of gestures with his hand, only the faint shadow of a shushing gesture, but it was enough to stop Nava at once.

"What if it had been a boy, not a girl?" the colonel asked. "Would that have made a difference?"

"If it had been a—" A sweaty sheen had popped out on Nava's forehead. "But the forensic report, it said—"

"I understand," Marmolejo said kindly. "But now it

seems the report may have been in error. Professor Oliver is going to look into that. Would you foresee any problem with reopening the matter if there is a reason; assigning some of your better men to it?"

"No, sir, absolutely not. With your permission, I would like to work on it myself."

"Very good. I will let you know. As we proceed on these matters, I trust you will show Chief Sandoval and Professor Oliver every courtesy."

"Of course. They have been extremely helpful, most obliging. We are most fortunate to have their expert counsel available to us."

"Thank you, Sergeant."

Nava, attuned to understanding a dismissal when he heard one, rose, bowed, and took his leave, still sweating but looking relieved to get out of there in one piece. His expression said it all: Madre de Dios, *it could have been a whole lot worse.*

"And now, Chief Sandoval," Marmolejo said genially, "would you care for a little more of this excellent coffee?"

"Why yes, Colonel, I believe I would," said Sandoval, smiling broadly and extending his cup. "With maybe a little sugar this time. But only if it's not too much trouble, of course."

NINE

"ACTUALLY, a lot better than I anticipated," Gideon said, in answer to Julie's asking about how the session at the *Procuraduría General de Justicia* had gone. "It was a little rocky at first—those Oaxaca cops are a scary bunch—but once their colonel got into the act it all smoothed over. Sandoval practically fell in love with the guy." He smiled. "You know, on the way there, all he could talk about was what thugs and crooks and brutes they all are. But you should have heard him raving on the way back: 'A fine man, the colonel, a real gentleman. I can see things will really be different now.' Suddenly, he's the *policía ministerial*'s number one fan."

He stretched comfortably out in the wooden lawn chair. They were sipping white wine on the Hacienda's brick-paved interior patio, shielded from the late-afternoon sun by the wispy but sufficient shade of what Julie had informed him was a casuarina tree. "And what about your day?"

"Oh, Uncle Tony showed up with Jamie a couple of hours ago; that was the big event of the day. It's amazing, Uncle Tony's hardly changed at all—well, a little grayer, a little heavier—a lot heavier—but the same guy's still inside, only even more so: cocky, loud, overbearing, self-centered, pretty nasty sometimes—"

"A real charmer, huh? I can hardly wait."

"Well, it's true, he can be a little hard to take, but he's funny too. And generous, in his own way."

"'In his own way.' Now there's a phrase I've never understood. 'He loved her in his own way.' 'He was grateful in his own way.' What does it mean?"

"Oh, you'll like him, you'll see. It's never boring around Tony. He's unfailingly entertaining. In his own way, of course."

"I see. And what about Jamie? How did he strike you?"

"Jamie? He's gotten more than ever like Jamie—mousy, fussy, persnickety—"

"Well, he *is* a bookkeeper."

"Gideon, I'm surprised at you!" she cried, but she was laughing. "That is hardly the kind of hackneyed, stereotypical remark that I expect from a respectable professor of anthropology."

Abjectly, he bowed his head. "You're right. I don't know what came over me. Strike it from the record."

"Consider it done. But Jamie—I'm making him sound worse than he is. He's really nice, very likeable. Well, they all are, really. You'll see. . . ." She sipped her wine pensively.

"But?"

"But—I don't know, I used to envy them all so much, living this romantic, exotic life in Mexico. Now I find myself feeling a little sorry for them all. What a strange kind of existence they have down here, when you think about it. Carl, Annie, Jamie—Tony for that matter—they've lived here all or most of their lives, but they're not

Mexican and won't ever be Mexican. They're not really American anymore either, for that matter, except technically. They're foreigners wherever they are."

"That's true. Like the Man in the Iron Mask. Must be tough. The ones I've met so far, Annie and Carl, I noticed they both speak with a slight accent now, a kind of Mexican lilt. And my guess is that the Mexicans find their Spanish not quite right. It's almost as if they don't have a native language."

"And yet they do seem happy enough when you look at them. Or at least not *un*happy."

"Well, different people have different reactions. Me, I'm the way you are. I'd have a hard time living between two cultures like that." He got out of his chair and stepped over to a nearby hammock hanging between two posts. "I think I'm going to give this thing a try."

It was easier said than done, especially while holding a wineglass, but eventually he managed to get all his appendages safely in, while spilling no more than a couple of drops. "Mm, comfortable," he said. "So tell me about what the work is like. Not too overwhelming, I hope."

"Couldn't have been easier. One departure—a nice, quiet German family that's been here a week—and no arrivals, so all I have to worry about are the feminist professors. So mostly I just 'supervised.' And with Jamie here now, I can stop worrying about receipts, or check stubs, or reconciling the bank statement, knock on wood. Those professors, whatever else you might say about them, are very easy guests, nothing high-maintenance about them. No special requests, no complaints. Mostly they keep to themselves, but they've signed on for several of the hikes and horseback rides that Carl leads. Seeing them around Carl, they don't seem to be the man-haters you might think."

Gideon laughed. "I think Carl qualifies as an alpha

male. I understand they make allowances for alpha males. Look, if there isn't that much to do, do you think you'll be able to take a day off and go see Oaxaca with me? And maybe one or two of the archaeological sites? Couldn't Jamie cover for you for one day?"

"Oh, I think I could, in a day or two. One archaeological site will be plenty for me, thank you, but the Oaxaca part sounds good. I'd like to see the city." She thought for a moment. "Maybe even tomorrow, in the afternoon?"

"Ah, no, not tomorrow. I told the colonel I'd look at another skeleton for him. But maybe the day after?"

"*Another* skeleton. I'm shocked. Shocked."

"Well, he *asked* me. By the way, I have another shock for you, or a surprise, anyway. That colonel I've been talking about—who do you think he turned out to be? Three guesses."

"Mm, let's see. . . ." Julie sipped her wine and concentrated, looking up into the pale green, gently stirring branches of the tree. "Javier Marmolejo," she said.

Gideon almost choked on his wine. "How the heck did you come up with that?"

"It wasn't hard. I just mentally went over my list of all the Mexican policemen I know, and the total was one, and that one was Javier. So I took a wild guess. But how did he get to be a colonel in Oaxaca?"

It took five minutes to explain, by which time they had finished their wine. "Another?" Gideon asked, trying to sit up in the soft, moving hammock. "Assuming I can actually get out of this thing."

Julie glanced at her watch. "No, it's almost six. We're all having dinner in Uncle Tony's apartment. He likes to eat with everybody when he's here. He's read all about you, by the way, and he's really anxious to meet you. Really, I think you're going to like him."

"Oh, I'm sure I will. Cocky, loud, overbearing, self-centered, nasty . . . What's not to like?"

TEN

TONY'S "apartment" was in the Casa del Mayordomo, the one-time plantation manager's house, now divided into quarters for Carl, Annie, Tony himself, Jamie, and Josefa Gallegos, the housekeeping manager who was, Julie had told him, more of a charity case than an employee; she was Tony's aunt by marriage, the widowed wife of his mother Beatriz's brother.

Other than the upstairs bathroom and bedroom, Tony's unit consisted of one large, simple space with whitewashed walls that were hung with Mexican Primitive paintings. The room had been outfitted as a living room–dining room—a cove-like kitchen was tucked into one corner—with Mexican Colonial furniture, including a museum-quality, elaborately painted dinner table with the place settings—plate, spoon, fork (but no knife)—painted right on it.

Julie and Gideon were the last to arrive. When they got there the others were clustered near one end of the

table, where bottles of mezcal, wine, and beer were waiting (Gideon noticed that the painted surface had received
a thick coating of plastic or polyurethane to protect it
from spills) and from which hors d'oeuvres were being
served by Dorotea's two teenage nieces, who were her
kitchen assistants.

As Julie had implied, Tony had done some serious
prepping on Gideon, and on forensic anthropology as
well. With a few drinks apparently under his belt by the
time they got there, he had quickly collared Gideon and
pretty much appropriated him for discussion of matters
osteological.

Julie had said that, despite a few disagreeable personality traits, he was likeable, and he was: a big, blustery,
affable guy with a voice that sounded like the clatter of
the Eighth Avenue Express coming up through a grate in
the sidewalk. Physically, he was not an attractive man. He
bore a three-day growth of stubbly beard, trendy if you
believed the fashion ads, but as usual with men who had
a few too many chins and not enough neck, he wound up
looking more scruffy than macho. He was, as Julie had
said, considerably overweight, with the bulgy, button-
popping look that comes from having recently put on a
lot of pounds that haven't yet figured out where they are
eventually going to settle. His flushed, yellowish skin, and
the threadlike purple tracery of broken capillaries that
emerged from the stubble and crawled up his cheeks and
onto his nose spoke of the dedicated boozehound. But if
he was a drunk, he was a genial drunk, on this night at
any rate, and he had clearly taken a liking to Gideon.

"Hey, what are you drinking?" he said early on. "Is
that wine? Nah, put that crap down, you gotta try this.
You like mezcal?"

Gideon didn't know. "I've never tried it."

"Never tried it?" Tony was astounded. "Where've you
been all your life?" He led Gideon to the drinks table

and lifted one of several dark purple bottles with Hacienda Encantada labels. "Now, this stuff is special. This is made from maguey right on the property, the same plants they made the sisal from in the old days. I get it bottled at a distillery in Tlacolula. They only make a few cases a year. Okay, now do like I do."

Gideon did as instructed. The mezcal was poured into a shot-sized, cylindrical glass and placed on a saucer with four lime wedges and a cinnamon-colored spoonful of salt mixed with powdered chile peppers. A wedge of lime was dipped into the salt mixture, sucked on, and followed by a sip of mezcal. Four wedges, four sips. Then on to the next saucer. Because Gideon knew that tequila also came from the maguey and he had never developed a taste for tequila, he hadn't expected to like it, but mezcal turned out to have a rich, smoky taste, more like Scotch than tequila.

"It's good," he said truthfully, but turned down the offer of a third. Tony shrugged and poured one for himself. "Now, then," he said, arranging the salt and lime wedges to his satisfaction, "I want to talk to you—" A slurp of lime, a sip of mezcal. "—about, like, racial differences in, like, cranial form. . . ."

Ten minutes later, with Tony still monopolizing Gideon, the group sat down to dinner. "This guy," Tony declared to one and all, with his arm draped collegially around Gideon's shoulder, "this guy is famous. I Googled him; he's all over the Net. The Skeleton Doctor." The nape of Gideon's neck was jovially, if a little too vigorously, squeezed. "Right, Gid?"

"Actually," Gideon murmured, "not that it matters—"

"The Skeleton Doctor. They even had a TV show on him. On A&E."

"Well, not *on* me. I was just a small part of it. It was—"

"And there was a whole article on him in *Discover* magazine."

That much was true, but Gideon was getting uncomfortable. Tony was at the head of the table with Gideon on his left and Julie on his right. The rest, other than Jamie, who was chewing his lip and brooding over something, were smiling at him, or at least in his general direction, with apparent interest. But long-time professor that he was, he was an old hand at recognizing the glazed, overly bright stare and glassy smile of a captive audience. Tony Gallagher in full throttle was a hard man to ignore or to interrupt; no doubt even harder when he also happened to be *el patrón*.

In the end it was Tony himself who came to Gideon's rescue, interrupting himself in the middle of a sentence. "Hey, Jamie, why the long face, as the bartender said when the horse walked into the bar? You look like you just lost your best friend."

"Oh—sorry, Tony. It's nothing. I was just thinking . . ."

Jamie was much as Julie had described him, a skinny, narrow-shouldered man with Woody Allen glasses and a sad-sack, permanently worried, Woody-Allenish demeanor to match. Gideon couldn't help smiling, thinking of the wonderfully apt Yiddish word his old mentor, Abe Goldstein, would have used to describe him: *nebbish*. He had an aluminum cane hooked on the back of his chair, and it was obvious that he was still in some discomfort from his knee operation.

"Come on, little brother, out with it," Tony said amiably.

Jamie hunched his shoulders. "Well, it's just that I've been thinking about what you were telling me about on the way down, your new . . . installation. I put some working figures together, and honestly, I don't see how we can make it work. I mean, I'm not criticizing—"

"Oh yeah," Tony cried, "I was gonna get around to that." He removed his arm from Gideon's shoulder and rearranged himself in his chair. "Everybody listen to this now," he said, hammering on the table with freshened enthusiasm. "Jamie thinks I'm out of my mind, but you're gonna love it. This is Preciosa's idea, actually, and I think she's really got something this time." He looked proudly toward the foot of the table where Preciosa, his "current sweet patootie," sat smiling.

Only "sweet patootie" didn't come close to conveying Preciosa's looks. A tall, languid woman in her forties, exotic in a long-nosed, high-cheekboned way, over-made-up and overjeweled (six of her long, thin fingers bore rings, three of worked silver, and three with amethyst stones that closely matched her purple lipstick and eye shadow), she put Gideon in mind of one of those big wading birds, a heron or an ibis, exaggeratedly slow-moving and studiedly graceful. And, like a heron, endowed with an extraordinarily long and sinuous neck, so that her narrow head gave the impression of bobbing slightly on its slender support. As a physical type, she was as different from Tony as two people can be. Tony was one of those people who seemed to take up more space than he was entitled to, and to be made of something denser and heavier than plain flesh. The supple, lissome Preciosa seemed as if she could conform to any space available, like jelly, like smoke.

Gideon could see that identifying her as the originator of the idea to come did nothing to increase the receptiveness of Carl, or Josefa, or Jamie; instead, there was a flurry of exchanged, wary glances and even a few rolled eyes. Annie's feelings about her "harebrained schemes," it appeared, were widely shared. Like Tony, however, Preciosa seemed oblivious to the reception, responding to Tony's tribute with a slow, refined nod. Gideon had the impression that she might have enough English to get bits of the drift of what was being said, but not much more.

At this point Dorotea's nieces brought out chopped salads of avocado, corn, tomato, and jicama, along with bowls of cumin-scented dressing. Tony waited for them to finish setting them out, then made his announcement. "We—get ready for this—are gonna put in a *temazcal*." He looked around with an expectant grin, but the only response came from Carl, and it wasn't what Tony was hoping for.

"A what?"

Tony shoulders sagged. He looked at Carl disgustedly. "Aw, Carl—a *temazcal*, for Christ's sake. It's like sort of a—it's hard to—it goes way back to the Aztecs, it's—you tell them, Gid, you're the anthropologist."

Gideon put down the forkful of salad—the first—that was on its way to his mouth. "To tell the truth, it's not anything I'm all that familiar with, Tony, but I do know it's something that was found in a lot of Pre-Hispanic cultures—Aztec, Mayan, Zapotec, Mixtec—a kind of ritual sweat bath or sweat lodge, something like what you still see in some Native American groups. It was probably in use right here in the Valley of Oaxaca. I seem to remember that herbs were involved, and that the rituals were basically connected to healing. Is that the kind of thing you're talking about?"

"That's exactly what I'm talking about," Tony cried, his exuberance having returned.

"No, my love, that is *not* exactly what I had in mind," said Preciosa, whose English was just fine—better than fine: smooth, coldly formal, and elegantly accented. "Yes, of course we will have the traditional elements of fire and water and curative plants," she said with a boneless wave of her fingers, "and people will sit naked on woven *petate* mats to drink herbal teas and meditate. But there will also be a more modern focus on the healing powers of crystals and aromatherapy, both of which, I might add, will provide a welcome avenue to the sales of many a high-profit item."

She sat back, regal and smiling, like an opera star surrounded by adoring fans.

"Uh . . . did you say 'naked'?" Carl asked.

"Yes," said Preciosa, "it's the traditional way, but"—a condescending shrug—"if some people are too closed-minded for that, they can wear swimsuits if they choose. And don't look so worried, Carlos, my dear, there won't be any orgies. It's not at all like that."

"If you say so." Carl looked far from convinced.

"But what's it going to *cost*?" Jamie asked anxiously. "Have you taken into consideration the kind of facility it would require? You're not just talking about some simple concrete-block cube. The specialized plumbing requirements, the ventilation—"

Tony aimed a finger at him. "A new facility will not be necessary, my man. You know the empty room at the end of the storehouse that we don't use for anything—well, cleaning supplies and stuff? Well, Preciosa checked it out and says it'd be perfect: no windows, solid stone walls, and stone floor And the rest of the building's already plumbed, so how much could it cost to run pipes to it?"

"And ventilation?"

"Ventilation? We knock a couple of slits in the walls, high up."

"*Slits* in the walls? The health inspectors would never—"

He was cut off by a contemptuous laugh from Tony. "Hey, I can take care of the health inspectors, trust me. Look, the thing is, Preciosa says these things are making a comeback all over the place—but not here in the Valley, not yet. I checked it out for myself, and she's right, there isn't one; this would be the very first. It'll be a hell of an attraction, a hell of an income stream. Do you have any idea of what these weirdos pay for that aromatherapy crap? And it costs next to nothing to get. So—what do you all think about it?"

Not much, apparently. Tony's question received no answer at all for a good five seconds, until Carl spoke.

"It's your money," he said with amiable resignation. "As long as you don't expect me to take my clothes off and get into it myself, it's fine with me. One question, though—who's going to run this thing? I mean, you can't just have naked people running in and out and sitting around meditating together." He frowned. "Or can you?"

"Ah, that's the beauty part," Tony said. "Preciosa knows this healer, or teacher, or *curandero*, or whatever the hell you call him—they're actually certified—who'll run the sessions for us for half of what we charge, which is going to be a hundred and twenty bucks a pop. Valderano, his name is."

"*Valeriano, mi gordito,*" Preciosa corrected.

"Whatever. The point is, we don't have to worry about it, we just rake in the money." He rubbed his hands together. "So, anybody else got anything to say—anything *positive* to say?"

"Who's supposed to keep it clean?" was Josefa's mumbled comment. "Gonna need more help if you think it's gonna be me." Josefa, short, square-faced, square-bodied, and scowly (Gideon, seemingly in an animal-metaphor rut, was reminded of a slow, grumpy, old bulldog), was a woman in her sixties with a way of speaking that seemed not to be directed at any particular person, and rarely in response to any particular comment. She was like a radio that went on and off of its own accord.

"Aw, come on, you guys," Tony pleaded, his arms spread, palms up, "how about a little enthusiasm? Jamie, I showed you the figures. It's doable, isn't it?"

"I have serious doubts about those figures, Tony. This place isn't in the financial condition it was two years ago, you know. The exchange rate on the dollar, the money we put down the drain on the Swimming with the Fishes—"

"You wouldn't have lost money if you'd done it the way I said," Preciosa said hotly.

"And then the bad publicity we got on the mud bath

fiasco; that didn't help. We're still paying damages on that."

Preciosa impaled him with a ferocious look. "There wouldn't have been any fiasco, if you had just listened—"

"Knock it off, you two," Tony intervened. "How about letting me worry about all that crap, huh?"

"I was under the impression that worrying about 'all that crap' is what you pay me to do," Jamie said bravely.

"And you do a hell of a job, bro, a hell of a job," Tony said, but he was obviously getting bored with the subject.

Jamie wasn't interested in compliments. "I have to tell you, Tony," he said with a fretful, frowning shake of his head. "We are not in good shape, not anymore. I have my doubts about this. I have my *grave* doubts."

Tony responded with a snort of laughter. "You gotta excuse Jamie," he told Gideon with a doting glance at his brother. "He can't help it, that's just the way he is. He was born that way; it's in his genes. Remember that guy in the old *Superman* comics? Mr. Mxtlplx or something? With a little black rain cloud hanging over his head wherever he went? That's my baby brother all the way. There's always a disaster around the next corner."

"You could . . . you could use a few more of those genes yourself, Tony," Jamie ventured.

"I sure could!" Tony said happily.

"What are we all arguing about, anyway?" Carl asked. "You're the boss, Tony. If you want it, I figure we might as well get used to living with it."

More appreciative honking from Tony. "Damn right. Now you're getting the picture."

Clearly, he was used to having his parades rained on and perhaps was even amused by it. It was also clear that none of their opinions on the *temazcal* were, or ever had been, factors in the decision. The thing was settled, had *been* settled before he ever brought it up. The Hacienda Encantada would have the first *temazcal* in the Valley of Oaxaca, or more accurately the first *temazcal* in a thousand years or so. He would have preferred that they like the idea, but if they didn't, he'd have no trouble living with the fact.

He looked up with interest as Dorotea herself led her nieces in bringing in more food. "Hey, here comes the main course," he said, picking up a knife and a fork in his fists. "Whoa, look at that! Are you kidding me? Is that *caguesa*? My favorite dish in the whole damn world! Dorotea, you outdid yourself again."

Dorotea responded with an ungracious shrug and said something in Spanish; "You always did like peasant food," Gideon thought it was. This was not a woman who went out of her way to butter up her boss. Or anyone else, as far as he could see. Presumably she got away with it on the strength of her famous cooking.

Indeed, the *caguesa* turned out to be a pungent and delicious stew of chicken, tomato, and toasted corn, perfectly flavored with garlic and served with melt-in-your-mouth fresh corn tortillas and rice. Once a few spoonfuls had been put away, individual conversations resumed. With Tony and Julie reminiscing about family matters and members unfamiliar to him, he tried conversing with Josefa, who was seated on his left. ("I understand Tony is your nephew?" "Are you originally from Teotitlán?" "Have you always lived here?") But she was intently focused, first on cleaning her silverware with her fingernails and her napkin, then on eating her meal, and even when he tried the questions in Spanish, the only thing he got out of her other than *sí*s and *no*s was an unsolicited comment about Preciosa:

"I bet *she* no back next year," she said with satisfaction, jerking her head in that lady's direction. "She getting *old*. Look at them hands, all them veins, all them bumps. She get all the face-lifts she want, she still an old lady. Always you can tell from the hands." As before, the remarks were made, not quite to Gideon, but to some invisible person now a few feet behind him, now just in front of him, sometimes a few feet above him. He wondered if she might not be aware that she was expressing her thoughts aloud.

In any case, he had to admit (to himself), she did have a point. Preciosa's veiny, arthritic hands were a good twenty years older than her face. It was the sort of thing he *ought* to have noticed, or so he thought, but somehow he never did. He revised her age upward to the fifties, probably the late fifties. Well, he'd always had trouble judging a woman's age, at least when she still had flesh on her bones.

He gave up on talking to Josefa and tuned back in to the conversation between Julie and Tony. "I used to envy you all so much," Julie was saying. "I would have given anything to have grown up here on the Hacienda, the way you and Jamie did."

Tony, who had been guzzling steadily but seemed no drunker than before (nor any less, either), paused in shoveling stew into his mouth and gave a low, gravelly laugh. "Like Jamie, maybe, but not like me."

"Why? What do you mean?"

Tony looked puzzled. "You mean you don't know the story? Of my misspent youth? Sure, you do."

"No, she doesn't, Tony," said Carl, who was sitting on Julie's other side. "Don't you remember? She was just a wide-eyed kid back when she was working summers here. We all figured there was no point in loading all that baggage on her. You did too. So no, she doesn't know, and as far as I'm concerned, there's still no point."

"Yeah, you're right." Disappointed, Tony went back to eating.

"Now, wait a minute, you two," Julie said, putting

down her fork. "Just you wait one cotton-pickin' minute. I am no longer a wide-eyed kid, and I am certainly not innocent. I am a worldly, experienced, married woman. You should *hear* some of the things Gideon talks to me about. If there's something about this family that I don't know about, I want to hear it."

"Aw, Julie . . ." Carl began, and Gideon could see from her suddenly frozen expression that she was kicking herself, having suddenly realized that it might have to do with Blaze, a subject she now knew to be so painful to Carl. But it didn't, as Tony made clear.

"You're absolutely right," he said, perking up. "Time you found out what a hell-raiser your Uncle Tony was. Which reminds me, you're plenty old enough to drop that 'Uncle' shit now—hey, sorry, pardon my language. Anyway, it makes me feel a hundred years old, besides which I'm not your uncle in the first place, I'm your—" He scowled. "What am I to her, Gid? Anything?"

"Well, let's see," Gideon said. "Carl is her uncle, and you're Carl's brother-in-law, so that would make you her . . . nothing. You're not genetically related, and while some cultures would have a formal name for the relationship, we don't."

Tony nodded his satisfaction. "See? I'm nothing," he said to Julie. "Plain old Tony."

"You're on," Julie said, clinking glasses with him. "From now on you're nothing to me; plain old Tony." She was on her second beer, and the buzz was showing a little. There was something about beer that had always gone quickly to her head. "Now let's hear the story."

"Okay. First of all, I was a confirmed dope addict by the age of twelve . . ."

She laughed, thinking he was joking, as did Gideon.

"No, I'm serious," Tony insisted. "Jamie, was I a dope addict or not?"

"You were a dope addict," confirmed Jamie, who was

sitting two seats down, on the other side of Carl. "But it wasn't your fault, Tonio. What happened to you was a damned shame. You were just a little kid, how could you know what was going on?"

"Thanks, Jaime, I appreciate that."

Gideon had noticed earlier that they sometimes used the Spanish versions of their names when they were feeling affectionate or familial. Tony was Tonio, Jamie was Jaime, Carl was Carlos, Annie was Anita. "But the truth is the truth. Julie, Gideon, you're looking at the man who was the world's youngest speed freak. However, let me point out that from that point on in my life . . . from that point on, I went rapidly downhill." Another brief, rolling, belly-shaking laugh, but not as hearty as his earlier ones. This man sure laughs a lot, Gideon thought. It wasn't hard to take in small doses, but he'd be hell to live with. "Seriously, I was, like, nine years old when it started; ten at most."

He was looking at Julie and Gideon as he spoke, but once again he was really addressing the table at large. This time he had their honest attention. It might have been a familiar story to them, but apparently that didn't make it any less engrossing.

"You see," he said, "as a kid, I was kind of overweight."

"You mean, as opposed to now?" Julie asked with a giggle. She was a little under the influence, all right.

"Hey, watch your mouth!" Tony said, reaching out to tousle her hair. "No, I mean *really* overweight." He puffed out his cheeks to illustrate. "Remember, Jamie?"

"Not too well," Jamie said. "When you were twelve, I was only three years old."

"Oh yeah, I keep forgetting," Tony said. "It's because you're always acting like my older brother, not my younger brother. Anyway . . ."

Anyway, Vincent Gallagher, Tony's father, had been distressed, maybe obsessed, over his son's weight, Tony explained. The senior Gallagher had dreamed from the beginning that Anthony, his firstborn, would inherit and run the ranch some day, and a waddling, three-hundred-pound cowboy didn't fit the picture he had in mind. He had tried all kinds of remedies and had finally taken Tony to a weight-reduction specialist in Oaxaca, a doctor who had prescribed what was then the trendiest, most up-to-date reducing drug available: methamphetamine.

By the time he was eleven, he was well on his way to being hooked. Vincent sent him away for treatment, first to a rehab facility in Mexico City and then to one in Pennsylvania. Both times the cure had been pronounced successful; both times he had relapsed. By the second time, the use of meth had become a little more widespread, and Tony took up with another kid from a nearby village who had also developed addiction problems.

"Huicho," he said with a nostalgic smile. "Huicho Lozada. Now there's someone I haven't thought about for a long time. Jesus, he was in worse shape than I was, but we were both meth heads, plain and simple," he said. "Tweakers. And we got ourselves into a lot of trouble on account of it. I mean, a *whole* lot of trouble. Not as much as I got into later—now, that was *real* trouble—but enough." His mood had darkened. The others had grown more grave as well, except for Preciosa, who was smiling possessively at him, almost like a mother at her child.

He had run off at sixteen, unable to live with either the unavailability of the drug or the unrelenting pressure from his father about shaping up and eventually taking over the ranch. And then had come the "real" trouble. Life on the streets and in the twilight worlds of Oaxaca, of Miami, of Tijuana, of Cleveland; wherever a supply of methamphetamine could most easily be gotten. More than once he'd awakened in the gutter—literally—or in some filthy doorway, not knowing where he was or how he'd gotten there. He had robbed and been robbed, he had beaten people up and been beaten up, he'd been arrested five or six times—he couldn't remember how many or even where. And he'd been convicted and jailed twice, both times on drug charges, once in Las Vegas for sixty days, and then in Mexican prisons for almost four years, from the time he was twenty-one until he was twenty-five.

"How horrible," Julie said. "That must have been . . . I can't imagine what that must have been like."

"Sure you can," Tony said. "Just think about what you've heard about Mexican jails—you know, movies, TV—and what frigging nightmares they are. Okay? Got a mental picture? Now multiply it by a hundred. That'll give you a small idea. I'm here to tell you, once you survive that, you can survive anything. The only good thing was, I could still get meth on the inside, at least for the first two years, when they had me in Tijuana, and that was all that mattered—although, trust me, you don't want to know what I had to do for it."

But even that dismal comfort came to an end when he was transferred to the infamous Reclusorio Oriente, the high-security prison in Mexico City, for the last two years of his sentence. There it was either lick his addiction cold turkey or commit suicide. More than once he had been on the very edge of the latter, and of his sanity as well, but an older fellow prisoner, a grizzled Mexican double-murderer serving a life sentence, had taken an interest in him. It was thanks to that old convict's kindness, Tony said, that he not only survived the ordeal, but eventually walked out of prison free of drugs and determined to stay that way. And he had.

Tony's story had taken them through coffee and a simple, luscious dessert of *plátanos asados*—soft, tiny grilled bananas with cinnamon and cream, served family style.

"That's quite a story," Gideon said, helping himself to

another couple of bananas and dousing them with cream. "It's not often that people can turn their lives around like that."

"I'll say," said Julie. "I had no idea, Uncle Tony. I mean plain old Tony." She reached over to give his hand a squeeze.

"Well, I don't want to brag," Tony said, "but, what the hey, it's true. I did come a long way. And I owe it to two people: Lalo Arenas—the old guy in prison; he's dead now—and my father. My father—" He knocked twice on the table for emphasis. "My father never lost faith in me. Never."

"That's so," Jamie put in. "I was only a kid, but I remember, while you were gone all those years, Dad used to tell us—Blaze and me—'Don't you worry about your big brother Tony; he'll be all right. He just has to get it out of his system, that's all. He'll be back.'"

"Yeah," said Tony quietly (for him). "Dad was great. He died while I was in jail, you know, and when I found out he left the ranch to me, I couldn't believe it. I mean, talk about faith. There I was, rotting away in this hell-hole, a loser through and through. I hadn't even bothered to get in touch with him for years . . . and he trusts me with his precious ranch."

"You were his firstborn," Jamie said. "He loved you. From the day you were born, you were the one who was going to inherit." If there was any resentment behind the words, Gideon couldn't see it.

"Yeah, that's true," Tony said with a wondering shake of his head. "And his trusting me like that was what really turned me around. I *had* to deliver. Still, it was a little tricky when I first came back. I still feel bad about . . . I mean, I feel like part of it's my fault that—" He shot a brief, wary glance at Carl. "Well, never mind, doesn't matter anymore."

"Your fault that what?" asked Julie, not nearly as perceptive as she would have been without the beers.

"I said never mind, okay?" Tony barked at her, abruptly, surly. He slapped his napkin down on the table and stood up. "Shit. Look, it's been a hell of a long day. What do you say we call it a night?"

"BUT what did I say?" a stricken Julie asked Gideon as they walked back to their room in the cool night air.

"Julie, I have no idea. Well, *some* idea—it had something to do with Carl; I could see that much."

"It must have been something about Blaze, then," Julie said, shaking her head. "Honestly, I don't remember everybody being so sensitive before. You really have to watch your step around here, don't you?"

"Like walking on eggshells," Gideon agreed. "All the same, I think the guy owes you an apology. That was really uncalled for."

"Oh," she said, sighing, "that's just Tony. It's just the way he is."

ELEVEN

EVERY forensic anthropologist will tell you, and every homicide cop too, that after a while you become hardened to looking at the remains of murder victims; you can divorce yourself from them as once-living human beings and view them simply as cases, clues, evidence. When you go home at night, you put your thoughts of them aside and relax or get on with other things.

With one exception. No one ever gets used to looking at murdered children. No one manages to completely overcome the internal shudder of sadness and horror—of despair at the wickedness of people—when dealing with the remains of a murdered child. There is always a desire for vengeance mixed in with it too—for justice, certainly, but mostly, if you are being honest, for vengeance. You want to do every possible thing you can to put the bastard away. Forever. And if he should resist arrest and get the bejesus beat out of him by somebody his own size, well, gee, wouldn't that be a shame?

These were very much Gideon's feelings as he stood looking down at the contents of the one-by-three-foot fiberboard carton containing *Caso Número* 08-Teo dV 1-1, now tenderly laid out by him on two sheets of newsprint atop the desk in one of the unoccupied cubicles at police headquarters, a few yards down the corridor from Marmolejo's office. The carton had been waiting for him when he arrived, and when he removed the lid, a single glance had convinced him that Orihuela had been right in classifying the remains as those of a teenager; the bones were small and gracile, and at least some of the epiphyseal unions were incomplete. Not as unsettling as a baby would have been—a baby, so utterly trusting and defenseless, was the worst—but plenty bad enough; a fresh young life, innocent and unworldly, barely started and bursting with promise, cut off before it could be lived.

In this frame of mind he thought it best to put off opening the neatly folded brown paper sack labeled *cráneo*, in which the patent evidence of murder would be found. In merely lifting it out of the carton, he had been made aware of the fragile, shattered pieces inside, crackling like so many broken eggshells. Better to work his way slowly up to that.

He pulled up the stool that had been provided at his request, had a sip of Marmolejo's excellent espresso that had likewise been provided, put the sack to one side and settled down for a closer look at the rest of the skeleton. Score another one for Dr. Orihuela: he could tell the difference between a right and left clavicle and even between a right and left fibula. One might think any physician, especially a forensic pathologist, would be able to do that, but one would be wrong. Yes, an orthopedic surgeon, say, had better be familiar with every muscle insertion point, every foramen, every fossa, on the human tibia. But as for differentiating between a right one and a left one, they had available to them a foolproof, sublimely simple method for doing it: the right one was the one in the right leg, and the left one was the one in the left leg. Medical doctors simply aren't trained in working with bones that don't happen to be enclosed in bodies and at least roughly in their appointed place, and why should they be? When would a doctor have to deal with an isolated, bodyless bone? Never. That was what anthropologists did.

But this particular doctor had gotten it right. There were, as he had reported, a left clavicle, a right innominate (the right half of the pelvis); the long bones of the left leg—femur, tibia, and fibula; and, in another paper sack, twenty-two of the twenty-six bones of the left foot. (Orihuela had prudently described them as hand *or* foot bones, and hadn't specified the side, but this was understandable; it had been a long time before Gideon himself could reliably distinguish between many of those almost identical little bones without an atlas at hand.)

Why this particular assemblage of bones? Why the right hip and the right collar bone, but the left leg and foot? Why the top and bottom of the body but nothing, other than a single clavicle, a collar bone, in between—no ribs or vertebrae, no scapulas, no arm bones? Why no sacrum, why no sternum? Who knew? Gideon could speculate, but after all the time these remains had lain in the mine it wouldn't be much better than guesswork. The elements, the bugs, the animals had all had their chance at mucking up things over the years.

The years they had lain in the mine. Here, Gideon thought, was one place he might question Orihuela's judgment. Yes, the bones showed the kind of pitting and superficial flaking that he too might associate with five or so years of exposure in the semiarid climate of inland southern Mexico. (Or two, or twenty; bone weathering was one of the many wildly variable after-death phenomena.) But how much "exposure" was involved in lying at the bottom of a mine shaft? There might or might not be rain, depending on exactly where the body was situated, but there would be no sun to broil the bones, no wind to abrade them, no big temperature or humidity swings to swell and shrink and crack them. So if the remains had really been in the mine all that time (not that there was any guarantee of that), the weathering process would have been greatly slowed. These bones might be considerably older than five years. Sergeant Nava had said they had tried to identify the girl, if it was a girl, from missing-persons records that went as far back as eight years. Gideon would be suggesting to Marmolejo that they might do well to take that back as many as four or even five decades. He jotted a note to himself on the breast-pocket pad he'd brought with him.

Next, also putting aside the sack of foot bones, he went over the innominate, clavicle, and leg bones for signs of injury, old or new, and of disease or abnormality or anything else that might individuate them and thus help the police in identifying them. As Orihuela had said: there was nothing.

That left ancestry (formerly known as "race"), sex, and age, preferably to be determined in that order because girls' and boys' skeletons matured at slightly different rates. (Girls' skeletons matured earlier.) So it was helpful to know the sex before trying to determine the age; and since sexual characteristics differed somewhat between racial groups, it was helpful to ascertain the race before trying to determine the sex. Ancestry, sex, age.

Ancestry he already knew he had little chance of determining. Not on this assemblage of subadult bones. It might be that when he opened the sack with the skull and the mandible, he might find that the incisors were "shovel shaped," which in this part of the world would suggest, but hardly prove, Native American ancestry. In any case he wasn't yet ready to face that particular dismal litter of human debris. Besides, he didn't need the race to determine the sex. He already knew the sex.

Once again, Orihuela had been on the mark. Subadult or not, the sexual characteristics of these remains were unmistakable, and they were those of a female.

The "too much chewed" right innominate bone—the right half of the pelvis—made that absolutely clear. The bones of the pelvis, for obvious reasons, offer more differentiating criteria between the sexes than any other skeletal element in the body. Indeed, the pelvis is the one skeletal element from which the sex can be determined with 100 percent reliability. Women are built to be capable of having babies. Men aren't, and the distinctions are hard to miss or to get wrong once you know what to look for. There is the shape of the greater sciatic notch, of the obturator foramen, of the auricular surface of the ilium, of the ilium as a whole. All these things were observable despite the heavy gnawing around all the edges, and they all yelled "female" at Gideon, as they would have at anyone else who knew what he was doing.

That the skeleton of a teenage girl—thirteen to fifteen, if Orihuela was correct—should show the sexual differentiation of a woman of twenty was, as Gideon had told Marmolejo, unusual; something you didn't expect to run into every day, or every month, and its uncommonness bothered him. Generally speaking, skeletal maturation and sexual differentiation progressed in concert. You wouldn't expect one to outstrip the other by five years, or even three. Like any scientist, Gideon was more comfortable when his data performed the way they were supposed to, when they fit the prevailing model; and these remains definitely didn't. However, he understood well enough that while something like this was anything but common, it wasn't unique either, or even "abnormal."

Human variability wandered all over the map, and, like

most kinds of variability, the results were almost always in the ubiquitous form of the bell-shaped curve. Whatever characteristic you were measuring, the great majority of people could be counted on to cluster near the center, in the great, humped body of the bell. But there were always those who didn't fit—bigger, smaller, fatter, thinner, more developed, less developed—the people with the traits that constituted the "tails" on either side of the bell, tapering down to nothing as they became more and more extreme and infrequent. What he had in front of him now was apparently an example of someone out near one of those extreme ends of the bell-shaped curve of subadult sexual differentiation. If something has, say, a one-in-a-hundred probability of occurring, then it was reasonable to expect to encounter it every hundred times or so. And he had looked at hundreds, maybe thousands, of skeletons. He was probably long past due to come across one like this.

So why worry?

But worry he did; the more extraordinary your findings, the more you had to wonder if there might be something you were misinterpreting, something more or less than met the eye, something that would easily explain away apparent discrepancies or inconsistencies. Something, even, about which you were flat-out mistaken. Well, he wasn't mistaken about the sex, of that he was sure. So that left the other end of the equation, the age. She was a subadult, all right; Gideon had already seen that for himself with a glance, but where in that category did she fit? If she were at the eighteen-year-old end, then the sexual differentiation wouldn't be so extraordinary, no more than a year or so premature; not much to trouble oneself about. But if she were, as Orihuela had estimated, at the other end, the thirteen-year-old end . . .

With good reason, forensic anthropologists aren't supposed to prefer any particular outcome of their investigations, but forensic anthropologists are as human as anybody else, and Gideon knew that the younger she was, the more his findings on sex differentiation and skeletal maturation would be at odds with each other. Bell-shaped curves notwithstanding, thirteen-year-old girls weren't supposed to have pelvises like twenty-year-olds. There wasn't much he could do about it except to warn himself in no uncertain terms that he was not to let what he preferred or didn't prefer affect his analysis.

Having given himself a talking-to along these lines, he belatedly realized that his back needed a break. He got off the stool to stand up, work his shoulders, and massage the kinks out of his neck. He'd been crouched over the desk for over an hour now. Having borrowed one of the Hacienda's vans, he had arrived at the *Procuraduría* a little before two, where he was received at the foot of the basement steps with full military honors—salute, clicked heels—by Donardo, the hulking cop who had been notably short on courtesies the day before. It was obvious that Marmolejo's admonitions to Sergeant Nava had been promptly passed on down the line. Donardo had shown him to Marmolejo's office for a cup of espresso and a leisurely chat before Gideon got down to work.

Now, wanting a breather for both body and mind, he walked down the hall to beg another coffee from Corporal Vela, Marmolejo's adjutant, then returned with it to the bones. His aim was to come up with a probable age range of his own that would either confirm Orihuela's estimate or refute it. The odds that he could do one or the other, and do it with confidence, were in his favor. The younger a person was, the more precisely his or her age could be determined from the skeleton. In a child under three it could often be narrowed down to a couple of months one way or the other. After thirty-five or forty, you'd have a hard time pinning it down to anything less than a ten-year range. But for a teenager, if you knew what you were doing and you had enough of the right bones in front of you (and Gideon thought he did in this case), you ought to be able to come up with a reliable—and defensible—age range of no more than three years, perhaps even two. That's what he was shooting for.

The age of a person in her teens is established mostly by gauging the degree of growth in the long bones—the arms, legs, ribs, and collar bones. A bone grows by depositing new osseous material at both ends of the shaft, the "diaphysis." But beyond each growing end, all long bones have a sort of cartilaginous cap, the "epiphysis," which cooperates by moving outward to accommodate the lengthening bone. With time, however, the epiphyses ossify and slowly fuse to the shaft. When the fusion is complete, the bone is done growing. And when the last epiphysis has fused to the last shaft, that's it; you're all "grown up."

How long it takes from the time fusion begins until the time it's complete and the segments are firmly, permanently attached varies from bone to bone, but for each individual bone the process moves forward through known, identifiable phases and is completed by a predictable age. Thus, by comparing the progress of fusion in the bones (there is a standard five-stage model that most anthropologists use), a fairly narrow age range can be determined with reasonable confidence—always assuming, of course, that one is working with a set of remains that aren't too awfully far out along the tails of that bell-shaped curve. But all you can do about that is to knock on wood and hope for the best. And hedge your bets if you have any doubts. Whatever you do, however competent you are, you are going to get one wrong once in a while.

Gideon had four usable long bones to work with: the left collar bone (which might not seem to be one of the "long" bones, but is, physiologically speaking), the right femur, or thigh bone (the lower end only; the top had been chewed away), and the two bones of the lower leg: the thick, sturdy tibia and the slender fibula. Still, he thought that was enough to do the job.

He began with the clavicle, the collar bone, which he expected to give him an upper end of the age range. The clavicle is one of the last bones to fuse, the process typically not even beginning until about age eighteen. Thus, if the bone showed no evidence at all of fusion, as was indeed the case with this one, you were pretty safe in saying the individual was no older than eighteen. Okay then, as expected, she was no more than eighteen.

But he could do better than that. The leg bones develop on an earlier timetable than the clavicle does. In girls, while they vary from epiphysis to epiphysis, *all* of them are completely fused by the age of eighteen, when the clavicle is just getting started. But in examining the ones before him, Gideon found that, while all had begun the process of fusion, nothing was past the halfway point to completion. That meant, if the usual standards held (an appropriate place to pause for that knock on wood), that this young girl had never made it to eighteen at all, and very probably not past sixteen. So that lopped two years off the top end of the range.

What about the bottom end? As he'd just noted, all of the epiphyses of the knee and ankle joints had started on their way to attachment. But those of the knee didn't typically even *begin* to attach until fifteen or so. So, if "typically" held, this girl had to be at least fifteen and was probably no more than sixteen. Orihuela had missed on that score.

Fifteen to sixteen, a two-year range, and he didn't see how he could narrow it any more than that without *really* going out on a limb. He would have felt better with a seventeen-to-eighteen range, but—

"And why," Marmolejo's interested voice asked from the entry to the cubicle, "would seventeen to eighteen be better than fifteen to sixteen?"

Gideon was surprised to find out that Marmolejo had been standing there, but not at all surprised to learn he himself had been talking out loud. It was an old, comfortable habit, conversing with the skeletons, and he had long ago given up trying to break it; not, to be truthful, that he had ever tried very hard.

"Better in the sense that the skeletal maturation and the secondary sexual development of the skeleton would have been in sync, instead of one being well behind the other," Gideon explained. "It'd just be less unusual, that's all. Less peculiar."

"But you are satisfied that it is indeed a female?"

"Oh, no question. Orihuela was right about that."

"And the age? Fifteen to sixteen? How confident are you of that?"

A moment's hesitation this time, and a shrug. "Pretty confident."

"Pretty confident," Marmolejo repeated, head cocked in that thoughtful-monkey way he had. "Am I wrong, or is 'pretty confident' somewhat lower on the scale of certainty than 'Oh, no question'?"

Gideon smiled. "You're right, but that's my story and I'm sticking to it—at least until I look at the cranial remains. Oh, and there's one other thing I can tell you that I'm 'pretty confident' about. I think Orihuela may have underestimated the time since death. In the mine, the bones were largely protected from the environment. The weathering process would have been very slow. He estimated five years. I'd say twenty to forty is more likely. So when you go looking for evidence of what might have happened, take that into consideration."

Marmolejo nodded, not looking happy with this information. "Very good. Anything else?"

"Sorry, that's it for now. Haven't come up with anything that qualifies as a rabbit yet. Give me another hour or so, though; you never know. I'll stop by your office when I'm finished." He glanced at his watch. "Probably about four. Okay?"

By now Gideon felt ready to deal with the bag containing the mandible and skull, and as soon as Marmolejo had gone he unfolded and opened the sack. When he began lifting out the contents he found that the jawbone was almost whole, with only the right mandibular condyle, the ball-like process that forms the "hinge" of the jaw, snapped off and missing. On the cranium *per se*—the braincase—some of the sutures had pulled apart, giving it a warped look, but it was still essentially bowl-shaped and whole. But the facial skeleton—my God, it was as if it had exploded. It must have been in fifty pieces, not counting the dust-like sediment that had settled at the bottom of the bag.

After twenty minutes of work, with a little thought, a little trial and error, a little piecing of them together, he was able to identify thirty-one of the pieces; the rest were too small, mostly particles and fragments of the thin, curling, complex structures of the inner face—the ethmoid, the sphenoid, the lacrimal portion of the pterygoid. Some of them might even be rodent bones. Some parts of the facial skeleton were missing altogether, probably carried off by animals or eaten on the spot. He set the smallest pieces aside and concentrated on the recognizable chunks.

Much of the damage was postmortem, the "too much chewing by animales" of Dr. Orihuela's report. Very few bony edges failed to show some signs of carnivore gnawing. But the perimortem damage, the destruction that had been inflicted at the time of death, was as bad as you were likely to find on a human face. The maxilla, the main bone of the face, running from the eyes to the palate, had suffered what was known as a Le Fort I fracture, broken roughly in half by a side-to-side fracture that ran through the base of the nasal aperture, so that the palate and the upper teeth were separate from the rest of the face, like some grotesque parody of an upper denture. Both zygomatic bones—the cheekbones—had been crushed into crumbs just under and inside the bony orbits of the eyes. The inner and outer rims of the orbits had also been splintered and broken, with pieces missing. The nasal bone no longer existed and the sinuses behind them, on both sides, had been fragmented as well. That, along with the knocking-out of upper front teeth and the shattering of their sockets, was the major damage. There was plenty of minor damage too, all of it adding up to a confirmation of Dr. Orihuela's *fuerza despuntada*, although "blunt force" hardly conveyed the horrific extent of the destruction. Someone had smashed this kid in the face, judging from the damage probably right in the middle of the face, and more than once—probably more than twice—with something really heavy: a lead pipe, or a crowbar, or maybe a baseball bat.

The blows would have driven most of the skeleton of the face deep into the brain. He tried to visualize what they would have done to the fleshed, living head of a young girl. Then he tried not to visualize it. But certainly, the report's probable cause of death could now be considered confirmed. Nobody could have lived through that.

Other than that, there wasn't much these bone fragments could tell him beyond what he already knew. The unclosed cranial sutures were no help in aging, except to verify that she hadn't reached her mid-twenties. The sex criteria were all either neutral or female.

The deciduous teeth had all been shed, and all of the permanent teeth (those that hadn't been knocked out), except for the third molars, had come up. That was another nod in the direction of a minimum age of fifteen, because fifteen was generally accepted as the age at which the second molars were fully erupted. As for the state of development of the third molars, the upper jaw could tell him nothing because the back parts of it were gone. Not so in the mandible, however, and there he found that, while the third molars were not fully in place, they *had* broken through the bone and were a good third of the way up.

Predicting the age that wisdom teeth will erupt is risky business, since they are the most unpredictable of all the teeth, often not coming in at all. But a range of seventeen to twenty-one is a pretty safe bet. If these cranial fragments and teeth had been all that he'd had to work with, that would have been his guess: seventeen to twenty-one—which would have fit nicely with the advanced sexual maturation. But in this case he also had the long bones, and they suggested fifteen to sixteen.

Taking everything together, which was what you did when you had data that didn't fully match up (which is what you usually had), he was inclined to stick with his fifteen-to-sixteen estimate. The process of epiphyseal fusion was more reliable by far than the eruption of the wisdom teeth. As for the accelerated sexual maturation, that was just one of those things that you ran into from time to time, and, he supposed, maybe not all that surprising if the girl was sixteen.

And that, he thought, hoisting himself off the stool for another stretching break, was probably all he was going to be able to . . . He hesitated, frowning. *Wait a minute, wasn't there something about . . .*

He sat back down and picked up the mandible again, then the lower fragment of the maxilla, the one with the palate and the teeth. *Of course.* Four of the premolar teeth were missing. Normally, people have eight premolars or bicuspids, sets of two, left and right, upper and lower, between the canines and the molars. But this girl had only one in each place; none of her second premolars had come in. They hadn't been knocked out or been lost on account of disease; they'd never developed in the first place.

Naturally, he'd noticed it earlier, but with his attention, emotional and intellectual, riveted on the horrible maiming of the face, he hadn't really registered it until now. The condition was called hypodontia, and it was of forensic interest, both because it was rare—the incidence of one or more congenitally missing teeth ran at about 5 percent in most populations, but the probability of *all four* second molars being missing was—well, he didn't know what the incidence was, but it was surely under 1 percent. And it was of interest because it was genetically linked; it ran in families. This, he thought with satisfaction, could well be the most important thing he'd turned up in terms of coming up with who the girl was. With some legwork and a little luck, she might yet end up with a better resting place than a cardboard box in a government warehouse in—

"Gideon—"

This time Marmolejo's unexpected presence behind him made him jump. "Jeez! Javier, you have to stop sneaking up on me like that," he said irritably. "Get some leather heels or cough or something."

"You have my abject apology," Marmolejo said unconvincingly. "I came to tell you that four o'clock won't be possible. I'm on my way to a meeting in the office of the *procurador general* himself. The subject is the promotion of cooperation and teamwork between our various state and federal police agencies. This assures that it will be an extremely contentious meeting, and probably lengthy as well, so I may not be available for some time; perhaps as late as five. Or if that doesn't work—"

"Five is fine. I'm running a little slow anyway."

Marmolejo came a step closer and peered with interest at the bones. "Have you found anything more?"

"Actually, yes."

He explained about the missing teeth. Marmolejo was gratifyingly impressed. "You see? I knew you would find something. Congenital hypodontia, that is new to me."

"And on the age, move my 'pretty confident' up to 'very confident.'"

"But still short of 'Oh, no question'?"

"If you mean, would I bet my life on it? No, but it's the best you're going to get out of me. The epiphyses don't lie. She was fifteen or sixteen years old, or if you want to play it completely safe, make it fourteen to seventeen. I'll see you at five."

When Marmolejo left, Gideon stood up and stretched again, walked up and down the corridor a few times, turned down an offer of more coffee from Corporal Vela—it was getting to the time of day where a highball or a glass of wine would be more welcome—and returned to the cubicle to finish up.

There was nothing left but the bones of the feet, which he had not yet laid out properly. For whatever reason, in forensic analysis, these bones figure less than any of the others. There is less interest in them, less known about them, and less research done on them. Gideon wasn't sure why, but he thought it might simply be that feet just aren't that exciting, at least not to most people. Still, they had to be examined; as he had told Marmolejo, you never know what you're going to find.

The tarsus, composed of the four largest ankle bones, was missing, but everything else in the foot was there: the three smaller cuneiforms, the five metatarsals, and the fourteen phalanges that made up the toes, even the four tiny ones at the ends. That was unusual, and he assumed that the foot, like the foot of the mummy, had been encased in a shoe.

Almost the moment he began to lay them out anatomi-cally for a proper examination—no easy task; they are confoundingly similar—he ran into a shock. He found himself holding what he thought was a left first metatarsal in his right hand, and what he was sure was *another* left first metatarsal in his right hand. This was not as it should have been. The first metatarsal is the bone in the sole of the foot that leads to the first toe—the big toe—and like the toe itself, it is by far the strongest, bulkiest of its fellows, twice the thickness of any of the others, and therefore the easiest to recognize. Most important, we are entitled to only one apiece, not two. Two first metatarsals indicate two separate individuals just as surely as two jawbones do.

All alone in the cubicle, with no one to see him, Gideon Oliver blushed. He had just committed the simplest, most sophomoric error of omission that a forensic anthropologist can make. The very first thing to be established—how often had he drummed this into his students?—when faced with a pile of bones, is how many people one is dealing with. Well, strictly speaking, the first thing to be established is whether or not the remains are human, but figuring out whether you have one person or more than one is every bit as elementary. The fact that he'd been assured by the police that the carton contained a single individual was no excuse and he knew it. Cops weren't anthropologists. Doctors weren't anthropologists.

Everything he'd come up with, everything he'd told Marmolejo, was now in doubt. Were the legs and skull from one person or two (or more)? To which one did the clavicle belong? Or was that a *third* person? Why *wouldn't* the skeletal maturation and the sexual differentiation be out of joint if he were dealing with two or more people? How could he have been so careless, so cavalier . . . ?

In the midst of all this self-recrimination, he became aware that his own left thumb was trying to send him a message. Something didn't feel right about the metatarsal. Why was its head so smooth? Why couldn't he feel the grooves for the sesamoids? He took a closer look. The other end of the bone was peculiar too. Where was the prominence for the *Peroneus longus* tendon? What were those facets for the cuneiforms doing there? They should have been . . . they should have been . . .

It took him longer than he'd have liked to admit to realize what the problem was, or rather what it wasn't. He'd made a mistake, all right, but not the inexcusable one he thought he'd made. The thing was, the bone he was holding in his left hand wasn't another first metatarsal at all, it was the *second*, but greatly thickened, so that its bulk gave it the initial appearance of a first metatarsal.

Whew. One person, after all, and not two.

All the same, he finished laying out the foot bones now, as he should have done to begin with, just to be sure. And, happily, there they all were, with not a spare in the bunch. Other than the four missing ones from the tarsus, there were precisely enough to make one human foot; no more, no less.

One foot with a peculiar, grossly enlarged second metatarsal. Again, he picked it up, turned it round and round, fingered it, studied every ridge and fossa. Aside from its size, it was perfectly normal. The bulkiness wasn't the result of disease or trauma; it had been caused by muscular stress . . . and he was fairly sure he understood exactly what kind of stress it had been, although he needed to check a few sources to be certain.

He was also fairly sure that the age estimate he'd given Marmolejo was going to suffer a significant revision.

He couldn't help smiling. Marmolejo was going to love this.

TWELVE

WHEN the colonel got back to his office a little after five, he found Gideon getting up from Corporal Vela's computer. The colonel raised his eyebrows inquiringly.

"Just looking up a few things on the Internet," Gideon explained cheerfully.

The eyebrows settled down and morphed into one of Marmolejo's familiar, foxy expressions. "I know that look," he said, leveling a finger at Gideon. "You've come up with a rabbit, after all."

Gideon grinned. "I think I just might have," he agreed.

GIDEON, having been breathing bone dust for several hours, wanted some fresh air, so they went outside and sat on one of the peeling metal *Libertad* benches that lined the brick plaza out front. It was late afternoon now, with a drowsy sun on its way down, and the people going in and out of the *Procuraduría*, or just hanging around the vicinity, seemed mellower than they had earlier. Several pairs of people, mostly men, sat chatting and laughing on the other benches, or on the rims of the rusting fountains, and others were wolfing down tacos and Cokes in the clusters of plastic chairs that had been set up around umbrellaed food carts at the edges of the brickwork. Near the benches, three or four shoeshine stands—green-awninged metal chairs on wheels—had been set up. All had waiting customers.

It was all a little exotic and unfamiliar to Gideon, of course, but tinged with an everyday, life-goes-on normalcy that he found welcome. As always, it was restorative, even slightly surprising, to come out into the daylight after a session with the pitiful remains of a murder victim and find the sun shining and the world going along as usual.

"So, then," said Marmolejo. "Tell me." He sat peering at Gideon, very upright as usual, with a hand on each knee, and the toes of his tiny, perfectly buffed shoes barely touching the bricks, more than ever like a wise old monkey. Or perhaps better yet, a meerkat, erect, alert, attentive, intelligent.

"Umm . . ."

Marmolejo frowned. "Why do you hesitate?"

"I'm hesitating," Gideon said, "because I don't know which would be more fun: stringing you along bit by bit, or boggling your mind by giving it to you all at once."

"All at once, I think."

"Good enough. I was wrong about the age, and Orihuela was even more wrong about the age. She wasn't a girl, she was a grown woman—"

Marmolejo was not a man whose surprise plastered itself across his face, but this time it couldn't be missed. "A grown woman—"

"—who happened to be—"

"One moment please. Kindly wait until my mind stops boggling. All right, go ahead."

"—who happened to be a ballet dancer."

Marmolejo stared at him. "Do you mean to say you know *who* she was?"

"No, only what she was. You'll have to figure out the who."

"When you say ballet dancer, do you mean a professional ballet dancer?"

"Professional? That I don't know. Maybe. Serious? Yes."

"A grown woman, a ballet dancer," Marmolejo repeated. Hm." He continued to sit there inscrutably, meerkat-like, unmoving and silent, his chin slightly uplifted as if he were sniffing for the scent of outsiders on the wind.

"Uh . . . Javier, would you care to hear the brilliant manner in which I reached this new and startling conclusion, or aren't you interested?"

"Of course I'm interested. I said nothing because I knew I had no choice in the matter in any case. Go ahead, please. Tell me."

Gideon smiled and stood up. "No, I'll show you. Come on, let's go back to the bones."

"IT wasn't really so brilliant," Gideon said. "In fact, I was pretty slow to put things together. It was this bone here." He laid his finger on that enlarged second metatarsal, which had been put back in its place relative to the other foot bones, so that they were looking at an entire skeletal foot. "As you see, it's the longest of the metatarsals, which is normal, but ordinarily it'd be about the same thickness as these other three that lead to the smallest three toes, and only half as thick as this first one that goes to the big toe. But this one is huge, just about as thick as the first one."

"I see. And from this you infer?"

"That she engaged often, and over many years, in some kind of activity that put continuing heavy stress on this particular bone, which reacted to it, as bones do, by thickening up to better withstand it."

"And this activity you mention, this would be ballet dancing?"

"Right."

"Ballet dancing and only ballet dancing? Nothing else could account for it?"

"As far as I know, no. Nothing else stresses the second metatarsal and only the second metatarsal; or rather, I should say, nothing that anybody has found so far. That's what I was checking on the computer to make sure when you saw me there."

"I see." He scratched delicately and thoughtfully at his cheek. "From dancing *en pointe*, I presume."

"So you'd think—so I thought—but as a matter of fact, no, that isn't what does it. If it was, only female dancers would be affected, because they're the only ones who go around on tippy-toe, but male and female dancers get this equally. No, it's from dancing on what they call half- and three-quarter point, which is what they're all on most of the time. In that position the metatarsals act like an extension of the leg, and since the second metatarsal is the longest one, it takes most of the punishment. As I've just learned, something like sixty percent of professional dancers have second metatarsals like this one."

"All right, she was a dancer. But why have you changed your mind about her age? What happened to your previous certainty?" He sat himself on the one chair in the cubicle and turned his eyes up toward the stained acoustic-tile ceiling. "Let me see . . . 'The epiphyses do not lie,'" he said, deepening his voice in imitation of Gideon's. "Isn't that the way you put it?"

"Did I say that? Well, then maybe I overstated it a bit,"

Gideon admitted. "It's not that they lie, but sometimes they do hoodwink you a little, and this was one of those times. Young female ballet dancers—gymnasts too, by the way—are notable for having delayed skeletal maturation. Apparently, there's something about that kind of training that slows it down, or it might be that having slower skeletal maturation gives you an edge of some sort; nobody's really sure about the cause, but everybody agrees that it's a fact. According to the study I was reading when you came back, the average delay is about three years. So—"

"So," said Marmolejo, "your previous estimate of fifteen to sixteen now becomes eighteen to nineteen?"

"That's it. The emerging wisdom teeth lend some support to that too, by the way."

Marmolejo stood up and came again to the desk to look down on the bones. "Let me see if I can summarize. What we now believe we have before us is a woman eighteen or nineteen years of age—"

"Give or take a year either way to play it safe."

"—who had undergone serious ballet training, and whose dentition displays a condition known as congenital . . . ?"

"Congenital hypodontia involving the second premolars. I'll write it all up for you, Javier. You'll want to see if you can get some DNA samples from the bones too. If so, you'll be a long way toward identifying her."

Marmolejo nodded and looked quizzically up at Gideon. "This is quite a different story from the one you told me with so much certainty not much more than an hour ago. I mean no offense, my friend, but you were quite confident of your 'facts' then. How confident are you now?"

Gideon grinned. "Pretty confident," he said.

Marmolejo just rolled his eyes.

THIRTEEN

BY the time Gideon got back to the Hacienda at a little after seven P.M., dinner was problematic. Tony and Preciosa had gone to a concert in Oaxaca, so there was no obligatory family meal in the Casa del Mayordomo. And, at the request of the women professors, some of whom were also going into the city, Dorotea had served dinner at five thirty and started cleaning up with her nieces at six forty-five.

When Gideon and Julie peeked into the kitchen to see what the situation was, Dorotea, up to her roughened elbows in suds and dirty dishes, glared challengingly up at them. Words were not necessary; the look spoke for itself: *Just you* dare *and ask me to cook up something especially for you.*

"What now?" Gideon asked once they had backed apologetically out.

"Well, there are two sit-down restaurants in the

village, but they wouldn't be seating anybody as late as this; they're mostly there for day-trippers. But Jamie told me about a new place—well not a place, exactly; they set up a bunch of tables on the sidewalk in front of the village market, across from the church. The food's supposed to be great."

"Sounds good to me. Can we walk there?"

"Oh, sure, it's practically at the bottom of the hill, right in the middle of town. It's called Samburguesas."

"Hamburguesas?" This was the Spanish word for hamburgers.

"No, Samburguesas. It's a pun. The guy who does it, his name is Sam, and he serves—"

"Hamburgers, I get it. Okay, let's go. I guess I'm about ready for a burger."

IF there was anything that passed for night life in Teotitlán, it had to be Samburguesas, which was jammed with laughing, gossiping people happy to have an excuse to be out in the fresh air on a warm December evening. The place was like a cross section of Teotitlán society. There were grizzled, mustachioed, solitary old shepherds or farmers in from the hills, in sombreros and loose white working clothes; trendier young weavers in plaid shirts and designer jeans; and groups of young and old women, almost all in traditional dress, with their hair in long braids down their backs, and wearing *huipiles*— wraparound, apronlike tunics—over their housedresses, and *rebozos*—wide, multicolored cotton shawls—draped over their shoulders. Many of the younger ones used their *rebozos* as little hammocks in which to carry sleeping infants. A little away from the crowd, on the grass of the church plaza across the street, were the teenage boys and girls, mostly (like teenagers anywhere) hanging around and eyeing each other from same-sexed groups, the boys unconvincingly cocky and show-offy, the girls flirty and giggling. A few of the luckier ones had already paired off and were lounging on the grass farther away and out of the light.

Sam (they presumed he was Sam) operated from a stand under an awning on the side of the market building, serving *hamburguesas* and tacos as fast as he could make them, at five pesos each, about fifty cents. Despite the name of the place, almost everyone at Samburguesas was opting for the *tacos al pastor*, which smelled and looked heavenly, and Gideon and Julie did the same. Sam would deftly shave marinated pork from the sides of a *trompo*, a top-shaped vertical spit like the Middle Eastern roasters used to cook *gyros* meat, lay it over two stacked, warm, freshly made corn tortillas, and neatly top the whole with a slice of grilled pineapple.

With their paper plates of tacos in one hand and warm-ish cans of Mexico's most popular soft drink (Coca-Cola) in the other, they managed to snag a newly vacated folding table facing the old church tower, now floodlit as the night grew darker. Gideon cleared the table of the previous diners' leavings, came back, and sat down.

"Did you see Tony today?" he asked while they used plastic spoons to lay on condiments from the platter on the table: cilantro, lime, salsa, guacamole, chiles. "It seems to me he owes you an apology for last night. I was wondering if he made it."

"Yes, you said that before. No, I didn't see him, but if I did, I wouldn't expect one. He flies off the handle once in a while, but basically he's a good guy. He just—"

"Takes a little getting used to, yeah. You said *that* before. I'm sorry, that doesn't cut it as far as I'm concerned. Here you are, using your vacation time to help out—"

"Oh Gideon, I appreciate your taking offense on my behalf, but I really think you're overreacting. Some of your academic-type friends take some serious getting-used-to too. Audrey, for one, or Norton, or the huge one with the pince-nez—"

"Well yes, that's true enough—"

"Or if you want to talk about *really* creepy, what about Harvey—my God!—or Lyle—!"

"But that's different. They're—" He laughed. "Okay, point taken. I'll take Tony as he is."

For a while they busied themselves with their seriously overloaded tacos, the eating of which required the use of both hands, all of their focus, and the copious application of paper napkins, which were soon piled in a messy clump in the middle of the table.

"Oh, I have a little bit of news," Julie said, when they paused to wipe their chins and take a couple of breaths. "Annie's going to be back tomorrow morning. They settled on the divorce agreement in one day. She said, and I'm quoting, 'El Schmucko didn't have enough to make it worth fighting about.' She also said, 'He sure doesn't look like Robert Redford anymore.' That last was said with a certain amount of satisfaction, I should add."

"Good for Annie, but what does that mean for us? Are we going to be heading home?"

"Well, they said we were welcome to stay as long as we want, of course, but I think we should stick to our original plan—go home at the end of the week."

"That's fine with me. So then are you going to be free for the next few days? Can we do some touring?"

"Not altogether, no. I— Oops." She leaned quickly forward as a strip of salsa-drenched pork disengaged itself from the taco and plopped onto the table. Another napkin was produced from the dispenser to clean it up. "I promised to help Jamie with the quarterly accounts—I guess Annie is hopeless at that kind of thing, even worse than I am—but he says we can probably wrap it up in a couple of mornings, maybe only one. So I'm hoping to be available, yes, but not until tomorrow afternoon, anyway."

"That works out perfectly," said Gideon. "I need to write up a report for Marmolejo in the morning, on those bones I was working on today. I know what: maybe we can drop it off personally—I know he'd like to see you—and then continue on into downtown Oaxaca; have lunch out, maybe. There are supposed to be some first-rate restaurants."

"Maybe," said Julie, wiping her chin, "but I bet they won't be as good as Samburguesas."

"You're probably right." He swigged some Coke from the can and got up. "I'm still hungry. I'm going to get another taco. Want one? My treat. You can buy tomorrow."

AFTER dinner they walked contentedly back up to the Hacienda in the dark, their flashlight throwing weird, flitting shadows on the adobe-brick and concrete-block walls that lined the steep alley.

"What did you think of Preciosa?" Julie asked out of nowhere.

"Preciosa? I don't know, seemed okay to me. A little strange, maybe. And I can understand why Annie calls her Preciosa the Pretentious."

"How old would you say she is?"

Julie, Gideon had learned, had a bit of an obsession about women who employed face-lifts, dermabrasion, Botox, and the rest of the antiaging arsenal in their own obsessive, futile pursuit of staying young forever. The idea of it simply irked her; she didn't like to see them getting away with it when she herself was honestly taking age as it came. It also irked her that Gideon typically couldn't spot a face-lift when he saw one. So when she asked him that particular question—"How old would you say she is?"—in that particular tone of voice, it was inevitably with the purpose of setting him straight about some artificially enhanced actress or acquaintance that she thought might have him fooled.

"Preciosa?" he said. "Oh . . . late fifties, maybe sixty or so."

She was surprised. "I would have thought you'd have said thirties or forties."

"Are you kidding? No way," he said, then added: "The hands. You can always tell from the hands."

FOURTEEN

THE next morning Gideon sat out on the patio in the feathery shade of the casuarina tree, typing the report into his laptop, with a mug of Dorotea's delicious, cinnamon-scented coffee on the little table beside him. It had been plunked down without his requesting it, along with what he liked to think was a grumpy apology for sending him off dinnerless the previous evening. ("As long as you're sitting there, I suppose you expected me to make you some coffee.") Grumpy or not, he was keenly appreciative.

He also appreciated the music that was drifting up from below; the village marching band, which seemed to play several times a day: all trumpets and brass. The music this morning was slower than he'd heard before, quite funereal, in fact, something like the bands that play for a New Orleans funeral, but even slower, and with a mariachi lilt instead of a jazzy one. This one was a funeral procession too, he supposed; pretty appropriate background music for the work he was doing.

At a little after ten, he hit the Save button, copied the report to a flash drive, and went looking for Julie. When he checked the dining room, he saw Tony and Preciosa breakfasting with a few of the women professors. Tony beckoned him affably over, but Gideon refused stiffly. He hadn't meant to be rude, but he was still irked at the way Tony had jumped all over Julie at dinner the other night, and he couldn't help showing it.

Julie was with Jamie, at a table on the front terrace, going over a mess of accounts and receipts spread out in front of them. They were in a secluded corner that looked not out at the town, but down on the dusty corral twenty feet or so below, where Carl and Juanito, his Mexican helper, were saddling up horses for a morning ride for the women's group. Gideon stood near their table for a moment, leaning on the terrace's low stone wall, watching Carl and Juanito and savoring the smells of salty horse-flesh, old leather, and sweetly fragrant alfalfa feed. Carl glanced up at him and waved. "Gonna ride out along one of the arroyos this morning. Just half an hour, forty-five minutes, to get them comfortable with the horses. Want to come? Take no time to saddle one up for you."

"Thanks, no, not this morning," Gideon said. *There's room for only one alpha male on a ride like that,* he thought with a smile, *and it's not me.*

When Julie caught sight of Gideon her face lit up, producing a lovely, melting glow all through his chest. Was there anything sweeter in his life than seeing her uncontrived pleasure on unexpectedly seeing him? If there was, he couldn't think of it.

"Hi, honey!" she said. "Come join us."

"Well, you're obviously working. Why don't I—"

"No, no," Jamie said, beginning to gather the papers to him. "Enough, already. Thank you, Julie, we can finish up this afternoon."

A quick, wincing exchange of eyebrow-shrugs between

Julie and Gideon sent the same message both ways: *There went their plan to go into Oaxaca together.* "Tomorrow?" Julie mouthed, and Gideon nodded.

"Anyway," Jamie went on, "Annie'll be arriving at the airport, and I'm going to have to get going in a minute. Carl"—he gestured at Carl, manfully, gracefully cinching a saddle on a fidgety mare—"is tied up with a guest ride, so it's up to me."

"What about your knee, Jamie?" Gideon asked. "Can you drive all right? If not, I'd be glad to pick her up for you."

"No, it's not a problem. The vans all have automatic shifts, so I don't use my left leg. Have a seat, Gideon, will you?"

"Julie, I'm glad I found you!" It was Tony, striding toward them from the dining room, still chewing. "I owe you an apology. I was on you like a ton of bricks there the other night, and I had no business doing it. A few too many beers, I guess."

Tony rose a couple of notches in Gideon's estimation.

"I had no business prying," Julie said. "I had a few too many beers too."

Tony took a chair from another table, pulled it over, and straddled it wrong-way-round, with his elbows leaning on the back. The denim over his massive thighs was stretched tight with the strain. "You see—"

"Tony, it's all right, you don't have to," Julie said.

"No, I want to." He looked at his brother. "Or did you fill her in already, Jamie?"

Jamie shook his head, looking down at the papers he was continuing to arrange. "Not me."

"Okay, then." Tony took a rasping breath, gathering his thoughts. "It's like this. What I started to say—"

Gideon got up, murmuring. "I guess I'll go—"

Gruffly, Tony waved him back. "Just sit, will you? I got no deep, dark secret here. I just didn't want to talk about it in front of . . ." With his chin he gestured at Carl, still busy below with the horses, and well out of hearing range.

"It's like this. . . ." he said again and had to stop for another noisy, sighing breath. Deep, dark secret or not, he was having trouble getting it out. "See . . . well, in a way I'm responsible for what happened. With Blaze, I mean. When she . . . when she . . ."

"Tony, you are not responsible for what Blaze did," Jamie said with a patient resignation that suggested they had been through this many times before. "Nobody thinks that. Even Carl doesn't think so. You're the only one."

Tony ignored him. "See, the thing is," he said mostly to Julie, "things were messy. See, my father made Carl the executor of the will, with full power of attorney—"

"Technically, it wasn't power of attorney," said Jamie. "It was—"

"Well, whatever the hell you want to call it," Tony said with exasperation. "It meant that he was running the damn ranch for the two years it took me to get out of jail and show up. Okay?"

Jamie was silent.

"And you know Carl, he was working his ass off, and not doing too bad, either, considering it was just a horse ranch at the time. He was the boss man, and Blaze, she was the boss lady. And then, all of a sudden, after all that time, in walks the black sheep brother, who never gave a damn about the place, fresh out of jail, to take it all away from them. How could they *not* be ticked off?" Unexpectedly, he chuckled. "And if that wasn't bad enough, I was so big-headed I actually *fired* him, remember?"

"Well, for about five minutes," Jamie said.

"More like five days."

"You fired *Carl*?" Julie said, her eyebrows going up.

Tony shrugged. "Yeah, I did. Amazing, huh? See, I just—well, I wanted him out of my hair, you know? I mean, he was already sending me all this advice about how I should and shouldn't do things when I got back. I figured he'd cramp my style—I didn't know him then, you understand. So I sent him this letter telling him I was gonna let him go. I knew this guy Brax, you see—I forget his whole name—"

"Braxton Faversham," Jamie said.

Tony smiled. "Braxton Pontleby Faversham, right. Is that a name or what? Anyway, he grew up on this ranch in Oregon, so he knew all about that stuff, and I just figured I'd be better off with him as my head wrangler instead of Carl. But, I don't know, the more I thought about it, the lousier the idea got. My father really thought a lot of Carl, and I didn't really know Brax all that well. Besides," he said, laughing, "who ever heard of a head wrangler named Braxton Pontleby Faversham? So I changed my mind, told Carl I wanted him to stay. But the whole thing—he couldn't have liked it."

"Tony, that is simply not fair," Jamie said. "Have you ever once gotten even a smidgen of resentment from Carl?"

"Well no, not from Carl," Tony admitted, "but, you know, Carl's pretty good at keeping his feelings to himself. But be honest, how else could he feel? How would *you* feel? One day he's the boss of the whole shebang and the next day he's just another hired hand, taking orders from the jailbird son—the jailbird son on account of whose happy arrival his wife has just taken off with some sleazy ranch hand."

When Jamie opened his mouth to protest, Tony shushed him. "Anyway, it wasn't really Carl I was talking about, it was Blaze. And Blaze—I know you agree with me, Jamie, even if you won't admit it—Blaze was pretty damn hot-tempered, even as a kid. You'll never make me believe she didn't resent it when I came back. She must have thought I was gonna boot her out or something."

"Well, what did she say when you showed up?" Gideon asked. It wasn't his business, but he'd gotten caught up in the tangled story.

"She didn't say *anything*," Tony said. "She didn't stick around long enough for me to get there. That's my whole point. About three days after she finds out I'm on my way—two days before I show up—she's gone, along with What'shisname—"

"Manolo," Jamie supplied.

"With Manolo."

"Manolo and sixteen thousand dollars cash, the entire ranch payroll," Jamie said bitterly, and to Julie and Gideon: "Did you know he robbed me at *gunpoint*? It was the worst experience of my life. It was nightmarish, what with his waving the gun in my face and talking that way, without moving his mouth, like something out of *Night of the Living Dead*." At the memory a shudder ran visibly up his body and ended by making his head jerk. "I couldn't understand what he was saying, and he was getting more and more wild. He was like . . . I thought for sure he was going to shoot me."

"And you think," Julie said to Tony after a moment, "that she ran off with this guy because she couldn't stand losing the ranch to you?"

"That's exactly what I think."

"But I don't understand. She didn't just leave the ranch, she left *Carl*. Why would you feel responsible for that?"

"Well, maybe it wasn't *only* because of me. . . ."

"It wasn't at *all* because of you," Jamie insisted. "Tony, you'd been residing elsewhere for years—"

Tony laughed. "'Residing elsewhere.' Don't you love it?"

"You have no idea what Blaze was like. She was just so darn . . . She *should* have been in heaven. She had this beautiful little baby of her own—Annie—and as far as Carl was concerned, she walked on water; he couldn't do enough for her. But she just couldn't be happy, she simply didn't have it in her. Manolo wasn't the first . . . the first other man she was involved with, you know that."

"Yeah, I guess," Tony said listlessly. "But you know, Blaze and I never got along real well, even when we were kids. I don't know what it was. I think maybe she resented me because she thought the old man, you know, liked me best of all."

"The old man *did* like you best of all," Jamie said without rancor. He looked at his watch, straightened the papers, slipped them into a folder, and grabbed his cane. "Oh my goodness, Annie will be arriving in less than an hour. I'd better be on my way. Thanks again, Julie, we'll finish up easily tomorrow."

As he left, Dorotea appeared with a platter loaded with four more mugs of coffee and a plate of nougat-and-almond bars.

"*Gracias, mamacita,*" Tony said, brightening and snatching one of the bars off the plate before she could get it to the table. "Ah, *turrones*, my favorites! Still warm too."

"What isn't your favorite?" Dorotea said in Spanish and stomped back to the dining room with the empty platter.

"Dorotea's personality doesn't change much, does it?" Julie said, smiling.

"Heart of gold," said Tony, chomping away. "Best cook in Mexico. Wait till you try these." He shoved the plate at them.

Indeed, they were luscious. Feather light, but moist and chewy at the same time, and subtly sweetened with honey, they ranked right up there with the best confections he'd ever tasted. And that coffee! He was beginning to see why Tony and the others so willingly put up with the woman's crabbiness.

"What did Jamie mean," he asked after a couple of blissful swallows, "about Manolo talking weirdly? Did he have some kind of impediment?"

"Not before Carl gave him one," Tony said, laughing. "Busted his jaw in two places."

"Carl *hit* him?" Julie exclaimed. "It's hard to imagine that. He's always so in control, so calm."

As if to illustrate her point, a smiling, serene Carl, looking handsome and very much at home on horseback, was heading slowly out through the corral gate, followed by a line of devoted, mounted females. *Like a gaggle of imprinted ducklings scurrying after mama,* Gideon thought. *Well, maybe not quite.*

"Not when his wife is screwing around on him, I guess, pardon the language," Tony said. "I guess he did feel bad about it, though. He paid for getting the guy's jaw wired."

Another *turrón* slid down Tony's gullet, and then another, the last of them. ("You guys weren't gonna eat this, were you?") He finished his coffee, pulled over the one Dorotea had brought out for Jamie, and started happily on it as well.

"And Blaze was never heard from again?" Julie asked. "She never even wanted to hear about her daughter?"

"Nope, never."

"She just up and left with her boyfriend? No note, no anything?"

"No nothing," Tony said. "I mean, I hadn't got here yet—I didn't show up until a couple of days later—so all I know is what everybody tells me. Blaze used to go into Oaxaca for lessons once a week, and she'd stay overnight—Wednesday, I think, and come back on Thursday. So one week she leaves for her lesson as usual—this is, like, one day after this creep Manolo gets kicked off the ranch by Carl—only she doesn't show up the next morning the way she always does. And that happens to be Thursday, the morning Jamie brings back the payroll from Tlacolula. So Jamie gets in the van with a suitcase full of cash as usual, and starts driving back here, and as soon as he gets to a deserted stretch of road, Manolo jumps up and sticks a gun in his ear—he was hiding on the floor in back—grabs the cash, and drives off in the van, leaving the poor kid standing out in the desert, shaking like a leaf. I don't think he's ever gotten over it, even though there's no way it's his fault. He had to bum a ride on a manure wagon to get back."

"And then?" Gideon asked.

"There isn't any 'and then.' Good-bye Manolo, good-bye Blaze, good-bye payroll. End of story. Hey, look who's here!"

Jamie and a broadly smiling Annie were coming across the terrace toward them.

"How the hell did you guys get back so fast?" Tony said, getting up and holding his arms open for Annie, who responded with her own enthusiastic hug.

"Tony, it's so good to see you. I'm so glad I didn't miss you!"

There were a few minutes of chatter, mostly to explain that Annie had caught an earlier flight than expected and had taken a taxi to Teotitlán rather than wait for Jamie. The taxi had pulled into the Hacienda's parking lot just as Jamie was starting out for the airport in one of the vans.

"What happened to the *turrones*?" Jamie asked. "What happened to my coffee? I saw Dorotea bring it all out. I was gone, what, ten minutes, and it's all gone?" He shook his head. "Never mind, if I put my mind to it, I think I can figure it out."

Tony hunched his shoulders. "I was hungry."

"*Turrones?*" Annie said. "Did I miss *turrones*?" She was back on her feet and headed for the kitchen. "Maybe she made a few more."

Smiling, Tony watched her go. "One thing we got in

this family, we got healthy appetites," he said approvingly, then called after her. "Hey, bring out whatever she's got in there. We could use some more coffee too!"

"What kind of lessons was she taking?" Julie asked Tony.

"Huh?"

"You said Blaze went into Oaxaca for lessons every week. I was just wondering what she was taking."

"Oh hell, I don't know. I think it was some kind of—"

"Dance," Jamie said. "Blaze'd been taking ballet lessons since she was nine. She was really serious about it too; practiced three solid hours every morning, seven days a week, even right after Annie was born. That's one of the reasons I couldn't believe it when she actually—"

It had taken all this time since the word "dance" for Gideon to find his voice. "She was a *ballet dancer*?" he croaked.

Jamie looked at him, puzzled. "That's right, a good one. We all expected her—"

"How many teeth did she have?"

Now everybody looked confused, including Julie.

"How many teeth?" Jamie echoed with a hollow laugh. "I have no idea."

"Tony, do you know?"

"No, how the hell would I know how many teeth she had?" Like the others, he'd been thrown off by Gideon's sudden intensity. "What's this with teeth?"

"How many teeth do *you* have?"

"How many—I don't know, how many teeth does anybody have?"

"Mind if I peek?"

Tony looked at him peculiarly, then shrugged. "What the hell, help yourself." He opened his mouth and Gideon peered in.

"No, they're all there. Damn," he added softly.

"Damn?" Tony echoed. "What do you mean, *damn*? Why shouldn't I have all my teeth?"

A thoughtful look had settled over Jamie's face while this was going on. Gideon could see that his tongue was poking at his teeth.

"What about you, Jamie? Are you missing any?"

"Well yes, it's odd that you should ask. Four of my teeth never did come in. I forget which ones. Not the important ones; the second somethings."

"Premolars," Gideon said. "Bicuspids."

"That's it, bicuspids. But what in the world—"

"I don't have all mine either," Annie said, having arrived with a plate bearing a few more *turrones*. "Mine never came in either. It runs in the family. Doesn't really cause any problems, though. Who needs bicuspids? Why are we talking about teeth, anyway?"

Gideon sighed. "I have some news for you, folks." Boy, did he have some news. He looked up at Annie. "Annie," he said gently, "maybe you'd better sit down."

FIFTEEN

HE couldn't blame them for refusing to accept it at first. He was having a hard time accepting it himself, and he was new to the story of Blaze's abandoning her child and running off with Manolo to Juárez, or whatever it was. He'd never heard of either of them before last Sunday, three days ago. But these others—Jamie, Tony, Annie— they had lived with the tale for almost twenty years; it was established family history by now, validated by time and by retelling. Besides that, they all remembered the *policía ministerial*'s onerous investigation, only a year earlier, of the "little girl's" skeleton that had been discovered in the mine.

And now, just because Gideon Oliver, after a few hours' perfunctory work, without instruments or laboratory facilities of any kind, concludes that the police pathology experts from Mexico City were dead wrong, that the "little girl" was actually a big girl, they were supposed to accept it as proven fact? And even more unimaginable, that out of all the unidentified skeletons in Mexico it could possibly be, it was that of their own Blaze? They were supposed to swallow that as well?

With all due respect, other than Julie they did not; not at first. But slowly he explained, and slowly they came around; first Tony, then Jamie, and finally, most reluctantly, Annie. The probability of a nineteen- or twenty-year-old woman, who happened to be a ballet dancer *and* who shared a rare genetic condition of missing teeth with Annie and Jamie *and* who had been found in this remote, barely populated region only a few miles from the Hacienda Encantada *and* for whom no identification had ever been made *and* who had been killed at about the right time—the probability of such a person's being anybody *but* Blaze Gallagher Tendler was simply too implausible for them to hold on to in the face of Gideon's coherent exposition.

The fresh *turrones* lay untouched and cooling on the table throughout. Once it had all sunk in, Tony was the first to speak. "Let me get this straight. You're saying she never ran away with that guy? You're saying she was *murdered*? There's no doubt about that?"

"None. Her face—" He had almost forgotten for a moment that he was talking to Blaze's two brothers and—especially—to her daughter. "None," he said.

"How was she killed?" Annie asked dully.

"Blunt-force trauma." Gideon hoped she'd let it go at that and was relieved when she merely nodded and looked down at her hands. He wouldn't have looked forward to telling her that her young mother's beautiful face had been pulped with something along the lines of a baseball bat.

"So he actually *killed* her," an incredulous Jamie said. "Manolo?"

"Who the hell else?" Tony said bitterly. "The sonofabitch. Robbing the frigging payroll and taking her away from Carl wasn't enough payback for him." He shook his head slowly back and forth. "And all this time we thought . . ."

"No," Annie said dully, "Manolo wouldn't have killed her. Why would Manolo have killed her?"

"Hey, honey," Tony said kindly, "maybe this is something it's not so good for you to be talking about right now. This is kind of a shock to everybody, you most of all. You sure you don't want to go unpack or something, get your head clear? We can talk about it later."

"Forget it," she said stonily. "I'm staying. So why would Manolo have wanted to kill my mother?"

Jamie answered diffidently. "Well, so he could have that sixteen thousand dollars all to himself; he could have lived on that for five years. Or maybe it was just to get back at your father, I don't know. But my point is, once he had the money, why would he want to take her with him? You can't seriously think he was in love with her?"

Julie shook her head. "But even so, as Annie said, why would he want to kill her? He could just as easily have taken off with the money without murdering anyone."

"Could be he just didn't want to leave any loose ends behind," Tony suggested. "She must have known about his plans, about where he was going. She could have put the police on his tail."

"So he could have changed his plans and gone someplace else, anywhere he wanted," Julie persisted. "Sixteen thousand dollars—he must have felt like a rich man. So why go out of his way to kill her? Why would he risk a murder charge hanging over his head, instead of a simple robbery? Besides, if he was worried about the police hunting him down, he'd have killed you too, Jamie. Right then and there, on the road, it would have been the easiest thing in the world. You were the only eyewitness, the only one who could identify him for sure as the person who robbed you."

Jamie's eyes widened slightly and his Adam's apple jigged up and down. "Yes, you're right," he said in a hushed voice. "That's certainly true."

"What do you think, Gid?" Tony asked. "You know more about this kind of stuff than any of the rest of us. You got an opinion?"

"I don't see that knowing something about bones gives my opinion any more weight than anyone else's, but on the face of it, Manolo would probably be at the top of my list."

"What about you, Tony?" Jamie asked. "What's your theory?"

"I don't have a theory. How could I? I wasn't around until a couple of days later and I hardly know anything about Blaze other than what I've heard here. The last time I saw her she was, like, fourteen. But don't worry, the police will come up with plenty of theories."

"The police," Jamie groaned, rolling his eyes. "God help us, do you mean to tell me the police have to be involved in this? After all these years?"

"I don't see any choice," Gideon said. "I have to tell Colonel Marmolejo about it, and he'll certainly put somebody on it. I'm seeing him later today, so it won't be long."

Jamie frowned. "Damn. That's terrible."

Annie flared angrily up. "Terrible? What the hell is the matter with you, Jamie? Don't you want to see whoever did it caught? Don't you want to see him punished?"

Jamie was shocked. "Well yes, of course I do, Annie, how can you even ask that? I just hate to see this terrible old business dragged out in public again after all this time. Besides, I'm afraid . . . you know."

"No, I don't know. Tell me. Afraid of what?"

"Well . . ." he fidgeted in his chair. "The police are going to ask a whole lot of questions, and the first one is going to be: who had any reason to want her dead? Am I right, Gideon?"

"Maybe not the first, but it won't be very far down the line."

"All right, then," Jamie said, addressing all of them, "and who is the person that had the most reason to hate Blaze, to be out-of-his mind enraged at her?"

Brows were knit in thought for a fraction of a second, and then Tony abruptly exploded. "For Christ's sake, are you honestly suggesting that Carl . . . that Carl murdered his own wife? I don't believe this!" He was halfway out of his chair. His blotchy red face, thrust out at his brother, had blotched and purpled even more; his nose was flaming.

Predictably, Jamie quailed. His hands came up as if to ward off the assault. "No, Tony, come on, give me a break, I'm not accusing Carl of anything. Of course not! Why is everyone picking on me? I'm just saying what the police are bound to think. I'm just saying we have to be very careful what we say to them, that's all."

"Oh." Tony sat back down. His color subsided. "Sorry, Jaime, I didn't mean to fly off the handle. You're right, we better give this some thought."

"Look, folks," Gideon said, "this is your affair and I don't want to interfere, but I've been involved with a lot of police investigations, and my advice is not to try to protect Carl or anyone else; in fact, not to 'try' to do anything. Just answer their questions as truthfully as you can. Otherwise, you'll wind up making trouble for yourselves *and* for Carl."

"Yeah, but you're talking about American police," said Tony. "Down here it doesn't work the same, trust me."

"Well, I know you know more about that than I do—"

"Do I ever," Tony said with a harsh laugh.

"—but if Colonel Marmolejo is involved in it, I think you can count on decent treatment. And don't try conning the guy—trust *me* on that."

Tony smiled, keeping his thoughts to himself.

"Speaking of Carl . . ." Julie said, gesturing with her chin toward the corral gate, through which Carl was leading the straggling line of ladies back from their short ride.

"Whew," Jamie said. "Who's going to tell him about this?"

"I'll do it," Tony said, grim-faced, beginning to push himself up.

"Uh-uh," Annie said, putting a hand on his arm to keep him in his chair. "I will."

They watched her go down the stone steps to the corral, watched her go up to Carl as he dismounted, and saw Carl's tanned, lined face go through a parade of expressions that would have been comic under other circumstances: pleasure at seeing his daughter—she'd been away three days—followed by frowning concentration, then disbelief, then denial, then anger, and then something like despair, all in the space of ten seconds, all without having let go of the reins. Then he closed his eyes and turned away from his daughter, leaning his face against his horse's neck. Annie, looking stricken, began to stretch a hand toward him, but pulled it back.

"I think I better go down there too," Tony said.

Jamie grabbed his cane and got up with him. "Me too. The poor guy, can you imagine?"

When they'd gone, Julie said with just a trace of irony: "No one's ever going to be able to say that you don't know how to stir things up, Dr. Oliver."

"Well, what was I supposed to do, not say anything? Just let them keep thinking she ran off with the guy and never bothered to come back?"

"Of course not. Why are you angry?"

He blinked. "Am I angry?"

"Yes. Well, a little."

He shrugged. "I guess I am, a little. I think maybe

it's more guilt than anger. I know you're going to tell me I'm being silly, but I feel bad about digging up something like that when nobody asked me to, and especially about dumping it in their laps that way—*plop*. I should have been a little more sensitive about the way I broke the news."

"You're right, I'm going to tell you you're being silly. You did fine," Julie said staunchly. "You were as surprised as they were, so it just popped out. You know, when they think about it a little more, they may come to see it as good news."

He gave a short laugh. "I don't see how."

"Maybe good isn't the right word, but what I mean is, now Annie isn't left believing that her mother totally abandoned her, never bothering to get in touch again or find out anything about her in almost thirty years."

"That's a point."

"And Carl . . . now he knows that Blaze never did run off from him."

"He knows she *intended* to."

"Does he? Now I'm starting to wonder about that too. Did she *tell* him she was leaving him? Did she leave a note? As far as I know, she didn't do either. So how do we know for sure that the story about her running away with Manolo has anything to it? How do we know that she had anything to do with the robbery at all?"

"I don't know," Gideon said, getting interested. "How *do* we know?"

"That's the question. Did it just get pieced together after the fact—everybody saying, 'Well, she's gone, and he's gone, and the payroll's gone, and we know they had a thing going, so they must have been in on it together.' Well, maybe yes, maybe no. There's a lot we need to find out, Gideon."

"No, there's a lot Marmolejo or whoever he puts on the

case needs to find out," Gideon corrected. "Let's not stir
the pot any more than I already have."

"And another thing," Julie continued placidly on,
"what makes us so sure *Manolo* really left? What makes
us think he wasn't killed too?"

"Why would we think he *was*?"

"For the same reason Blaze was—the money. Maybe
somebody killed them both for the money."

He shook his head. "Well sure, maybe, but that's about
as hypothetical—as speculative—as you can get. There's
nothing at all that points to it that I can think of."

"Okay, I grant you there isn't. But half an hour ago
you could have made the same point about Blaze: there
wasn't a shred of evidence to suggest she hadn't taken off
with Manolo."

"Except for that little matter of her skeleton."

"But until Mr. Skeleton Detective came along and
stuck his nose in, everybody assumed it was some little
girl, which made it impossible for it to be Blaze. How do
we know there might not be some other unidentified skeleton out there that will turn out to be Manolo's?"

"Because there isn't. These were the only unidentified
skeletal remains Marmolejo's office had. Nobody's found
any others."

"Maybe, but that doesn't mean they're not out there.
The fact that something hasn't been found hardly proves
its nonexistence, does it? What evidence is there that he
hasn't been killed?"

"That he *hasn't* been killed? Other than having him
walk in the door, how can there be evidence—whoa, this
is getting pretty deep. Are we getting into epistemology
here?"

"Look, nobody found what's turned out to be Blaze's
skeleton either, until just last year, and Blaze has been
dead almost thirty years. How can we be sure someone

isn't going to find another skeleton out there in the desert a month from now, or a year? Or tomorrow?"

"We can't, of course. But are you suggesting that the possibility that something as yet unfound should be considered probable evidence of its existence?"

Why, they weren't sure, but they both started laughing. "Let's call it a draw," Gideon said.

"All right, but I'm going to mention my theory to Javier when I see him. He can do what he wants with it."

"No reason not to, but you don't have a theory, Julie. A theory requires at least *some* observed facts from which to draw reasonably reliable inferences that can then—"

"Okay, my hypothesis."

"You don't have a hypothesis, Julie. Even a hypothesis has to be founded on *observed* phenomena that—"

She was rolling her eyes. "Okay already, my speculation! All right?"

"You don't h—"

"My conjecture! My supposition! My *unverified* supposition? My blind guess? My shot in the dark?"

Gideon stroked his chin contemplatively. "I would accept blind guess, yes."

She made a face and threw a balled-up napkin at him, and they broke into laughter again. "Oh, the joys of being married to a pedant," she said.

Below, Carl, Annie, Tony, and Jamie were speaking rapidly in a tight, earnest little cluster near the horse.

"I sure hope they're not putting their heads together to cook up some kind of story to protect Carl," Gideon said. "Marmolejo will see right through it. Besides which, I'll have to tell him whatever I've heard about it."

Julie nodded. "I know you will. When are you going to see him?"

"I think I should head over there now. I gather you can't come with me after all; Jamie said the two of you needed to finish up whatever you were doing this afternoon."

"Well, I should be free all day tomorrow. How about if we go into Oaxaca then?"

"You're on."

"Gideon," she said thoughtfully, "do you really think Javier will be interested enough to pursue this? I know, cold cases are what he's working on, but this one's positively freezing. It was almost thirty years ago."

"Julie, if I know Javier as well as I think I do, he'll be after this like a fox goes after a rabbit. He lives for this kind of thing."

SIXTEEN

IT appeared, however, that Gideon did not know Javier as well as he thought he did. Marmolejo heard him out with patient interest, but when it was done, he sat back, engulfed in his enormous chair, rolled his brown thumbs over each other, and said: "Well, my friend, I can't deny that you've produced your usual rabbit, but I'm afraid I don't see what I can do about it."

"What you can do about it?" Gideon exclaimed. "How about an investigation, for starters? Obviously, there's never been one, at least not on the right track, since no one even knew she was dead. And the people who were closest to her are all still right there, they've never been questioned about it. Surely, there's information to be gotten."

"I don't doubt it. Still—"

"What *do* you doubt? Do you think my identification might be wrong?"

"No, but—"

"I thought cold cases were what you were here for. What, is this *too* cold for you?"

"Yes, exactly. There would be no point. You see—"

"No point?" Gideon was having a hard time understanding Marmolejo's reticence. This was utterly unlike the man, whom Gideon knew to be the most dogged and resourceful of policemen. "How can you possibly say there's no point?" he said in exasperation. "I don't understand you."

Marmolejo merely sat there, quietly smiling at him, not with his mouth but with those exotic Mayan eyes, opaque and strangely piercing at the same time.

"What?" Gideon said.

"I'm permitted to speak now?"

"Go ahead."

"An entire sentence? Perhaps even two?"

"Who's stopping you from—" Gideon stopped, laughed, and relaxed back into his chair. He'd been propped tensely on the front edge of it. "Sorry about that, Javier. I apologize. Sure, go ahead. What the heck, take three if you really need them."

Marmolejo soberly leaned forward, elbows on the desk. "I gather you aren't familiar with our statute of limitations."

Gideon shook his head. "No, but surely there's no statute on murder."

"Ah, but there is: fourteen years. After fourteen years, cases cannot be prosecuted. This death would seem to have occurred thirty years ago."

"That's crazy. Every . . . country excludes murder from its limitations statutes."

"Every country but Mexico," Marmolejo said bleakly.

Gideon had almost said "every *civilized* country." Now he was glad that he hadn't. "But Javier, statute or not, surely you want to look into this—a brutally killed young wife and mother, a—"

"Of course I *want* to, Gideon," Marmolejo said with just a tinge of exasperation himself. "Unfortunately, I am bound by the parameters of certain policies and procedures. How can I justifiably devote public resources to the pursuit of an investigation that can have no legitimate juridical outcome?"

Gideon nodded. "Okay, you're right. I can see that."

Marmolejo looked at him suspiciously, closing one eye as if he were studying him through a microscope. "If you can see that, may I ask what that small, secretive smile is about?"

"That small smile—I didn't realize it was secretive—is strictly in admiration of your English. I mean: 'How can I justifiably devote public resources to the pursuit of an investigation that can have no legitimate juridical outcome?' I don't know a lot of native English speakers that would put it quite so eloquently. In writing, maybe. Not talking."

"I take that as a compliment, and I appreciate it, but I would appreciate it still more if you attended to the *substance* of my words."

"I'm sorry," Gideon said, clamping down on the smile. "And what, pray tell, is the substance of your words?"

"The substance of my words—of the words that I was about to utter—is that I would greatly prefer that *you* don't look into it either. I wouldn't want to see you put yourself at risk, especially for something that is beyond prosecution."

"Me? What can I do? I'm only going to be here a few more days anyway."

"Even if you were to ferret something out, even if you were to identify her murderer, nothing could be done about it, you understand?"

"Sure."

Marmolejo peered at him with narrowed eyes. "Gideon, I would rest easier if I had your explicit promise to refrain from investigating the matter on your own. No good can come of it."

He was right, Gideon knew. If the murderer were identified, what good would it do? Nothing could be done about it, or at least nothing legal. And what if it should turn out to be somebody close to the Gallaghers, or even in the family? That would be horrible, an impossible situation, impossible to remedy satisfactorily.

"Okay, I promise," he said. "Honestly."

That seemed to satisfy Marmolejo. "All right then." He smiled. "Unfortunately, it looks as if you must gird your loins and face up to the dreadful prospect of simply relaxing and enjoying yourself for the remainder of your stay. Go and see some ruins. They always please you."

"I will, Javier."

BUT not just yet. After a quick lunch with Marmolejo at one of the taco stands on the *Procuraduría* plaza, he drove not to one of the area's archaeological sites, but back to Teotitlán. However, instead of continuing through the village and up to the Hacienda, he parked in the open area between the market and the church, where Samburguesas had been set up the evening before. On the other side of the church was police headquarters, in the plain, one-story, ochre-colored building that held the village municipal offices. PALACIO DE GOBIERNO, the sign beside the one door somewhat grandly proclaimed.

That Sandoval himself was not in his office could be seen from the outer room, and a grizzled cop in uniform—dark blue trousers, matching T-shirt and light-weight blue tunic (no handgun tucked into the belt or

anywhere else)—informed Gideon that the chief would
be back soon, in ten minutes or so. Maybe twenty. Could
be a little more.

Gideon didn't mind waiting; he'd seen nothing of the
village and this was an opportunity. He strolled the main
street—almost every doorway opened into a weaver's
gallery—for ten minutes before he was driven indoors by
the sun. Back at the police station, he found that Sandoval
had not yet returned. He spent the next fifteen minutes
visiting the old Spanish church, then checked back. No
Sandoval. Then twenty minutes at the little community
museum, looking at the weaving exhibits and the archaeological relics, and back to the police station to inquire
again. No Sandoval. Maybe ten minutes, the old cop, who
was starting to look irritated, told him. Maybe twenty, he
yelled after the retreating Gideon.

Gideon decided to give him ten more minutes, enough
to walk around the block that held the church. He was
glad he did. On the church's south side was a small *zona
arqueológica*, a forty-by-twenty-foot swath of exposed
excavation. Earlier, he had seen the Zapotec reliefs
embedded in the white stuccoed wall surrounding the
church plaza, but he hadn't realized that the church itself
had been built on *top* of a destroyed Zapotec temple. The
archaeological zone made that beautifully clear, expos-
ing a carved-stone corner from the base of the ancient
temple, with the two bell towers and the twin red domes
of the "new" church rising almost directly from it. It was
marvelous, as perfect an example as he'd ever seen of the
Spanish colonial practice of demolishing a native temple and using its ruins as the foundation for a Catholic
church, thereby accomplishing two important purposes
at once: making use of ground that was already sacred;
and, more significant, demonstrating the power of the
Christian deity over that of the native gods.

It was all interesting enough to keep him happily there for thirty minutes instead of ten, so that by the time he got back to the police station Sandoval had actually arrived. The chief, volubly apologetic over Gideon's having had to call more than once, was stammering out his excuses: an important meeting with the mayor to discuss a critical traffic revision; then the weekly meeting of the village council, at which he was required to present a summary of police activities; then the troublesome matter—

"Flaviano," Gideon said when Sandoval was forced to stop for breath, "didn't you say the other day that someone had once found an old Zapotec skeleton in the same mine that they found the skeleton of the girl last year?"

At the unexpected question, Sandoval blinked. "Yes, that's right." A quick breath, expelled through his mouth, showed that he was relieved. Gideon wasn't going to involve him in more complicated relations with the police. Those old bones had nothing to do with him. But just to make sure Gideon understood that, he added: "That was eight, ten years ago, *long* before I was the police chief."

"You said it was quite old, maybe a thousand years."

"Yes. Well, *I'm* not the one who said so. Dr. Ybarra, he said so."

"Dr. Ybarra?"

"Sure, the *médico legista* before Dr. Bustamente. Oh, a very good man, much more easy to get along with than . . . well."

"How did he know?"

Sandoval's brow wrinkled. "How did he . . . ?"

"How did he know it was ancient and not modern?"

"I don't know nothing about that, but Dr. Ybarra, he would know such things; a real scientist, an educated man, not like . . . well."

"Would it be possible for me to get in touch with him?"

Sandoval smiled. "Not before you enter the next world, my friend."

"Ah. Well, do you have any paperwork on it?"

"No, why should there be paperwork?" He was starting to get nervous again. Mother of God, was he going to get dragged into this somehow, after all? "What is this about, Gideon?" he asked nervously.

"Well, I've been thinking about Blaze's murder—"

Sandoval did another of his classic, pop-eyed double takes. "Blaze's *murder*? You mean Blaze from the Hacienda? I thought she ran away somewhere!"

"So did everybody else," Gideon said, realizing that of course Sandoval had no notion of what Gideon had only figured out for himself not much more than four hours ago.

So that took some explanation, and although the more he explained, the more stunned the chief's expression became, Gideon thought that he had gotten the basic point through. The bones that had turned up last year were not those of some anonymous "little girl"; they were the earthly remains of wild, young Blaze Gallagher Tendler, sister of Tony and Jamie, wife of Carl, mother of Annie.

"I don't understand," Sandoval said.

"Nobody understands," Gideon said. "Yet." He was on the verge of asking another question about Blaze, but his pledge to Marmolejo held him back. He had promised not to investigate what had happened to her and, being a man of his word, he wouldn't.

But he hadn't promised not to look into what had happened to *Manolo*. Sure, at Marmolejo's insistence, he'd agreed not to probe into "the matter," but the matter under consideration at the time had been Blaze's death, not Manolo's. Marmolejo's interpretation of this admittedly hairsplitting distinction might differ (*would* differ, he was pretty sure), but Gideon thought he could talk his way out of it. It was merely a question of semantics, after all, a "what the meaning of *is* is" kind of thing.

In any case, it was Manolo that he was interested in now. Julie's conjecture this morning, her "blind guess"— "What evidence is there that he *hasn't* been killed?"— had snagged itself a perch in his mind, had clamped there with birdlike little talons, and had been nagging away at him ever since. What evidence *was* there that he hadn't been killed, right along with Blaze? The only evidence, if you could call it that, was that his body had never been found, and there were no unaccounted-for remains anywhere in the area.

Except for one ancient Zapotec skeleton, which, as it happened, had been found in the same mine in which Blaze's skeleton had turned up a decade later. But *was* it an ancient Zapotec skeleton? Did Dr. Ybarra, educated though he might have been, know what he was doing when it came to something like that?

The odds were that he did. And the likelihood that it was Manolo was pretty minimal, to say the least. Besides, even if it did turn out to be him, there was nothing to be done about it; the fourteen-year statute of limitations would apply. So there really was no point in looking into it. Still, since Gideon was here in Oaxaca anyway, and since he had nothing else on his agenda at the moment . . .

"This skeleton," he said, "do you know where it is now?"

"Sure, the man who found it—I wasn't the chief then, you understand, so I had nothing to do with it, but I remember—the guy who found it, he knew he couldn't take it back to Canada with him, so he gave it to this guy, Beto, who has a bar in Tlacolula. La Casa Azul."

"And that's where it is now?"

"Yeah. Well, the skull is. He has it on a shelf behind the bar, with, you know, a candle on it, and all that candle stuff, all different colors, dripping down over it. I saw it once."

"I'd like to have a look at it, Flaviano. Could you show it to me?"

Sandoval shrugged. "If you want, sure, but you don't need me. La Casa Azul's real easy to find. It's right on the main street. And the skull, it's right there on the shelf, where anybody who wants can look at it."

"But I'm probably going to want to take it down, handle it. And I'd like to see the rest of the skeleton too. Could you at least give Beto a call and arrange that?"

"Sure, you bet," Sandoval said expansively. "I'm glad to help." He could hardly believe he was getting out of it so easily. "I do it for you right this minute."

But it wasn't quite as easy as that. "He don't have it anymore," Sandoval said as he hung up. "Beto, he sold the skull to another guy."

"Oh boy," Gideon said softly.

"No, no, you can still see it anyways. This other guy, he runs a museum in Oaxaca, in the city. Beto says he's got it in a glass case, all cleaned up."

"Great. And what about the rest of the skeleton, is that in the museum too?"

"No, Beto don't remember what happened to that. He thinks maybe he threw it out."

Gideon sighed. Still, the skull was the critical element in what he hoped to find out. "Do you know where I can find the museum?"

Sandoval did. The Museo de Curiosidades was located only four blocks from the Zócalo, on Calle las Casas. He had been there once with one of his young nephews who had a ten-year-old's taste for the bizarre. The boy had heard about the place and couldn't wait to see it, and Sandoval had taken him there for his tenth birthday.

"It's a pretty weird place, Gideon," he said, shaking his head. "You know, shrunken heads, baby mummies,

Aztec knives, that kind of stuff. It's in this rundown old *casa*, all dark and smelly. Checho, he loved it, but to me it gave the creeps."

"Sounds like my kind of place," Gideon said. "I'll stop in tomorrow morning."

"No, it's only open in the afternoon, from noon till four, I think. The guy that runs it, he's a little strange."

SEVENTEEN

"THEY'RE *not going to investigate it? They're not going to do anything at all?*"

It was the first time Gideon had seen Carl show anything that might qualify as emotion, and he was showing plenty of it. He had risen from his chair and was leaning tensely forward, hands on the table, eyes blazing. An artery pulsed at each pale temple.

Gideon had arrived late for the family dinner, served this evening not in Tony's quarters, but out on the dining terrace. The feminist professors had gone home, and the only other diners were a Canadian family of three and a lone Albuquerque gallery owner who had come to Teotitlán to buy weavings for his shop. The four guests were sitting inside, so the Gallagher clan had the darkening terrace all to themselves and were already well into dinner when Gideon got there. A buffet had been set up and they all waited politely while he helped himself to a couple of wedges from a *clayuda*—a crisp, pizza-sized, wood-oven-blackened tortilla topped with beans, sausage, and cole slaw—shrimp enchiladas slathered in now-tepid mole sauce, and a longneck brown bottle of Cerveza Montejo.

However, he could sense their impatience to hear the upshot of his meeting with Marmolejo, and he'd barely sat down next to Julie and taken his first bite of *clayuda* before the barrage of questions erupted. What did the colonel have to say about Blaze? How did he act? What did he think? Where would he go from here? Would the police be coming to Teotitlán to get depositions or would they all be required to go into Oaxaca? When would the investigation begin?

Gideon managed to down a couple of swallows of beans and sausage and a single swig of beer, then held up his hand to cut them off. It would, he thought, be best to go right to the hard facts. There would be no investigation, he told them in so many words. Blaze had disappeared twenty-nine years before. The statute of limitations had expired fifteen years ago.

That had taken a few seconds to sink in, and then Carl had exploded. "They can't get away with this," he was yelling now. "I don't give a . . . I don't care about any goddamn statute of limitations, I'm not just going to let this lie. There has to be somebody else to talk to."

But he didn't look as if he really believed it and neither did anyone else. All the air seemed to go out of him and he flopped limply back down. Annie, sitting beside him, covered her father's hand with her own. Others picked mutely at their food.

"Maybe it's for the best," Jamie said quietly.

"I know somebody in the *policía ministerial*," Preciosa offered in her smooth, queenly manner. She was wearing a flowing, loose, long-sleeved blouse of black silk that made the movements of her arms and veined, long-fingered hands more sinuous and elegant than ever.

Carl looked hopefully at her. "Who?"

Josefa snorted. "Always she knows 'somebody,' this one," the old woman muttered to no one in particular.

"Somebody *important*," Preciosa said with barely a contemptuous glance at Josefa. "Somebody with more power than this Marmolejo person, somebody with whom I can say I have a certain amount of influence."

Tony looked at her admiringly. "She always knows somebody," he said with a totally different implication than Josefa's. "Who do you know, honey?"

"His name is Colonel Archuleta, a very old friend of my family, very high in the police, very powerful. Maybe you've heard of him. I will speak personally with him."

Archuleta, Gideon remembered after a moment's thought, was the corrupt, high-ranking cop Marmolejo had booted out. "I'm afraid your friend's not there anymore," he said. "Colonel Marmolejo has replaced him."

"Ah." Preciosa gave him a thin-lipped smile, but the look in her turquoise-shadowed eyes told him he had not made a friend of her. Looking at her, he realized with a kind of awe that her rings, and there were at least as many as she'd been wearing the other night, were not the same ones. Those had been set with amethysts to match her purple eye shadow. These were all jade and turquoise, to set off tonight's blue-green eye shadow. Did the woman have a different set of jewelry for every shade of eye coloring? Did she actually take them with her when she traveled?

"Hey, maybe we could get a private eye to look into it," Tony said. "Preciosa, honey, you know any *investigadores privados*?"

"As it happens, *amorcito*—"

"Ah no," Tony interrupted with a sudden wave of his hand. "What are we doing? What could a private eye find out now? Where would he even start? Why do we want to shake everything up again, upset everybody? What would be the point?"

"The point?" Carl cried. "The point? How about justice?"

"Carl, if the police can't act," Jamie said reasonably, "how are you going to get justice? What are you going to do, take the law into your own hands?"

Carl glowered down at his plate. "How about finding out what really happened? Doesn't anybody care about that?"

Annie, her hand still on his, said, "We all care, Pop, but they're right. It's too late, too much water under the bridge. Let it go."

Carl jerked his head in frustration. "Just drop it? Never know who did this terrible thing, or why, or exactly what happened? I mean, sure, Blaze had problems, she wasn't perfect, but you know, she was barely twenty years old, just a kid, really. She was your *mother*, Annie. To just let it lie without doing anything at all, as if it never happened . . ."

Gideon hadn't yet mentioned his plans to look at the skull in the museum and was unsure whether or not he should. Identifying the skeleton as Blaze's had wound up providing more hurt than help, as far as he could see, and he wasn't sure how this would turn out. Still, he thought he owed them the information.

"Well, actually," he said hesitantly, "I am looking into it a little more, or at least there might be a connection."

Six pairs of eyes swiveled in his direction.

"There was an old Zapotec skull found in the same mine some years ago. Anybody familiar with that?"

Head shakes all around, except from Josefa, who was concentrating on picking her teeth.

"And it occurred to me that maybe it wasn't really ancient, that maybe it was modern." He told them about his conversation with Sandoval and how he'd learned it was now in the Museo de Curiosidades in Oaxaca. "I thought I'd go look at it tomorrow afternoon."

"I don't understand," Annie said. "What does that have to do with my mother's death?"

"I don't know that it does. For all I know, it really is a thousand-year-old skull. But if it's modern, then we have the skeletal remains of *two* people found in the same mine. If this one shows signs of violence too, the possibility increases that they were killed at the same time."

"That's true," Tony said. "They don't get that many murders around here. Hell, till you showed up, I thought they didn't get *any*."

"All right, let's say this one does show that there was a second murder," Jamie said thoughtfully. "Let's say it even seems to have happened at the same time. What would that mean? Where could you take it from there?"

He didn't really have a good answer. The truth of it was that he wouldn't be able to take it anywhere. There was that statute of limitations to contend with, and besides that, he would be leaving in a couple of days. The truth of it was that he was doing it for no deeper reason than curiosity. But of course he couldn't say that. And if he told them he was motivated at least in part by wondering if it might be Manolo, there would be a new round of incredulous questions—*Manolo! Why would it be Manolo? How could it be Manolo?*—that he didn't feel up to contending with. By now he was deeply sorry that he'd brought the subject up at all.

"Well, you never know, it might turn up something," he said lamely.

It was as anticlimactic as it deserved to be, and he could sense the energy going out of the atmosphere again. After a few seconds Carl sighed and spoke quietly. "I want her . . . her remains back. I don't want her lying in a box in some warehouse."

"Gideon, couldn't you arrange that?" Julie asked.

"Of course," Gideon said. "I'll talk to Javier."

* * *

"OHO," Julie said when the others had left. "I gather you don't think it was such a blind guess on my part after all, about Manolo's getting killed too? That's why you want to look at the skull, isn't it?"

"Well—" Gideon began from the buffet table, where he was pouring coffee.

"*Isn't* it?"

"Well, on having given your idea some thought," he said, "I'm willing to upgrade it from blind guess to unverified supposition. Or, what the hell, even *reasonable* supposition, how's that?" He came back with two fresh mugs and sat down.

"Oh, that's big of you."

"I'm going to go to Oaxaca to look at it tomorrow afternoon. Think you'll be free? The skull business shouldn't take up that much time."

"I think I will, yes. Jamie says another couple of hours should wrap things up, so I should be done by then. And I'd love to go into town. We can have lunch, and I can look for presents for people while you do your skull thing. Maybe we can stop in and say hello to Javier."

The Oaxacan night had come on by now, warm and fragrant. Only along the tops of the hills on the horizon was there any remaining red glow from the sunset. Pockets of lights shimmered on the distant hillsides across the valley; tiny communities that were unseen in the daylight. From the village below came waves of radio music and laughing conversation—dinnertime at Samburguesas?— and from the opposite direction, off somewhere in the barren hills that rose immediately behind the Hacienda, they could hear the predators of the night at their work: the hollow, periodic *hoo-hoo-hoo* of an owl, the *screee* of a nighthawk, the woofing howls of a band of coyotes.

"Gideon," Julie said, sipping at the steaming coffee, both hands around the mug, "does it seem odd to you that no one except Carl wants to pursue it? That they're all content to just—well, to just forget about it?"

"Actually . . . no."

"But you've always said that what the families in cases like this want more than anything else is closure. Why don't these people want it?"

"But really, they've gotten it. They got it today, as much as they can reasonably expect to ever get. They don't have to wonder about Blaze anymore. They don't have to wonder if she'll ever show up again. They know she didn't run off with Manolo, they know she was killed and left in the mine. And now they'll get her body back. That's closure. Who killed her, and why—that's unlikely ever to come out now, and they know it. They're better off putting it behind them."

The coyotes' howling turned into increasingly excited barking, then frantic yawping, then, slowly subsiding, into silence. They'd run down their prey. They were feeding. Straining his ears, he imagined he could hear them tearing bone and flesh, and greedily wolfing down gobbets, and snapping at each other.

Julie shivered. "It's getting cold. Let's go in."

EIGHTEEN

THEY were on the terrace again early the following morning, taking in the cool, fresh air and just finishing working their way through one of Dorotea's breakfasts— hibiscus juice, cubed melon and papaya, a tender, perfectly cooked vegetable frittata, and toast, jam, and coffee— when Tony appeared, rumpled, yawning, and scratching at the stubble on his cheeks.

"Okay if I join you?" he asked, having already plopped heavily into a spare chair.

"Sure," Julie said. "Where's Preciosa?"

Tony snorted. "Preciosa's not exactly what you'd call a morning person. Hey, *mamacita*," he called in Spanish toward the open window of the kitchen, "the big boss is here and he's hungry. How about some breakfast?"

"I see you, I see you," was the mumbled reply. "It's coming, it's coming."

"Coffee first."

"You'll get it when you get it."

"What a sweetheart," he said, grinning. "Not a grouchy bone in her body. So, Gideon, you like it here? Having a good time?"

"A great time, Tony, and the Hacienda's beautiful."

"Yeah, but are you finding anything to do for fun, aside from looking at bones? It's not like there're a million things to do around here."

"Well, true, but that's not such a bad thing. This morning I was thinking about spending some time at one of the archaeological sites."

"Oh yeah? Gonna go up to Monte Albán?"

"No, I've been there before, and anyway, I didn't want to make a long drive. I thought I'd just go down to Yagul. It's the closest one."

"Yagul? You know, it's funny. It's like fifteen miles down the road, but even though I grew up right here where we're sitting, I've never been there myself. When I was a kid, I wasn't interested, and after I came back . . . well, I just never got around to it. It's like how New Yorkers are always telling you they never got around to going to the Statue of Liberty. But one of these days . . ."

"Well, why don't you come with me? I don't expect to stay very long, maybe a couple of hours. We'd be back by noon at the latest."

Tony looked as if he was considering it, but then he shook his head. "No, I better not. I got all kinds of stuff to do around the place. If I don't finish finally rewiring the meeting room on this trip . . ." He rolled his eyes, signifying Gideon knew not what. "What the hell. Ah, hey Maribel, that's my girl," he said with a grin as one of Dorotea's young nieces came out with a full breakfast on a tray and set it out on the table for him. A slight movement of Tony's hand along with an incipient little flinch and a stifled giggle from Maribel suggested that a slap on the bottom would have been administered had Julie not been there.

"So, Julie," he said after a swallow of coffee, a fond look after Maribel, and a sigh of pleasure over either or both, "what about you? How's it going? They're not working you too hard, are they?"

"Not at all, Tony. It's been fun. I have some things to finish up with Jamie this morning, and I think that'll be it. At noon I'm going into Oaxaca with Gideon."

"Oh yeah, to look at an old skull, huh? Whoa, that sure sounds like a *ton* of fun."

"Well, I have a hunch I might get a good meal out of him too, if I play my cards right."

Tony arranged his plates to his liking with surprisingly meticulous care: juice and melon on the left, frittata in the center, coffee and toast on the right; plates then nudged until they were all equally spaced. Then he was ready to eat. "Hey, Gideon, tell me something," he said as he buttered the toast. "I've been thinking about that skull. I've been trying to figure it out, and I don't get it. What's the point of looking at it? Where's it gonna get you?"

Gideon was fresher this morning, and it was something he didn't mind talking about, especially since it was only to Tony and not to Carl and the others. "It was something Julie said yesterday. She was wondering if it might be Manolo."

Tony's eyebrows went up. "Manolo? The guy Blaze . . . ? You think somebody killed them *both*? Jesus Christ, where did *that* come from?"

"It was just a thought," Julie said. "Nobody ever did find out for sure what happened to him, and there was a lot of money involved. Down here, it would have been a fortune. I couldn't help wondering if maybe somebody killed the two of them for it."

"Yeah, but . . . look," he said, slathering jam on the toast, "let's say for the sake of argument somebody really did kill them both. How would you know it's *him*? Wouldn't you need to know what he looked like?"

"It'd help, but it's not strictly necessary."

"I suppose you could ask Carl or Jamie; they'd probably remember, but don't forget, it's been thirty years. Me, I can't help you out there, I never even saw the guy. Missed him by a couple of days."

"I don't really need to know what he looked like, Tony."

Chewing away at his frittata, Tony frowned. "So how . . . ?"

"Easy. I just look for maxillomandibular fixation paraphernalia."

The chewing stopped. "Maxillo . . . ?"

"I look to see if his face is held together with pins and wires and plates."

" Ohhh, I get you. Yeah, good point. Carl busted his jaw for him, didn't he?"

"Right. And since he was never seen again, he was probably killed—if he was killed—within a few days of having it fixed, so they wouldn't have taken out the wiring yet."

"But wait a minute, Gideon," Julie said, her brow wrinkling. "The Zapotecs wouldn't have known how to wire broken jaws, would they?"

"I doubt it. As far as I know, that's a nineteenth-century invention."

"That's what I thought. So if they saw wires in this skeleton's jaw, wouldn't they have known right away that it couldn't be ancient?"

"Not necessarily. The Aztecs, Mixtecs, Mayans, and the rest of them may not have known how to work with a living skull, but they sure knew how to work with a dead one. There are mosaicked skulls, and turquoise-decorated skulls, and skulls ornamented with loads of silver or polished pyrite . . . *and* skulls that actually have the mandible reattached. It's possible that that's what they assumed this was." He shrugged. "I figure it's worth a look anyway."

"Okay, yeah, I can see all that," Tony said, "but even so, even if it *is* him, where does it get you? The cops can't do anything, can they? It's over fourteen years." He shook his head. "Stupid law."

"You're right," Gideon said. "They can't."

"So what's the point?"

Julie finished the last of her coffee and put down the cup. "The point," she said, "is that Gideon has never met a skeleton he didn't want to know better."

Tony laughed his gravel-on-a-tin-drum laugh. "Well, what the hell, *chacun à son goût*," he said surprisingly: French for *each to his own.*

NINETEEN

YAGUL.

Contrary to what he'd said to Tony, he wasn't here simply because it was the closest site. He had been a twenty-year-old junior at UCLA when he'd first come across its name in a Mesoamerican prehistory survey course, and it had been one of the factors that had turned him into an anthropology major. "An intermittently occupied Mixtec-Zapotec site of limited archaeological significance," his textbook had called it, "located in the eastern Valley of Oaxaca, a remote area of central southern Mexico, and thought to be concurrent with Mitla (of which it is sometimes considered an inferior imitation) and Monte Albán, more important settlements to the north. Its most notable feature is a ball court with fretted stone mosaics of a conventional style, believed to be second in size only to the far more impressive court at Chichén Itzá."

This decidedly lukewarm description notwithstanding, the deliciously exotic sound of it, *Yah-goohl*, had stirred his youthful and adventurous soul. It was the kind of word you might expect to hear from the first Venusian to visit Earth when he stepped from his flying saucer and held up a two-fingered, vaguely hand-like appendage in greeting: "Yah-goohl, Earthlings."

A little something of its magic was lost when he learned that it was Zapotecan for *dry stick*, but it had remained a symbol of the strange, prehistoric, fascinating places that a career in anthropology might take him. *I will stand among the ancient stones of Yah-goohl someday*, he had told himself, and with such travels in mind he had started out in the sub-discipline of archaeology. But within a year it had been evolution, bones, and physical anthropology that had snared him for good, so that, until Julie had brought up the idea of coming to Oaxaca a few weeks ago, it had been more than two decades since the site had even crossed his mind.

And now here he was, taking it all in from a rise at the edge of the otherwise empty parking area at the end of a rough, two-mile-long dirt road, pretty much in the middle of nowhere, surrounded by scrubland and dry river beds; not a sign of modern humanity in sight, other than a ramshackle booth at the entrance with a hand-painted wooden sign: ENTRADA 10 PESOS. But no one was in the booth to collect the fees, and it looked as if no one had been in it for a long time. Obviously, Yagul didn't get enough visitors to make it worthwhile. That was equally clear from the potsherds that littered the ground, just sitting there for the picking; you didn't find those at Monte Albán or Teotihuacan.

He'd Googled the site earlier to refresh his memory and located plenty of material (what was there that *didn't* have plenty of material on Google?), so he'd known what he would find, but still, it was bigger and more interesting than he'd expected. There were three main areas. In the center was the famous ball court, as well as the

imaginatively named "Palace of the Six Patios," originally probably civic/religious offices, but now a roofless,
moldering warren of stuccoed stone-and-clay walls and
foundations. From this central area, stone steps led up a
sizeable hill to the walled "fortress," which probably *had*
been a defensive compound. And in an area east of the
ball court was a group of sunken tombs.

The best thing about it, he thought with selfish pleasure, was that he had it all to himself. No iron-lunged tour
guides with yellow umbrellas, shouting commands at
their obedient, beaten-down herds; no yelling kids scram-
bling over the stones and crying when they skinned their
knees; nothing noisier than the sound of his shoes on the
stony pathways, and an occasional whisper of breeze sighing through one of the runty trees that had sprouted here
and there around the ruin. But it was still early, barely
nine o'clock, so it was likely that other people would be
showing up as the day wore on. He decided to hit the
tombs first, before that happened. They were a labyrinth
of semi-subterranean chambers that were bound to be
small and cramped, best seen without company.

They were as dank and stuffy and constricted as he'd
imagined, but every bit as interesting too, made all the
more atmospheric by the sparse shafts of daylight, filled
with slowly swirling dust motes, that provided all the illu-
mination there was. He spent a blissful half hour prowl-
ing from chamber to chamber—mostly on his knees; the
openings were only about three feet high—examining
and touching the geometric stone mosaics and the strange,
Olmec-style heads carved in bas-relief on the walls, and
in general happily communing with the spirits of people
long, long gone.

When he crawled blinking into the sunlight, he practically bumped into a pair of hairy, bowling-ball-calved
legs topped by green walking shorts.

"Hey, here you are!" came from two feet above the shorts. "I was looking for you."

"Tony!" Gideon got to his feet. "I thought you couldn't make it."

"I figured, what the hell, the wiring waited this long," Tony said. "And Preciosa isn't gonna be conscious until eleven anyway, and if she has to get breakfast herself, no big deal, she can handle it. So what's in there, the tombs?"

"Yes, want to have a look?"

"Do I have to crawl around on my hands and knees like you were?"

"Afraid so."

"I'll give it a skip, then. What else is there to see? What's this ball court you were talking about?"

"I was just going to head for it. It's right over there."

"Okay if I go with you? Maybe I'll learn something."

"Sure, come on," he said affably, but the truth was he'd have preferred to be alone. For once in his life he wasn't in the mood to lecture. He wasn't really there as an anthropologist, he was there delivering on a promise he'd made to himself a long time ago. Anthropologist to the core he might be, but there was an almost mystical side to him that surfaced every once in a while—a long while—and this was one of those times. He didn't want to talk or to think with any rigor about the archaeology of the place, he wanted simply to bask in its antiquity and foreignness, to walk paths that had been trodden by the sandaled feet of the Mixtecs and Zapotecs before him, to take pleasure in passing his hand over stones that had been laid in place well before the birth of Christ, by people who, despite the best efforts of science, would remain forever mysterious and unknowable. Still, if Tony was making the effort to learn, Gideon could be counted on to make the effort to instruct.

The ball court at Yagul consisted of an open, flat, rectangular field of play about two hundred feet long. Second in size to the one at Chichén Itzá it might be, but it was a distant second. The court at Chichén was a good three times longer, or as the guidebooks never tired of saying, "as long as two football fields." Still, it was an impressive structure, bordered on both sides by masonry walls that were nearly vertical to about hip height, where there was a narrow horizontal "bench," and then sloped back and up from the playing field, to be topped by flat stone platforms about thirty feet above the playing surface. At one end of these walls, as usual, there was a flight of stone steps up to a landing, where they turned ninety degrees and continued to the platform at the top. Also as usual, the steps varied wildly in height, from eight or nine inches to a foot and a half. Tony had trouble with his balance negotiating some of them—had he had something to drink between breakfast and now?—and Gideon had to give him a steadying hand, but eventually they made it to the top with Tony breathing heavily.

Once they got there, they stood at the corner of the platform, looking down on the playing field, while Gideon told Tony as much as he remembered about the ancient game. Which wasn't much.

It had been enormously widespread in pre-Columbian Mesoamerica, he explained. Well over a thousand courts had been found so far, wasn't that amazing? Different cultures had varying versions, and nobody today could say for sure what the rules were, but judging from reliefs and from a modern variant of the game, it was something like a combination of volleyball and soccer, with the object being to keep the ball in play, but using only the hips, although in some later versions the forearms were used, or even rackets—

"Didn't they, like, used to sacrifice the losers?" Tony asked. "Cut their heads off right in front of the crowd?"

"Not down here, no. That was only in the Mayan and Veracruz cultures."

"Oh." He was disappointed.

"But it was a brutal game all the same," Gideon said to cheer him up. "The ball wasn't like a volleyball or a soccer ball. That is, it was about the same size, but it was hard, solid rubber, weighing a good five or six pounds. Imagine getting hit in the face with that when you weren't expecting it. Players would get really beaten up by them. According to one of the Spanish chroniclers, some of them were killed when the ball hit them in the head or the chest."

"No kidding," Tony said. "That's interesting." But it seemed to Gideon that his interest was wandering. He was restless. Enough lectures for one morning.

"Why don't we head up to the fortress?" Gideon suggested. "Supposed to be a terrific view from up there."

"Yeah, later, but the ball court's cool. Tell me some more stuff."

Gideon shrugged. "I don't know that much more. There's some evidence that the game was sometimes used as a proxy for war. For example, one of the missionaries claims he saw a game between the Toltec king and three of his rivals, with the winner becoming the ruler of the whole empire."

"You're shitting me," Tony said. "The whole empire?" But it was increasingly clear that his interest had wandered. He was preoccupied with something. He was oddly animated too: jumpy, on the edge of something. Gideon had the strong impression that he was getting up his nerve to say something, to ask Gideon something.

"Tony, is there something on your mind? Anything wrong?"

"Wrong? No, I got a lot on my mind, that's all. Business stuff. But this is interesting. So who won the game? Did the Aztec king win?"

"Toltec, not Aztec," Gideon couldn't help pointing out, as if Tony gave a damn. "But I'm afraid I don't know who won."

"Shame," Tony said distractedly, and then, half to himself: "Toltec, not Aztec. Got it." His eyes darted haphazardly over the site. Gideon had the extraordinary impression that he might be on the verge of tears. *What was going on here?* "That round stone in the middle down there," Tony blurted. "What's that for? A goal or something?"

Whatever was bothering Tony, that old stone wasn't it. But Gideon wasn't much of a psychotherapist; he was supremely uncomfortable, and not very good, at digging into the reluctant psyches of other people. If Tony had something to say, it was going to be up to him to say it.

Gideon turned to look down at the stone, a crudely carved disk about a foot thick and two feet across. "No, that was probably a marker dividing the two sides. The way they—"

He heard something halfway between a sob and a grunt. Surprised and concerned, he turned. What happened next was so astounding, so utterly unexpected, that his reaction was completely instinctive. Tony, face contorted, was rushing toward him with his arms outstretched. Gideon batted with his right arm at Tony's extended arms, catching him heavily in the shoulder. The blow sent Tony off to one side, but his momentum carried him one, two lurching, twisting steps onward to the edge, where he teetered briefly, then, arms windmilling, making chimp-like hooting noises, his feet went out from under him and over the edge he went. The last Gideon saw of him were his eyes, wild and rolling and furious.

The whole thing had taken less than two seconds.

TWENTY

TONY fell, not toward the playing field, but to the side, where the stone staircase came up, his body flumping heavily onto the landing where the steps turned. It was a drop of no more than nine or ten feet, but a violent contortion—almost as if he intentionally wrenched himself off the landing and into the air—sent him over the edge of that as well, and he plummeted another twenty feet to the stony ground. There he landed on his back, and this time he lay still.

For a moment Gideon was frozen, so utterly thunderstruck that he couldn't move. *What just happened?* When he'd first seen Tony barreling into him, he'd thought for a millisecond that Tony *had* burst into tears, that this was an anguished embrace, a plea for help.

But only for a millisecond. If Gideon hadn't been turning at the time, Tony would have smashed into his unprotected back and it would have been Gideon who had been launched into space and would now be lying there thirty feet below. But what on earth had made . . .

He jerked his head to shake the cobwebs loose and started quickly down the steps. Tony was moving a little now, he could see: a gentle, circular motion of his left forearm, fingers slightly curled, like an orchestra conductor calling forth a slow, *pianissimo* passage. He had drawn up his knees too. He didn't seem to be in pain. There were no obviously broken limbs, and Gideon could see no blood. He knew better than to think there were no grave injuries, however; nobody could fall ten feet onto a stone platform, and then an additional twenty feet onto hard, stony ground—flat on his back both times, which meant he had to have struck his head as well—and then walk away as if nothing had happened.

When he reached Tony, he saw that he was right. Tony's eyes were open and they followed Gideon, but the rims of both eyes had brown residue on them, a sure sign of intracranial hemorrhaging. He had taken out his cell phone on the way down, but he didn't know Mexico's equivalent of 911. Instead, he dialed the Hacienda. Annie picked up on the first ring.

"Good morning," she sang, "*buenos días*—"

"Annie, this is Gideon. I'm at Yagul. Tony's had an accident, a fall—serious—"

He caught the shocked intake of breath. "Serious? What do you mean, serious? He's not—?"

"He's alive, but I think he's suffered a brain injury. Can you get an ambulance here?"

"Yes, of course. Is he—never mind! I'll call right away. My God—" She clicked off.

Gideon knelt beside him. Tony's eyes continued to follow. There was a glob of blood in one nostril, and a thin trickle from his right ear. The nasal blood might be nothing, but the bleeding from the ear—that was another bad sign.

"Tony," he said softly. "What was that about?"

Tony looked at him with an expression of mild curiosity. He made no attempt to speak. His arm was still making its slow circles. Gently, Gideon took hold of his wrist and laid it on his chest. It stayed there.

"Tony, can you hear me?"

No reply. Tony was watching Gideon's lips. The pupil of his left eye was a pinpoint; the other seemed normal. Another indicator of an injured brain. There wasn't much doubt about it now.

Tony was mostly on his back, but his head and hips were twisted to opposite sides. The position looked unpleasant, but Tony didn't look uncomfortable. Gideon knew better than to try to straighten him out.

"Do you know who I am?"

"Creo que sí." I think so. Gideon waited for a name, but none came.

"Do you know who you are?" he asked quietly.

"Quién sabe?" he said, sounding too weary to care. *Who knows?* Then his eyes rolled up and his eyelids fluttered a few times and closed.

"Tony?"

No reply. Gideon put a hand on his chest to make sure he was still breathing. He was, but raggedly. The trickle of blood from his ear now ran all the way to the back of his head and dripped slowly onto the ground. The blood at his eyes and nose was about the same as before.

Gideon settled down on the ground to wait with him, his mind whirling. *What the hell just happened?* Several groups of visitors had arrived by now and although everyone else kept well clear of the two men, a Mexican tour guide came up to ask if there was anything he could do.

"Not unless you're a doctor," Gideon said.

The man had seen the entire terrible incident, however—how the other man had tried to push him off the platform—and he offered his name and telephone number if a witness were needed. Gideon, realizing for the first time that a witness might indeed be a very good thing to have, gratefully accepted his business card: *Vicente Abelardo: Tours Arqueológicos, City Tours, Bike Rides y Otros.*

The ambulance, a brand spanking new orange-and-white van from the hospital in Tlacolula, came bouncing up to them, right onto the edge of the playing field, spraying dust and gravel. At almost the same time another one of the Hacienda vans pulled up, with Annie at the wheel and Julie in the passenger seat.

The two ambulance attendants were professional and quick. A few brief questions that he was able to understand and answer in Spanish: How long has he been unconscious? Was he conscious at all after the fall? Has he vomited? Convulsed? Shown evidence of pain? Shown any movement below the neck? Gideon answered them all and added his observation about the difference in pupil size.

They glanced at each other, saying nothing (what could they say?), then got swiftly down to work, while Gideon moved off to the side with Annie and Julie to watch. Tony's head and neck were immobilized in a plastic cradle with head and chin straps, and then he was expertly slid onto a board, strapped to it, and hauled into the back of the ambulance. Tony's lips were moving as he was lifted, but his eyes stayed closed. The doors slammed shut, and they were gone in another explosion of dirt and gravel. When the ambulance had gotten there, most of the other visitors to the site came to gawk, but now they rapidly dispersed, murmuring among themselves. It had turned into an exciting day for them, after all.

"Julie, would you mind driving back with Gideon?" a distracted, lip-biting Annie asked. "I want to go to the hospital to be with Tony."

"Of course, go ahead."

She started to leave, then stopped and took Gideon's hand. "Thank you for taking care of him."

He smiled weakly but said nothing. In fact, everything

had happened so quickly since they'd arrived that Gideon hadn't told them what had really happened. He said nothing now, either, as he and Julie walked to the van, other than to ask her to drive.

She looked at him curiously—he generally enjoyed driving more than she did—but got into the driver's side and turned on the ignition. They followed the ambulance and Annie's van down the dirt road until they came to Highway 190, where the ambulance flicked on its siren and raced south toward the hospital, with Annie closely following, like an airborne bird sheltering in the "wake" of the leader of the flock. Julie and Gideon turned north, toward Teotitlán. Only then did either of them speak.

"It must have been pretty bad," she said. "I don't think I've ever seen you so . . . I don't know . . . it's like you're in shock. *Are* you all right?"

"Sure, I'm all right. Look, when you get to the Teotitlán turnoff, don't take it. Let's keep going. I need to talk to Javier about this."

She looked doubtfully at him. "I don't understand. Why would Javier—"

"Julie, it wasn't an accident. Tony tried to kill me up there."

"He tried to—" She swerved rapidly to the side of the road and pulled up on the shoulder. "Did you just say what I think you said?"

"I'm afraid so. He tried to shove me off the platform. He wound up going over the edge instead."

"But why? That's crazy!"

He spread his hands. "I don't have a clue."

"My God. Tell me what happened."

"There's not much to tell. I was answering one of his questions about the ball court, and I had my back to him, and I heard—I don't know what I heard—a sob, maybe, and I'd been worried about him anyway because he'd been acting strangely."

"Strangely how?"

"Tense, nervous, preoccupied . . ." He gestured at the ignition. "Could we get going again, please?"

"Gideon, at this point, I think I'm more shaky than you are. I mean, if you hadn't been turning around . . . if you . . ." She let out a breath. "Do you feel up to driving? I think it'd be safer."

"Yes, I'm okay. The adrenaline rush is over, and so is the knees-like-jelly follow-up. I'm me again."

"I never had the pleasure of the adrenaline rush, I've gone straight to the knees-like-jelly phase. When I think what might have . . . *whew.*"

They switched seats, and then Gideon turned the engine on once more and edged out onto the highway.

For the next few miles there was only silence, and then Julie picked up the conversation where they'd left it. "Okay, so you hear what sounds like a sob behind you . . ."

"And I turn, and as I turn, here he comes at me, full speed ahead. I—well, I'm not sure what I did. I guess I sort of stepped out of the way and backhanded him—you know, a swipe with my arm to keep him off me—and over he goes, without a sound. Hit the landing on the stairs, bounced off, and fell the rest of the way down."

"And hit his head, obviously."

"I couldn't be positive at the time, but yes, obviously."

"And?"

"And nothing. I called Annie, and you know the rest."

She nodded. "How serious do you think Tony's injuries are?"

"Serious," Gideon said. "Put it this way: if he's lucky, he'll die, because I don't think his brain's going to be of much use to him from now on."

Another quiet nod, followed by a soft sigh.

"How are you feeling about this, Julie? I know you liked him. You must feel—"

"What I'm feeling," she said firmly, "is relief,

enormous, overwhelming relief that you're still here." She reached across to put her hand on his thigh. When he covered it with his own, he could feel it trembling. He curled his fingers gently around it. "What I'm feeling," she went on, and now the tremble was in her voice as well, "is thank God you acted the way you did, as quickly as you did. If something had happened to you . . . I can't even . . ."

He squeezed her hand, not trusting himself to speak, thinking for the thousandth time: *How fantastically lucky I am to have her, to be loved by this beautiful, marvelous woman.*

"What I'm feeling about Tony?" she continued after a moment, in a steadier voice. "I haven't sorted that out yet. Disbelief. Incomprehension. Bewilderment. What could he have been thinking? Was he crazy? What possible motivation could he have to do that to you?"

"Oh, I think I know what his motivation was."

She looked sharply at him. "I thought you didn't have a clue."

"Not to his *reason*, no, but to his *motivation*, I think so, yes."

"You'll have to explain that."

"His motivation was to prevent my seeing that skull this afternoon. What else could it possibly be?"

"Well—almost anything. I don't know, maybe it had something to do with your identifying Blaze's skeleton."

"I guess so, but that's already done; he couldn't do any-thing to change that. Also, he found out about that yester-day, at dinner. He's had all kinds of time to cook up some more subtle, less risky way to do me in between then and now—I don't know, poison, an accident, whatever. But he didn't. Then at, what was it, about eight o'clock this morning, he finds out I'm going to look at the skull this afternoon, and two hours later he's shoving me off a wall in a public place. I can hardly imagine a more desperate, clumsy, dicey way to try to kill somebody. Why was he in such a hurry?"

"Because he had no time to plan anything fancier," Julie said, nodding. "Because we were going into Oaxaca at noon."

"That's the way I see it."

"Yes, you're right, I think. But why was he so afraid of your seeing the skull?"

"Ah, see, that's what I meant about the *reason* part. That's the part I don't know."

AS usual, Marmolejo didn't seem to be doing much of anything when they got to his office. He was standing at one of the big mullioned windows, demitasse cup and saucer in his hands, tranquilly contemplating the peaceful scene in the plaza below. As always, he had on an embroidered white *guayabera* worn outside crisply pressed pants. His eyes lit up when he saw Julie, for whom he had a soft spot, and they quickly embraced, with the top of Marmolejo's head coming up to the level of her nose. He called for more coffee at once, and pastries as well, sat them down in the cozy grouping of leather armchairs in one corner of the big room, and started chattering happily about old times.

"Javier, this isn't exactly a social call," Gideon said.

Marmolejo's eyebrows rose. "I grieve to hear it." He waited expectantly.

Telling him about what had happened at Yagul took five minutes. Explaining to him who Tony Gallagher was, and the whole twisted story of the Gallaghers and their Byzantine history, took half an hour, most of it provided by Julie. Corporal Vela had brought in coffee and a plate of chocolate wafers. Only Gideon, suddenly ravenous, had eaten any of the wafers, wolfing down four of them, when Marmolejo called a pause to ask Vela to contact the hospital in Tlacolula about Tony's condition. The coffee had been drunk, and Vela had brought in another serving in fresh demitasse cups.

"And so you believe this attack occurred because he was afraid of what you might find when you looked at the skull?" Marmolejo asked as he spooned in his usual two teaspoons of sugar. "There was no history of animosity between you?"

"None. It's got to be the skull."

Marmolejo stirred, tapped the tiny spoon elegantly against the cup's rim, and laid it soundlessly down in the saucer. "And of what do you think he was frightened?"

"We talked about that in the car," Julie answered, giving Gideon a chance at another couple of wafers. "All we could come up with was that he was afraid that the skull would turn out to be Manolo's—at breakfast this morning, we told him that we thought it might be."

"And if it was? Why should that cause him concern?"

"Well, if he murdered Manolo—and if he killed Blaze as well—and wouldn't it make sense that the same person killed them both?—then . . ." She shrugged.

"Then what? Let's say he did kill them. Why should identifying the skull as Manolo's, if indeed it should turn out to be, bring suspicion down on Tony Gallagher in particular?"

"We couldn't come up with any reasonable answer for that either, Javier," Gideon said, swallowing a slug of coffee to wash down the wafers. "We also couldn't think of any reason for Tony to kill them in the first place. He wasn't a betrayed husband or a jealous lover, after all; he was Blaze's brother."

"I wonder if we're barking up the wrong tree altogether," Julie said thoughtfully. "Maybe your going to look at the skull doesn't have anything to do with what happened in Yagul. Maybe it *is* just an old Zapotec skull after all, and not Manolo's."

"That could be," Gideon said. "But my intuition's sure telling me otherwise. In any case, we'll find that out this afternoon."

At this point Corporal Vela came in with a sheet of paper for Marmolejo. "*Gracias*, Alejandro," he said, and scanned the few typewritten lines on it. "It's about Mr. Gallagher. The hospital says his condition is critical but has stabilized. He is in a coma designated as a five on the Glasgow Scale." He looked at Gideon. "Is this something with which you're familiar?"

"Yes, a little. The Glasgow Coma Scale—"

"Wait, start at the beginning," Julie said. "What *is* a coma? He was already unconscious when they took him away. When does being unconscious turn into a coma, exactly?"

"Well, there is no 'exactly.' A coma is just a state of protracted unconsciousness. A boxer who's knocked out and gets up a few seconds later wasn't in a coma. If he's still unconscious at the hospital an hour later, that's a coma. If he's still in it a month later, they usually reclassify it to 'persistent vegetative state.' If he's still in it a year later—well, then he's almost certainly never going to wake up."

"And this Glasgow Scale of five, what does that tell us?" asked Marmolejo.

"Not anything good, I'm afraid, as far as Tony is concerned. It's based on a bunch of basic tests: you know, can he answer a simple question with a yes or a no? Can he move a limb or nod his head if he's asked to? Does he react to being stuck with a pin? The scale runs from a three, I think, to a fifteen, with three being the lowest you can get."

"So a five," said Marmolejo, "would not be a very good sign."

"A terrible sign. If I remember correctly, three to five generally means the person has probably suffered a brain·

injury that's going to wind up killing him. Never going to regain consciousness."

"Can he live a long time like that?" Julie asked.

"Not likely, but it happens. Comas aren't very well understood."

"So," said Marmolejo, "wherever we find our answers to our questions, they are not likely to come from Mr. Gallagher himself."

"I think you can count on that," Gideon said. "Listen, Javier, I want to ask you something. You said nothing could be done about Blaze's murder because the statute's run out."

"Correct."

"And if this skull at the museum does turn out to be Manolo's, the same would apply to him."

"I'm afraid so."

"Well, doesn't what happened today change things?"

"I don't see how. Yes, of course we will look into it, but it's a completely separate matter."

"Is it? Here's this peaceful little village, Teotitlán, that supposedly hadn't had a homicide in umpteen years— umpteen *decades*—and now we find out that Blaze Gallagher, or rather, Blaze Gallagher Tendler, was killed thirty years ago, only no one knew about it. And today, one day after I identify her body, and only hours before I go to look at a museum specimen that might be her lover's skull, Tony Gallagher, Blaze's brother, tries to murder *me*. And what about that mummified guy I looked at the other day—"

Julie shook her head. "Where does he come into it? I thought he was just a drifter who happened—"

"Who happened to be seen heading up toward the Hacienda Encantada, and who was found dead, murdered, a few months later out in the desert. That adds up to two certain murders—Blaze and the drifter—one possible murder—Manolo—and one attempted murder—me." He had ticked them off on his fingers and now he held up his hand. "Four. Count 'em. Wouldn't you say that's quite a lot for this 'peaceful' little village? And wouldn't you say the Hacienda connection runs rather distinctly through them all?"

"And you think Tony was behind all of them?" Julie asked.

"I'm not ready to go that far. I can sure tell you he was behind *one* of them."

Marmolejo had been silent for a few minutes, having gotten up and gone again to the window, where he stood looking out with his hands behind his back. "I take your point, Gideon," he said without turning around. "I expect that we will indeed be taking another look at Blaze's murder, but I'm afraid it will be only to see what light it might cast on the attack on you. To her, the statute of limitations must still apply. If we should discover her killer, there will be nothing we can do about it."

Gideon shrugged. "Good enough. I understand. What about this drifter, though? He was killed only a few months ago."

"Oh yes, Manuel Garcia; we're proceeding with that, as we would have in any case. Now, however, I think we will be inquiring more deeply as to what business he had, if any, at the Hacienda. Oh, that reminds me—" He turned from the window. "I received the report of his autopsy from Mexico City this morning. Apparently, it confirms your findings in their entirety."

"Stabbed to death with a screwdriver?"

He nodded. "The chief examiner telephoned me to express his appreciation to you. Neither the screwdriver impressions in the bone nor the puncture of the chest wall by a rib was anything he had ever encountered or heard of before. He said he learned much, and that it was an honor to have 'collaborated' with *el famoso Detective de Esqueletos*."

"Well, please let him know that I appreciate that. Did the report turn up anything new?"

"I've yet to read it. It's still on my desk. Would you like to see it?"

"Gee, I wonder what the answer to that's going to be," Julie said to the ceiling.

Gideon smiled. "Sure, just for a few minutes, anyway."

Marmolejo went to his desk and got a thick, neatly opened envelope that he brought to Gideon. "I can show Julie around the building in the meantime, if she'd like. There are some interesting old corners that not many people get to see."

"I'd love it," said Julie.

They were hardly out of their chairs when Gideon, scanning the first page, asked with a distinct edge of excitement: "Javier, does *placas y tornillos de fijación* mean what I think it does?"

"*Placas* and *tornillos* are—"

But Gideon had already flipped to the sheaf of color photographs at the back. They had removed the mummi-fied hide of the head to expose the skull and mandible, and there were photos. "Never mind," he said, staring hard at the very first photograph. "I'll be damned. This whole thing gets weirder by the minute." He looked up at them. "I don't know what it's all going to add up to in the end, but there's one thing I can tell you right now. Julie, you were absolutely right. Whoever that skull at the museum belonged to, I'd be real surprised if it turns out to be Manolo's."

"And why?" a frowning Marmolejo asked.

"Because," said Gideon, slowly tapping the photo-graph, "that's who *this* is."

TWENTY-ONE

IN the space of a few seconds, with very little help needed from Gideon, it became as obvious to them as it was to him. The *placas* and *tornillos*—plates and screws—were clearly visible in the photos of the bared mandible: three narrow, inch-long metal bands, each secured with four screws, which had been inserted to hold together the jaw that had been shattered by Carl Tendler almost thirty years ago. The two fractures themselves were long-healed, but the plates and screws remained.

"But wait a minute," Julie said. "Didn't you tell Tony this morning that you'd know if the skull in the museum was Manolo's because they wouldn't have removed the wiring yet?"

"Right."

"'*Yet.*' The implication being that, eventually, it'd be removed. Well, he was killed only a few months ago. Why is it still there?"

"Oh, this isn't the wiring. The wires would have been

between his upper and lower jaws to keep them from moving. They were taken out long ago. If not, he'd have been eating his meals through a straw all these years. No, these plates are put in to keep the pieces in place while they heal—like splints or casts, only on the inside. To remove them would take another operation—two operations. So unless there's a problem—infection, say—they stay in for good."

"Ah. But how come *you* didn't see this when you looked at the body yourself?"

"Because it was covered with skin, which I wasn't about to try to remove. It took an autopsy to reveal this, and I wasn't doing an autopsy; I was just looking at the thing, helping Flaviano out."

"Well yes, this is all very interesting," Marmolejo said, "but right now I'm anxious to get started on what happened today." He steepled his fingers at his chin. "I will send a man to the hospital in the event Mr. Gallagher should speak after all. And I will have someone go out to the Hacienda this afternoon to conduct interviews; perhaps I'll go along. It may be that someone can throw light, even inadvertently, on Tony's actions. You know how important it is to gather information quickly, while events are still fresh in everyone's minds."

"Well," Gideon said, taking the hint and gathering himself together, "I guess maybe Julie and I will head over to—"

"And *I* guess maybe you'll head over to the interrogation room with Corporal Vela, where you'll make a detailed statement as to today's events while they are still fresh in *your* mind."

"Of course," Gideon said, "although today's 'events' lasted all of about two seconds. Listen, Javier, before we get started on all this, what about *this* guy, Manolo?" He brandished the file. "He was alive only a few months ago. The statute of limitations doesn't apply. You'll be looking into it, won't you? Besides, there's got to be a connection there to what happened to me, and to all the rest of it."

"Yes, naturally, we'll look into it. However, I think we need a bit more evidence than these *placas* and *tornillos* before we conclude that he truly is this Manolo. Other people have had broken jaws."

"Oh, sure. Probably just a coincidence that this particular guy, with a thoroughly healed fractured jaw—a total stranger—was seen wandering up toward the Hacienda a few months ago, and turned up dead just outside this peaceful, nonmurderous little village a few months later. What else could it be but a coincidence?" He looked up at Marmolejo from under arched eyebrows. "Yeah, right."

"Yeah, right," Julie concurred.

A few seconds passed and then Marmolejo sighed. "Yeah, right," he said from the side of his mouth, in a strangled American accent straight out of *The Sopranos*.

"WHAT sort of place are you looking for?" Marmolejo had inquired when they'd asked him to recommend a restaurant where they could have lunch in Oaxaca before going to the museum. "Did you want something on the lively side, in the middle of everything, with lots of noise and activity all around, or someplace quieter, more elegant, with real Oaxacan cuisine and ambience, of which few tourists would even be aware?"

They had surprised him by choosing the former, and so now they sat at an outdoor table on the arched, porticoed upper story of El Asador Vasco, the largest of the restaurants that bordered the Zócalo, Oaxaca's main plaza. They were glad they'd made the choice; what had happened at Yagul had shaken them both, and it was nice to be in a busy restaurant full of people chatting about normal, everyday things, and looking down on the green, well-kept public square, lively and bustling. There were strollers on the paths, sunbathers sprawled on the lawns, and sun-avoiders in the cool, dense shade of the laurel trees; there were street musicians, and vendors of baskets, of balloons, of herbs, of crickets (for eating), of colorful straw masks, of sliced fruits and sweets. A dozen or more of the mobile shoeshine stands with wheels and green awnings were doing a brisk business. At the other end of the plaza, an afternoon band concert was in progress, but only the *oompah*s of the tuba were audible at this distance.

Immediately below them was an old man playing the violin—Kreisler, Schubert, Dvorak—with such honeyed sweetness that Gideon had gotten up from the table to go downstairs and place a fifty-peso note in his open violin case. It was more than everything else in there put together, and the old man had shown his appreciation by asking what Gideon would like to hear. Gideon had told him that what he was doing was wonderful, and just keep doing it. The old man had taken him at his word: he'd been playing Dvorak's *Humoresque* at the time, and now, fifteen minutes later, he was still playing *Humoresque*, looking upward to bow to them at the conclusion of each repetition.

"I grant you, it's a pretty tune," Julie said with a strained smile as he started on his fifth run-through, "but maybe you should go down and give him another fifty pesos and ask him to play something else."

"I most certainly will not," Gideon declared. "I like it, and it seems to be making him happy. If anybody else doesn't like it, *they* can pay him to change."

They were done with their appetizer of manchego cheese with olive oil and toast rounds, and their entrées had just been set down: sea bass with a grapefruit coulis for Julie, and huge Gulf shrimp over garlic-drenched linguine for Gideon. It was after two o'clock—Gideon's deposition had consumed more time than expected—and the rich aromas practically had them salivating on the tablecloth. For a few moments, they happily shoveled in the food, only occasionally pausing for a sip of mineral water.

Julie suddenly blinked, struck by a thought as obviously as if it had hit her in the forehead. She put down her knife and fork. "That man . . . the drifter, the mummy . . . he really is Manolo."

"Oh, I think so. The probability that—"

"No, I just thought of something else. Didn't you say his name was Manuel?"

"Manuel Garcia. At least that's what he told Sandoval."

"That's what I thought. Well, Manolo isn't really a given name in Spanish. Would you like to guess what it's a nickname for?"

He put down his knife and fork. "Manuel?"

"Exactly. It's got to be the same man, Gideon."

He nodded. "It sure is one more piece that fits. What was Manolo's last name, do you know?"

"If I did, I've forgotten. But they'll know at the Hacienda. What do you think the odds are that it's Garcia?"

"Pretty good, I'd say. Sandoval thought it was fake, but now that's looking doubtful."

They finished their meals and sat back, contented, over coffee. "Thank God!" Julie exclaimed.

Gideon looked at her. "What?"

"He's finally stopped playing *Humoresque*. He's on to Mozart now—*Eine Kleine Nachtmusik*. You mean you didn't notice?"

"I guess not. I was thinking— if we've now identified Manolo, then what's that skull in the museum?"

Julie shrugged. "Probably just what it's supposed to be—some thousand-year-old Zapotec Indian."

"But why would Tony want to kill me over that?"

"*If* that's the reason he tried to kill you."

Gideon sighed. "What do you say we head on over to

the museum and have a look? Maybe we'll understand more in an hour or two."

EL Museo de Curiosidades was on Calle las Casas, only five short blocks west of the Zócalo, but in those few blocks Oaxaca went from urban chic to urban grit. Las Casas was a long, narrow, one-way street—if it had been shorter it would have been an alley—crowded with people and crammed with hole-in-the-wall shops and sidewalk stalls selling everything from rubber tubing and used automobile batteries to knock-off wristwatches and green high-top sneakers with pictures of Che Guevara or Daffy Duck on them. It was also the route to the second-class bus terminal, so it was choked with diesel fumes, and bumper-to-bumper with buses so old and beat-up that you expected to see them spewing nuts and bolts like cartoon cars.

The sidewalks were narrow enough to begin with, and with the encroachment of the curbside stalls, it was impossible to walk without continually shouldering aside people coming the other way, or being shouldered aside by them. Not once, though, did they encounter any rudeness or irritation; the locals had learned to live with it as a matter of course. Every now and then they got separated in the crush, but with Julie being half a foot taller than the average pedestrian, they had no trouble spotting each other over the heads of the crowd.

At the intersections, the pedestrian *Walk* signs made them laugh. They were, as Julie remarked, more *Run* signs than *Walk* signs. They allowed ten seconds to get across the street, and the dwindling seconds were shown: 10 . . . 9 . . . 8 . . . Underneath the numbers was the moving figure of a man. At ten, the start of the countdown, he was sauntering along, but by five he had broken into a run, and by two he was running like hell, arms and legs churning. The live pedestrians, they noted, did not follow suit. They started at a saunter and they finished at a saunter, whatever the count. This resulted in an unabated storm of horn-honking (the drivers were not as polite as the walkers), which had no effect on the street crossers, but added considerably to the general sense of clamor, closeness, and commotion.

They were glad to finally see the museum. It stood on a corner, an old one-story adobe house, much the worse for the two centuries or so that it had been in existence, to say nothing of the last six or seven decades of diesel fumes. Seeing it answered a question that had been bothering Gideon: If the skull was what was worrying Tony, why had he opted for murder rather than going to the museum in the morning, when it was closed, finding some way to break in, and stealing the skull? Sure, there would have been risks involved, but there had been even more risks doing it the way he did. And whatever the risks, who would choose murder over theft?

The answers were on the house itself. There were few windows in the thick walls, and every one of them had not only an iron grill over it but a steel security shutter, all of which were rolled down. And while the entrance door was probably as old as the building, it had been cross-braced with studded steel bars. A guided missile might have gotten the place open for you, but nothing less.

In front of the building was a small courtyard enclosed by high adobe walls and secured by a head-high gate of ornate metal grillwork, overpainted so many times that the twining leaves and stems and flowers were hardly more than solid globs of black paint. The heavy old padlock on the gate was in the process of being shaken to make sure it was closed, by a small, pale, waspish man in a dark suit and tie.

"We're closed," he said to them in dour, unaccented American English. "You'll have to come back tomorrow."

He was a bit of a dandy, or at least he would have been in 1965, when his threadbare double-breasted jacket and inch-wide tie were still in fashion.

"You're not open till four?" Julie asked.

"No," he said, his voice rising as if it were something he had already explained to them a dozen times. "Tuesdays and Thursdays, one until three. Saturdays, one until five. Mondays twelve until three, and Fridays, twelve until two. Look at the sign," he added irritably, gesturing at a small plaque so darkened by street grime and age that it was next to impossible to read.

"But it's barely three o'clock now," Gideon said. "Couldn't you let us in just for a minute?"

"Impossible."

"It really is important, and I don't think it'll take long. We'll be glad to pay your admission fees, of course."

Now the man was insulted. "It's not a matter of fees. Standards must be maintained."

"Well, sure, but—"

"I'm sorry. Now really, I must go, I must be on my way. Time is of the essence." And off he went around the corner, shaking his head.

Julie and Gideon looked at each other. "Now who does he remind me of?" Julie wondered, looking after the scurrying, still muttering figure.

"*Alice in Wonderland*?" Gideon guessed. "The Mad Hatter?"

They both laughed. "You might be right," she said. "Well, what now?"

"I come back tomorrow, I guess. Between twelve and three. Standards must be maintained."

"No, I meant us—what do you want to do right now? Do you—" The phone in her bag went off and she dug it out. They both went to stand right up against the wall of the building, out of the central flow of foot traffic, which until then had been parting around them and then coming together again, the way a stream does around a boulder. "Oh hello, Javier—" she began brightly, then quickly sobered. "Oh. Did he say anything before . . . Okay, I see. Yes, I appreciate that. Yes, of course I'll tell him. Thanks, Javier."

"Tony's dead," Gideon said as she put away the phone.

"Yes. He never regained consciousness."

"I—" He stopped speaking and shook his head.

Julie looked hard at him. "Gideon, you have nothing to blame yourself for. What else could you do?"

"I know that, Julie, it's just that . . ." But it was hard to sort out his feelings, let alone to put them into words. Of course Tony's death was Tony's own doing; of course it was inadvertent on Gideon's part. It had just happened, and Tony alone was to blame. Still, there was no avoiding the simple fact that Tony Gallagher, alive yesterday, was dead today. He would be mourned—and missed—by his family. And the unavoidable truth was that if Gideon Oliver had never come to Oaxaca, he would still be alive.

She squeezed his hand. "It was *not* your fault," she said firmly. "And the others aren't going to blame you, believe me."

He nodded. "I hope not." One more shake of his head, this time to clear it.

"I wonder if we'll ever find out what it was all about now," Julie said.

"Pretty doubtful. Javier's probably going to drop the whole thing now. From a legal point of view, there's nothing to be done. Tony's dead. There's nobody to be prosecuted."

"No, he's going to keep pursuing it; he made a point of telling me so, and he wanted me to make sure you knew."

"I'm glad to hear it. I guess he's gotten intrigued, and he needs to see how all the strands of this thing fit together. That sounds more like the old Marmolejo; none of this 'statute of limitations' baloney."

She nodded. "Anyway . . . back to what we do now. You want to head on back to the Hacienda?"

"Well, if you want to . . ."

"But you don't?"

"Not really, no. Marmolejo's people are probably out there talking to them right now, so everything's probably in an uproar. And they're going to be in a state of shock about Tony—that he's dead, and *how* he died. They'll have a million questions. I just don't feel up to facing that right now."

"Okay, I can understand that. Why don't we do some sightseeing and then have dinner here by ourselves? Then you won't have to face them until tomorrow, when it's all sunk in. And we can give ourselves a pleasant afternoon. I'd say we've earned it, especially you."

"Sounds like a plan," Gideon agreed

They threaded their way through the swarms (all the foot traffic seemed to be against them as workers apparently headed for the bus terminal for transportation out to their villages), back to the Zócalo, bought themselves a guide pamphlet (there wasn't anything that could properly be called a guide book) at one of the stalls, and spent the next four hours seeing the sights: the grand old Palacio del Gobierno, now a museum; the cathedral; the Museum of Pre-Hispanic Art. When that wore them down, they returned to the now-emptying Zócalo to drink coffee at an outdoor café and watch the sinking sun burnish the tops of the laurels and the arched porticoes of the surrounding buildings. Then they walked a couple of blocks to El Naranjo, the other restaurant that Marmolejo had recommended in the event they wanted "someplace quieter, more elegant, with real Oaxacan cuisine and ambience, of which few tourists would even be aware."

The place lived up to advance billing, a cool, quiet, skylighted interior courtyard in a well-kept colonial building, with Moorish arches, a seventeenth-century floor of green stone tiles, and a trickling stone fountain. And a full-sized orange tree (*el naranjo*) in the middle. They ate chicken with *mole coloradito*, drank local beer, and never once talked about murder, or skulls, or Tony Gallagher and his clan.

TWENTY-TWO

THE next morning, the Hacienda Encantada itself seemed to be in a state of shock. When they entered the dining room at eight thirty, they found no guests, no food on the buffet table other than a pot of coffee and an opened package of sliced white bread, and no Dorotea. In the nook at the far end of the room, at the table reserved for the Gallaghers, Carl and Annie appeared to be comforting a crying, mumbling Josefa, who, if Gideon remembered correctly, was Tony's aunt.

At the sight of Gideon, both Carl and Annie jumped up, with a flurry of questions, of expressions of shock and concern over what had happened to him at Yagul, and of contrition on Tony's behalf.

It was enough to fluster Gideon a little. "Hey . . . you two don't owe me any apologies; it wasn't your fault. I'm just sorry it had to end the way it did."

On that point, everybody agreed, and Annie went to the buffet table. "Let me get you both some coffee.

Sorry, not Dorotea's magic brew, just plain old straight coffee."

"Dorotea didn't come in today?" Julie asked.

"Dorotea didn't come in today, and Dorotea won't come in tomorrow, and Dorotea's not coming in next week. Dorotea quit."

"Quit?" Gideon asked. "After all these years? Because of Tony?"

"Tony? No, she didn't give a damn about Tony. She never could stand him. What'd you think, that was an act?"

I sure did, Gideon thought. "Well, then, why—"

"Because of Preciosa."

"Preciosa?"

"Yes, because—oh God, you don't even know, do you? Preciosa's getting the Hacienda. Tony left it to her."

"Preciosa?" Julie cried.

"I better get back to Josefa," Carl said, heading back toward the weeping woman.

"Yes, in his will," Annie said. "At least that's what Preciosa told us, and why would she lie? Tony's lawyer is coming from Mexico City to read it to us—Jamie's at the airport to meet her—so we'll have the official version before the morning's out."

"But why would Dorotea quit?" Julie asked. "The Hacienda will still be functioning, won't it?"

"Oh sure, but she refuses to work for Preciosa. It's not just Preciosa herself, either. The Hacienda's going to be a different place. No more dude ranch angle. She's already told Pop the horses are going. If he wants to stay on as a general caretaker, he's welcome." She looked back at him. "He won't, of course," she said sadly. "I'm not sure what he's going to do."

"That's awful," Julie said. "What about you? What about Jamie?"

"She didn't say. I guess for the moment, we have our

jobs. At this point, I'm not sure we'll want them. As for poor Josefa, she's out. Preciosa told her she's canned, gave her one week to find someplace else." Only at this point did Annie's eyes gleam with tears. "Damn. Now where's she supposed to go? Who's going to take her in?"

While talking, they had continued moving slowly toward the table, and now they could hear what Josefa was saying. "Where I'm gonna go? What I'm gonna do?" she was moaning—as usual, not quite directly at Carl, but at some invisible person somewhere in front of or behind him. She mopped at her eyes with a wadded, grungy handkerchief. "Old lady like me." Carl had her free hand in both of his big ones and was patting it and making impotent masculine sounds of solace.

"Oh gosh, this is terrible," Julie said. "Where's Preciosa now?"

"She's waiting in the meeting room in the old chapel, next to the office. That's where we'll meet with the lawyer."

Outside, a van pulled up and Jamie climbed out of the driver's seat. A stern-looking woman of fifty in a severely cut pantsuit exited from the other side. "Here she is," Annie said, lips pursed, "*Señora* María Elena García Navarro Sánchez, big-time *abogada*—our family lawyer. Oh, and look who's here," she said as the slide door in back eased open and a gaunt, hard, haggard woman with a cigarette wedged in her mouth climbed wearily down. "Conchita the Nutball—Tony's wife. Well, sure, why not?—I'm sure she comes in for plenty."

Julie stared. "*That's* Miss Chihuahua 1992?"

"Second runner-up," Annie corrected. "She's, um, changed a little since then."

"Just a bit, I guess. Wow."

"I guess that's what comes of living with Tony," Gideon said. The truth was, he'd completely forgotten that Tony'd been married.

The new widow remained beside the van, puffing fit-fully at the cigarette, but Jamie and the lawyer came in. Jamie was limping a little, but Gideon saw that he was getting around without his cane now.

Señora Sánchez did not waste time with greetings. "Who are these two?" she asked, meaning Gideon and Julie.

"My cousin and her husband," Annie said. "Julie was helping out while—"

"They are not included in the will. They cannot be present. I'm sorry," she told them sternly, "you will have to leave."

"Oh, we're meeting in the chapel," Annie said. "Preciosa is there already."

"Very well. May we go now, please? The will is complex. There are numerous provisions to explain. You are all mentioned in it." She turned and strode out. Jamie followed, and then Carl, with a final pat on the hand of the disconsolate Josefa.

"Well . . ." Annie said with a sigh. "Showtime."

"I'll keep an eye on things while you're all in there," Julie said.

"Not necessary," Annie told her as she headed for the door. "There's nothing going on. We've canceled bookings for the rest of the week, and gotten other lodgings for the guests we have. It's been crazy here. The police were all over the place yesterday afternoon and they plan on being back today."

Señora Sánchez, looking irritated, came back and opened the door. "Didn't you hear me say everybody? I need to be back at the airport at eleven."

"Yes, ma'am, sorry, ma'am," said Annie. "Here I come."

The lawyer glared at the wretched Josefa, who had stayed slumped in her chair, looking as sodden and bedraggled as her handkerchief. "You too. You are mentioned as well."

She had to repeat it in Spanish before Josefa understood, and when she did, she looked scared stiff. What new terrors awaited her in Tony's will? She shook her head no; she wasn't coming, she didn't want to know. But Annie came and helped her out of her chair. "Come, dear aunt," she said affectionately in Spanish, "Tony has left you some money to show his love. Who knows how much?" With her arm around Josefa, they shuffled off together.

"I wouldn't count on its being a lot," Julie said to Gideon. "How sad it all is."

"It sure is." He snapped his fingers, ineptly as usual. "I just thought of something." He ran to the door. "Annie? Do you happen to know what Manolo's last name was?"

He had to wait for her to think of the answer, and when it came, Julie couldn't hear it. "What did she say?" she asked as Gideon returned.

Gideon smiled. "She said it was Garcia."

WITH nothing to keep them at the Hacienda, they walked down the steep hill to the village and cast about for someplace to get breakfast. Pickings were slim to none, and they ate at El Descanso, where Sandoval and Gideon had had lunch a few days ago: melon juice, pink and frothy; eggs scrambled with beef, onions, tomatoes, and cilantro; fresh, hot tortillas; and coffee. Not quite Dorotea-class, but filling and good.

On the way out they had to stand aside for a group of six or seven sober, pensive men, mostly older, who were just coming in. The last in the line was Flaviano Sandoval, who looked anything but sober. The look on his face was a combination of happiness and relief, the sublime look of a defendant who has just heard the jury foreman say, "Not guilty."

"*Buenos días*, Chief S—" Julie began.

Sandoval held up his hand. "Not 'chief.' Never again 'chief,' *gracias a Dios*." He grinned at them. "You now address the executive officer of the village council of Teotitlán del Valle. As of this very morning." He couldn't stop grinning.

"Well, good for you—you made it!" Gideon said, enthusiastically shaking his hand.

"No more skeletons, no more bones, no more mummies, no more killings," Sandoval burbled. "What is today's agenda? Rerouting of the traffic on Avenida Juárez during festivals, and the design of new uniforms for the village band." He sighed. "It's wonderful."

Smiling, they watched him go to join the others. Gideon shrugged. "What the hell," he said, *"chacun à son goût."*

Afterward they strolled aimlessly around the town, which seemed wonderfully tranquil and slow-paced after the grit and clamor of Calle las Casas in Oaxaca. There was the occasional car, but there were also burros, and even a team of oxen pulling a wagon. Mostly the traffic, such as it was, was foot traffic: sombreroed men in white; braided, earringed women in their *rebozos* and aprons, some with bundles on their heads; nobody going anywhere very fast. At one point a troop of uniformed schoolchildren, led by their teacher, passed politely by, many with shy waves, and giggles, and garbled greetings: "'Allo." "'Ow you doing, pardner?" "You know him, Brad Pitt?"

By eleven, the sun was getting uncomfortably warm and they started on the twenty-minute climb up the steep, winding, cobblestoned hill to the shady protection of the Hacienda. Halfway up it, they had to jump to one side to

get out of the way of a black Mercedes that came careen-
ing down it, tires squealing on the curves.

"That's Tony's car!" Julie said.

"And that's Preciosa in it," Gideon said, as it rocketed
past. "I don't think she ever even saw us. I hope she doesn't
kill anybody before she gets wherever she's going."

"She didn't look happy, did she?" Julie mused. "Say,
do you suppose Tony didn't leave her the Hacienda after
all?"

It didn't take long to find out. When they reached
the Hacienda (having first stepped aside again for
another, slower vehicle, this one a Hacienda van bearing Jamie, Tony's wife, and the lawyer), they found Carl
and Annie, looking thunderstruck, sitting at one of the
umbrellaed tables on the terrace. Julie and Gideon slipped
into a couple of chairs beside them. "So what happened?"
Julie asked. "We saw Preciosa driving away. She didn't
look too pleased."

Annie was shaking her head. "Tony lied to her. He
didn't leave this place to her at all. He left her some
money and a little stock—it was all complicated—and
that's it; I think it comes to around, oh, twenty thousand
dollars altogether."

"Plus his Mercedes, obviously," Gideon said.

"Nope, he didn't leave that to anybody. Preciosa just
took it."

"What did the rest of the will say?" Julie asked.

"Well, when you sorted everything out," Annie
said, "almost everything went to his wife. The house in
Coyoacán, the investment portfolio. . . . According to
María, it all comes to somewhere between eight and ten
million dollars."

"You mean," Gideon said, "he left nothing at all to you
folks? What about Jamie, his own brother?"

"Not one . . . damn . . . thing," Carl said. "Hard to

believe, especially after all the work Jamie put into this place to keep it afloat."

"To say nothing of what you put into it, Pop," Annie said. Carl was stunned, but Annie was angry. "I can't believe it. What a miserable, ungrateful, lying creep. And then, what he tried to do to *you*!" she said to Gideon. "What was that all about?"

"Beats me," Gideon said. "I'm hoping Marmolejo can figure it out, but I don't honestly see much chance; not now, not anymore."

"So Tony's wife now owns the Hacienda Encantada," Julie said. "How do you think that's going to play out?"

"Oh no, he didn't leave the Hacienda to Conchita," Annie said, surprised. "What made you think that?"

"Well, you said she got everything—"

"I said *almost* everything. Not the Hacienda."

"All right, then who owns the Hacienda? Don't keep us in suspense."

Carl managed a small smile. "Our new boss," he said, "is *la señora* Josefa Basilia Manzanares y Gallegos."

Julie frowned. "And who is that?"

Carl's smile morphed into an easy laugh, in which Annie joined. "It's Josefa—our Josefa!" she cried.

For a moment Julie and Gideon were speechless. "But why?" Julie finally said. "I mean, yes, she's his aunt or something, but after all, Jamie's his brother, and—"

Carl answered with a shrug. "Who knows? The will said something about years of faithful service . . . something like that."

"Well, how about that?" Gideon said with a slow smile. "Two hours ago she's sitting there despondent about being thrown out, and now the whole place belongs to her."

"She must be overjoyed," Julie said.

"Au contraire," said Annie. "She's more miserable than she was before."

"Miserable! Why—"

"The poor old gal's scared to death," Carl said. "She doesn't want to own the Hacienda, she just wants things to stay the way they are. She asked if she could still keep her job if she owned the place."

"We told her she could keep it or not keep it, or do any damn thing she wanted," Annie said. "We told her we could run the place for her, if she wanted—which is what we've been doing anyway—and she could live like a queen and get waited on hand and foot. Or she could throw the bunch of us out, sell the place, and live like a queen anywhere she felt like—and get waited on hand and foot."

"I'm not sure we got through to her, though," said Carl. "We spent fifteen minutes carefully explaining everything to her, and she kept nodding her head and mumbling *sí, sí, comprendo,* like she understood, and then you know what her question was?"

Annie supplied the answer with an approximation of Josefa's piteous wail: "But they gonna let me stay in my room, or I gotta move to Tony's?"

TWENTY-THREE

AT a few minutes after one, Gideon stood in front of the small, gated courtyard of the Museo de Curiosidades. The gate was closed and latched, but the padlock had been removed. He lifted the latch and entered the courtyard. Once it had probably been a graceful patio, rich with plants and perhaps a welcoming fountain. Now it looked like the entrance to a junk shop, all weeds, cracked cement paving . . . and junk. On second glance, however, the junk proved to be exhibits, each with a small, faded, foxed, meticulously hand-lettered placard in English and Spanish. To the left of the big oak door of the *casa* itself was a weathered concrete bust of Kaiser Wilhelm I, complete with spiked helmet: "From the residence of Friedrich Pflegholz, German ambassador to Mexico, 1883–1886." To the right was the "sacred throne of Axayácatl, emperor of the Aztecs," an ugly hunk of basalt that an imaginative mind might have construed as being shaped more or less like a chair. Further along, attached to the *casa*'s wall by a chain, was a wooden "Chinese empress's bench."

If these were the guy's come-on exhibits, Gideon thought, it was no wonder he doesn't seem to be getting much in the way of visitors. Beside the door was a sign in English and Spanish that informed visitors that the entrance fee was thirty pesos and instructed them to ring the bell. Gideon did, and the door swung open to reveal a vestibule in which the man they'd seen yesterday sat at an old office desk, clacking away at a many-carboned document on an ancient, upright, manual Remington typewriter. *Sr. Henry Castellanos-Jones*, said the nameplate at the front of the desk.

"Yes?" he said, not pleased to be interrupted. He was wearing the same rusty suit, the same narrow black tie that he'd worn yesterday. Even sitting down, he had the suit jacket tightly buttoned.

"I'd like to see the museum."

"It's thirty pesos. I have no change."

"That's fine." Seeing no receptacle, he laid the bills on the desk.

"Would you like me to give you a tour? The fee is two hundred pesos."

"No thanks, I'd just like to wander, if that's all right."

"The choice is yours, but a tour would add a great deal to your visit."

"No thanks."

The man's thin lips turned down. "Very well. Please start in the room to your left, the drawing room, and continue around. That is the established pattern for the traffic flow." He returned his attention to his typing.

Gideon did as he was told, although he could see from the empty rooms ahead that traffic flow wasn't going to be a problem. The place was much as Sandoval had led him to expect, reeking of mildew and mold, probably from the old upholstered furniture and grungy carpets that appeared to be leftovers from the last person to reside there. The plastered walls were cracked and dirty, the ceilings water-stained and sagging. Lit mostly with low-wattage Tiffany-style lamps in various shades of brown, it was like walking around under a mushroom. Or inside a mausoleum.

Most of the exhibits, and there were many, were on dark, Victorian-era tables or in glass-fronted bookcases, and whatever else Gideon might say about them, he was ready to admit that it was the most eclectic and idiosyncratic museum he'd ever been in. The shrunken heads (actually, goatskin fakes) that Sandoval had told him about were there, and the Aztec stone knives (knockoffs, and poorly done at that) as well. There was also the withered brown arm and hand of "The Assassin Pedro Mendoza, Who Killed Beloved Governor Ocampo in 1901." This event rated an entire display case for itself. Along with the arm was the governor's ruffled shirt, complete with holes and blood, and the dagger that did the deed.

In general, though, the exhibits were more pedestrian, if no less odd: a "letter cancellation machine made in 1848, in use until 4/4/1911"; a "metal hamburger mold, circa 1931"; an "1860 Ashley Archimedean Eggbeater." If there was a pattern to the displays, Gideon couldn't make it out. The eggbeater shared a case with a "Czechoslovakian machine pistol from the Great War." The hamburger mold was housed with a porthole from a sunken ship and a "crystal ball used in crystal-gazing, late 1800s."

His quarry was in a glass-fronted case in the second room he came to, the former dining room, on a shelf shared with a baby shark in a Mason jar and a three-masted schooner made of matchsticks. It was only the skull—no mandible—and it rested in a saucer filled with straw. The legend beside it said "Sacrificed Zapotec princess, 1,000 years old." Gideon had to kneel to look it in the eye, so to speak, and even when he did, there wasn't much he could tell about it. It was male, not female—the supraorbital ridges and robust mastoid processes told him that much. There were streaks of green, blue, and red color here and there, probably the remnants of the colored candles that had once been mounted on its crown. The teeth, nestled in the straw, couldn't be seen. Was it really old enough to be Zapotec? That he couldn't tell.

There was a huge, irregular hole in the left side of the skull, involving parts of the frontal, parietal, occipital, and temporal bones. He was certain that this "open defect," as it was called in the bland jargon of forensic science, was postmortem. Bone is pretty much the same color through and through, so if it had been inflicted at the time of death its edges would have been the same color as the rest of the skull. But the edges of this "defect" were distinctly paler than the rest of the skull, indicating that the bone had been exposed to the elements for some time before the break occurred and the defect had nothing to do with the cause of death.

He returned to the desk out front, where the man was now struggling with another set of copies, trying to get the dog-eared carbons to go around the roller.

"Excuse me. You have a skull in the old dining room—"

"The Zapotec princess," he said without looking up.

"Yes. I wonder if it would be possible to take it out of the case. I'd like very much to have a closer look."

"No, no, no, no, no. It's against the rules."

"It's not merely out of curiosity. I'm an anthropology professor—"

"Rules are rules. If I let you break them, then I'd have to let everyone break them, wouldn't I? And then where would we all be? Where would it end?"

"I understand your point—"

The man looked up suddenly from his task. "Unless of course, you're interested in purchasing it?"

Gideon stared at him. "It's for sale?"

"Not ordinarily, no, of course not. But you, you're an anthropologist, a professional person. That puts an entirely new cast on things, you see."

No, Gideon didn't see, but having gone to all this trouble, he did want to have a better look at the skull. "Yes, I see that. Well, yes, I might very well be interested in purchasing it."

"In that case," said Mr. Castellanos-Jones, springing rabbitlike from his chair, "let us make haste. Time is money."

He grabbed a ring of keys from his desk, led Gideon to the case, and removed the skull with its saucer, laying them gently down on the only free corner of the ponderous, thick-legged dining table. "What do you think?"

"Hard to say," Gideon said, rotating it to see all sides.

"I can let you have it for one hundred American dollars, which is a professional-courtesy price, in that you are an anthropologist. . . ."

"Mmm . . ." Gideon was absorbed in his examination. When it had been in its case, he hadn't been able to see the rear portion of the skull, but now he could, and he had revised his earlier opinion. The hole had been inflicted after death, yes, but in a way, it probably was related to the cause of death. Extending onto the occipital bone—clear *through* the occipital bone—from the rearmost margin of the hole was a deep cleft—not a fracture, but a *cleft*—that had been hacked into the living bone. Ancient or modern, whoever this was had had his life ended by a wicked blow with something like an ax or a machete. And he guessed that the cleft had weakened the bone around it and possibly contributed to the later breakage.

"I see that the, er, imperfection concerns you," Castellanos-Jones said. "Yes, I had forgotten about that. Taking it into consideration, I can let you have it at a discount of, ah, umm, twenty-five percent? Seventy-five dollars, all told."

Gideon had turned it over and was now studying what was left of the teeth. They were in terrible shape, most of them rotted to nubbins, some to the size of corn kernels. That was probably what had led Dr. Ybarra, the *médico legista*, to declare that the skull was Pre-Hispanic. Nowadays, you only saw teeth like these in archaeological specimens, among peoples whose diets had consisted largely of stone-ground grains. Pulverizing corn between a *mano* and a *metate*, or between a stone mortar and pestle, also produced minute fragments of pulverized stone, and it was these fragments that could grind down tooth enamel, bringing on decay and gum disease, and turning the dentition into wreckage like this.

Ybarra had been right, he decided; this was not a modern skull. There was no conceivable connection to Tony. Reluctantly, he concluded that it had all been a wild goose chase. Whatever the reason Tony had tried to kill him, it had nothing to do with this "Zapotec princess."

"I should probably mention," said Castellanos-Jones, "that several other parties, one of them a prominent educational institution, have shown interest in this specimen. It may very well be gone by next week."

"Well, yes," Gideon said, placing the skull back in its saucer, "but I'm afraid I don't—" He stopped in midsentence, his forehead wrinkled, the image of the rotted teeth still in his mind. *Wait a minute. . . .*

"Opportunity missed is opportunity lost, you know. And opportunity seldom knocks twice. Why, whatever is the matter? Are you all right, professor?"

Gideon was staring so hard, so fixedly, at the skull that he had alarmed Castellanos-Jones. With staggering suddenness and mind-bending simplicity, everything had clicked into place. Why Blaze had been killed thirty years ago, why Manolo had been killed a few months ago, why he himself had damn near been killed yesterday. There were details missing, yes, but the overall picture had leapt into focus as crisply as if he'd turned the knob on a pair of binoculars. It was almost too crazy to be true, and yet . . .

"Yes, I'm okay," Gideon said. "Would a check be all right? I don't have seventy-five dollars with me."

"A check will be fine." He paused, smiling, with his hands neatly folded at his waist, like an old-fashioned department store floorwalker. "Would you like that wrapped?"

AN hour later Gideon pulled up in the parking lot of the Hacienda Encantada. He had tried calling Marmolejo, but Corporal Vela had answered, telling him that the colonel was in Teotitlán, at the Hacienda Encantada. That suited Gideon perfectly, and it was with building excitement that he climbed out of the van, carefully cradling the skull (he had declined Castellanos-Jones's offer to wrap it) in the palm of one hand, thumb lodged in the foramen magnum, the conveniently thumb-sized opening in the base for the entry of the spinal cord, and his other arm holding it protectively against his body the way a runner holds a football.

He saw Marmolejo at once. He was sitting at one of the larger tables on the terrace with Jamie, Annie, Carl, and Julie. Spread out in front of them were mugs of coffee and plates of mid-afternoon pastries: *turrones*, sweet rolls, and *galletas* (sugar, anise, and cinnamon cookies), the aromas of which made his mouth water.

"I see Dorotea's back," he said, approaching the table.

"Oh yeah," Annie answered. "Back and happy as a clam—well, as happy as she gets. She has no problem working for Josefa." She tilted her chin at the skull. "Who's your friend?"

"Ah, my friend, yes," Gideon said. "Well, that's an interesting story. But I don't want to interrupt—"

"There's nothing to interrupt," Marmolejo said. "I was simply partaking of the generous hospitality offered. Our business for the day is finished. Unfortunately, I fear we've come no closer to enlightenment."

"Oh, I think that with the help of my friend here—" He patted the skull. "—I might be able to provide a little of that." He pulled out a chair, sat, and set the skull on the table in front of him.

"Ouch," Carl said, looking at the jagged hole in the side. "Looks like somebody whacked him."

"Yes. With an ax or something like it."

Annie turned the skull to face her. "Alas, poor Yorick, I knew him well."

Gideon smiled. "You'd be surprised."

"Ooh, that sounds mysterious. What's it mean?"

Julie was eyeing him. "You look awfully pleased with yourself."

"Well, I think I have a surprise for you."

"Oh Lord, another surprise," Jamie said. "I don't know if we can handle another surprise."

"What is it, Gideon?" Marmolejo asked. "Is that the skull from the museum?"

"That it is."

"And is it an ancient Zapotec skull?"

"That it is not."

A couple of beats passed, and then Julie said. "And are you planning to tell us what it is anytime soon?"

"Well . . ."

With a sigh, Marmolejo addressed the others. "You see how we have to tease it out of him, how he lets it out one tantalizing morsel at a time? It's always this way. I believe he's doing it primarily for my benefit. Professor Oliver finds happiness in baffling the mind of the simple, hardworking policeman."

"Hey, this is pretty grim stuff I do," Gideon said. "I have to find happiness where I can."

"Well, you better tell us pretty soon," Julie warned, "or I guarantee you're not going to be happy very long."

Gideon laughed, but whatever they might think, he was not merely grandstanding, or at least not *only* grandstanding. What he had to tell them was going to knock them for a loop in any case—especially Annie, Jamie, and Carl—but he wanted to prepare them, to present it in the right way, and not simply dump it in their laps.

"Okay," he said, "but first let me make sure I have my facts straight. Tony came back and took over the Hacienda in 1979, is that right?"

"Right," Carl and Jamie said together, and then Carl added, "But it wasn't the Hacienda then. It was still a horse ranch."

"Okay. And he would have been how old at the time? Mid-twenties somewhere?"

"Twenty-five," said Jamie. He was born in 1954.

"Fine. And when he left home as a kid, he was how old?"

"Somebody tell me what this has to do with the price of tea in China," Annie grumbled.

"He was sixteen," Jamie said. "I was six or seven."

"So that was in 1970."

Jamie thought for a moment. "Yes. Sixty-nine or seventy."

"All right, that's what I thought. Let me get on with it then."

"God be praised," Marmolejo murmured, pleasantly enough.

"The reason this skull was thought to be very old," Gideon said, "was the condition of the teeth." He tipped it back for them to see the blackened, tarnished, cracked remnants of the dentition.

Annie winced. "Yuck, it hurts just to look at that."

"Believe me, it would have hurt more if you had them in your mouth. Now, until fairly recently, the only times you saw teeth like these were in people whose diet included a lot of stone-ground foods. So Dr. Ybarra, the local forensic examiner at the time, concluded reasonably enough that that's what it was."

"But," said Carl.

"Yes, but. Nowadays—for the last few decades—there's been another likely explanation for something like this, especially if you find it in a young person, and this guy is fairly young. And that is an addiction to methamphetamine, which is what we've got here; one hell of a case of 'meth mouth.'"

Meth mouth, he explained, went along with heavy methamphetamine use. There were plenty of reasons for it. First, the caustic, acidic mix of the drug itself corroded tooth enamel and gum tissue. It also decreased the production of saliva, which made things even worse because saliva both neutralized acids and inhibited the growth of cavity-causing bacteria. Also, the resulting thirst that went along with "dry mouth" often resulted in the consumption of sugary drinks that did their own nasty damage. Add to that the near constant teeth-grinding that was part of the addiction (this was the reason that meth addicts were called "tweakers") and the result was a toxic stew that could turn the teeth into horrors that looked just like what they had in front of them. Meth mouth. "Well, okay, but how can you be sure that's really what it is, and *not* an ancient skull?" Jamie asked. "I mean, if they look the same."

"Well, they don't look *exactly* the same, Gideon said. "With meth mouth, you get a distinctive pattern of cavities that aren't related to ordinary wear: on the buccal sides of the teeth, for example, and also between the anterior—"

"I think I see where Gideon's going with this," Carl said, frowning down at his coffee mug. "The other night, remember, Tony was talking about how he used to have a pal who had a worse problem with meth than he did—"

"Huicho something," Jamie said.

"And how they got into trouble," Carl continued. " A *whole* lot of trouble was the way he put it." He put a hand on the skull. "Is this him? Huicho? Is that where you're going?"

"No, it's not Huicho," Gideon said. "You're close, but not quite there. Look at the teeth again." He held the skull completely upside down for them. "Count them."

"Fourteen," Jamie said after a few seconds, and others murmured their agreement.

"But if he had them all, there'd be sixteen," Julie said. "And another sixteen in the lower jaw."

"Right. He's missing two teeth from his upper jaw. And if we had his mandible, I'd be guessing there were another two missing from that."

At that an almost visible current of uneasiness passed around the table. They had some dawning sense of where he was going, but couldn't quite see it clearly yet. Or couldn't believe it.

"Gideon, are you saying . . ." Julie said slowly, then gazed quizzically at him. "What *are* you saying?"

"The missing teeth are the second premolars. They appear to be congenitally missing. This, as you know, is an extremely rare condition . . . that happens to run in the Gallagher family. Blaze—Tony's sister—had it. Annie—Blaze's daughter—you have it. Jamie—Tony's brother—you have it. Only Tony, or rather the man you've been calling Tony for thirty years—didn't have it. But this man—" He tapped the skull. "He did."

For a long time they just sat there and stared at him, stared at the skull. None of them could bring themselves to say it, so finally Gideon said it for them.

"This," he said, his hand resting on the skull, "is Tony Gallagher."

"No, that's impossible," Jamie said with a nervous little laugh. "This is not Tony."

"This is Tony," Gideon said.

TWENTY-FOUR

HE gave it a little more time to sink in and then continued. "The missing premolars alone would have been enough to convince me—I mean, the chances of a man with that particular syndrome turning up in the vicinity of this particular little village, who *wasn't* a Gallagher relation, are minuscule to say the least. But throw that in with the methamphetamine addiction—which *your* 'Tony' didn't show any signs of—and then throw that in with the fact that Blaze was murdered, and that Manolo was murdered, and that—"

"*Manolo* was murdered?" Annie screeched. "What . . . how . . . ?"

Gideon had forgotten that they didn't yet know that part of it. "Okay, forget Manolo, I'll explain about that later, but there's also the fact that this guy here didn't just die; he was murdered too, and his skull was found within a few hundred yards of Blaze's, and those happen to be the only murders—literally, the only three murders—that have happened around here in the last fifty years, so—"

"No, Gideon, I just can't buy this," Carl said. "Look, I've been here on the Hacienda for almost forty years. I was here before Tony came back. And there is no doubt in my mind that the Tony who died yesterday was the same Tony who came back and took over in 1979. Believe me."

"I do believe you," Gideon said. "But you see, I don't think he was really Tony in 1979 any more than he was Tony yesterday."

"But . . . no, but . . ."

"Carl's right," Jamie insisted, his face flushed. "Look, Tony was my big brother. When I was growing up he looked out for me; I loved him. Are you saying I didn't know my own brother?"

"Look at it this way, Jamie. When Tony—the guy we've been calling Tony—came back here in 1979 he was a grown man. You hadn't seen him in almost ten years, right? He'd been only sixteen then. Do you really think you'd know one way or the other whether the man who showed up then was really the same teenager that had left back then . . . when you were just six years old?"

"Well—okay, maybe not, but my father certainly would have recognized his own—" His face fell. "No, dad had died a little while before."

"And I'd never seen Tony before he showed up in 1979," Carl added thoughtfully.

"And I was one year old in 1979," Annie said, no less soberly.

The three of them were beginning to accept it even though they didn't want to, but then Jamie perked up. "Wait, wait, wait—Blaze was older than me; she was only a year younger than Tony. There's no way some stranger could come in and make her believe he was her brother. He'd never get away with it."

"But Blaze never saw him. She was already gone when he got here," Gideon gently pointed out. "She was dead by then, although as far as everybody knew, she'd run off with Manolo."

"Sure," Jamie said, "but *he* wouldn't have known that. How could he take the chance . . ." The air went out of him. He sagged back in his chair. "Oh. *He* killed her?"

Gideon nodded. "That's the way I see it. She was the only one left who could know for sure that he wasn't really Tony. Well, Tony himself—the real Tony—would have known too, of course. So he got rid of them both, walked in in his place, took over, and was Tony Gallagher for the next thirty years."

"And the reason he tried to kill you," Julie said, "was to prevent you from finding out . . . well, what you found out—that he wasn't who he said he was."

Gideon nodded. "It fits, doesn't it?"

"Yes. I see." Jamie said miserably.

Annie flung her hands in the air. "Then who the hell was the guy whose hand I was just holding in the hospital? The guy that's *been* Tony for the last thirty years?"

"Annie," Gideon said earnestly, "I do not have a clue."

"Nor do I," said Marmolejo, who had been silent and ruminative for some time. "But I believe I know who can provide the answer. Where can I find the woman Josefa?"

"Josefa?" Annie said. "She's probably in the Casa del Mayordomo, in her room. But what makes you think she would know anything? She's just—"

"It was Josefa to whom this man willed your beautiful Hacienda, and not his brother, or his brother-in-law, or his niece, or the wife to whom he left everything else. Don't you find this curious?"

"Well, she's supposed to be some kind of distant aunt on my mother's side," Jamie said.

"Perhaps that's it," he said, rising and pocketing the little tape recorder that had been on the table, "but I expect there's something more to it than that."

BY the time Marmolejo returned half an hour later, considerable inroads had been made into the pastries, and Dorotea had come out with another pot of coffee. Gideon had explained about the drifter's being Manolo and answered, or tried to answer, a host of questions, but the overall mood was still one of dazed befuddlement.

Colonel Marmolejo, looking well satisfied with himself, took his former chair, daintily ate a cinnamon cookie, ate another cinnamon cookie, and poured himself some coffee.

"Excellent pastries," he said. "So light, so fresh."

"Now who's being tantalizing?" Annie said. "Come on, Colonel, spill the damn beans. What did she tell you?"

Marmolejo, who found Annie amusing, laughed and wiped his fingers on a napkin. "The name Brax—it's familiar to you?"

"Brax . . . Brax . . ." said Annie, frowning. "Yes, it is, but . . ."

Gideon had the same reaction. *Yes, it is familiar, but . . .*

"Josefa was unable to remember his last name," Marmolejo said. "Something like Stevenson or Halbersam . . ."

Oddly enough, it was Gideon who got there first. "Faversham!" he exclaimed. "Braxton Pontleby Faversham—Carl, wasn't that the name of the guy who Tony was going to replace you with back then, but never did? We were just talking about it the other morning."

"That's right," Carl said, and Annie nodded along with him. "Braxton Pontleby Faversham."

"Well, what *about* Braxton Pontleby Faversham?" Annie demanded.

"That's who the person you've been calling Tony for thirty years was," Marmolejo replied. "Braxton Faversham."

IT had taken very little effort to get the details out of Josefa—who was not exactly who they thought she was either, although Josefa really was her name. At first she had tried to stick to the cooked-up tale that she was Tony's (and Jamie's) aunt by marriage, the widowed wife of the brother of their mother Beatriz, but she had quickly gotten herself flummoxed in a maze of evasions and prevarications. And then the real story, as much of the real story as she knew, came tumbling out. In 1979 she had been a prostitute in Oaxaca—

"A prostitute!" Annie cried, delighted. "Our stodgy old Josefa, stumping around the place in her sensible shoes? Is that a hoot, or what? Can you just picture her—"

"Annie . . ." Carl said darkly.

"Oops, never mind," Annie said.

Josefa had been thirty-eight in 1979, old for a hooker, even in Oaxaca, and she was facing a dismal future. Already she'd been reduced to street pickups of drunks and kids, when she'd run into Brax outside a bar. He was almost penniless, but charming enough—a real American cowboy—to talk her into putting him up for a couple of weeks in her fifty-peso-a-night room, in addition to providing him with her customary services. Both of them outcasts, they'd become close and Brax had admitted to her that he'd been released a month earlier from the Reclusorio Oriente prison in Mexico City, where he'd served five years on multiple petty crime charges, and was in Oaxaca waiting for his friend Tony Gallagher, who had been let out only a couple of days earlier. They had met as inmates a year earlier and had become friends, two lost *gringos* in a Mexican hellhole.

But things were about to change, Brax said. Tony had learned that his father, who owned a horse ranch near Teotitlán del Valle, had died a year earlier. He had left the property to Tony, so despite knowing next to nothing about ranching and not having been anywhere near Teotitlán for almost ten years, Tony was coming to take it over. And his best pal Brax, who had grown up on a horse ranch in Oregon, was going to manage the place for him. It was a chance at a new life, a wonderful opportunity for Brax, who couldn't return to the United States because he was wanted for failure to pay child support. According to Josefa, he had pleaded with her to marry him and come live with him on the ranch, but desperate as she was, she had refused; she was almost fifteen years older than he was, and in any case, she knew marriage wasn't for her.

"Do you suppose that part's really true?" Julie asked. "About his wanting to marry her?"

"I don't know," Marmolejo said. "I have no doubt that at this moment she believes it."

"Now is that weird or what?" Annie said. "Can you imagine *Josefa* married to Tony?"

"To Braxton Faversham, actually," Jamie pointed out.

"That's right, I'm still trying to get my head around that. I keep forgetting that I never even met Tony Gallagher."

"Interestingly enough," said Marmolejo, "Josefa did. But she despised him on sight. *'Un hombre brutal,'* she called him. She also said—" (and this he accompanied with a deferential bow in Gideon's direction) "—that he had horrible breath, horrible, rotten teeth."

"That he did." Gideon had his palm resting on the skull. "You're lookin' at 'em now."

"She knew the ranch hand, Manolo Garcia, as well," Marmolejo continued. "He had just been fired from the ranch, and his jaw was wired shut, and he had no place to go, so on Brax's urging, she allowed him to use her room for a few days too, even though she was frightened of him—another *rufián*, just like Tony. He and Faversham talked and talked over bottles of tequila, secretive discussions from which she was excluded. And then, one day, to her delight, Manolo was gone, and so was Tony. They had vanished."

"Killed," Carl murmured. "By Faversham."

"It would seem so, yes." Marmolejo paused to slowly consume another cookie, anise this time, and to collect his thoughts before continuing.

Whether Faversham had planned it all ahead of time, or had come up with the idea in Oaxaca, Marmolejo was unable to say, but somewhere along the line he had formed an audacious new plan. He had learned a great deal about the ranch and about the Gallaghers from Tony during their years in prison. And Tony himself, after all, had not been seen at the ranch since he'd been a teenager; now he was a grown man whose hard life had left him much changed. What if Faversham "became" Tony and showed up at the ranch to claim his inheritance? They were about the same age, they both had brown hair and brown eyes, they both tended toward overweight. Would the Gallaghers really know the difference? Certainly not Tony's younger brother, Jamie, who had been a kid when he'd last set eyes on Tony. His father surely would have known his son, but his father was conveniently dead. That left Tony's sister Blaze . . . who would therefore also have to be conveniently dead for the plan to work. Tony, of course, would have to go too; that went without saying. Thus . . .

"Josefa actually *told* you all this?" Carl asked.

"No, no, these are extrapolations on my part. Josefa says that when she asked Faversham what had happened to his two friends, he told her that Tony had gotten cold feet. He hated horses, and he hated his rotten family, and to hell with the ranch. He had learned about some lucrative 'opportunities' in the drug trade and he and Manolo had headed north to get in on them. It's my belief that she knew nothing of the murders."

"Well, she sure as hell had to know that Tony wasn't Tony, and that she wasn't anybody's poor old auntie," Annie declared.

"Of course she did. Faversham, apparently grateful for the care she had extended to him, and perhaps feeling some affection for her, offered her a safe lifetime sinecure here, requiring only that she pretend that he was Tony and that she was a distant aunt. In her situation—an aging streetwalker faced with the most wretched prospects imaginable—she was only too happy to accept."

"What about Manolo?" Gideon asked. "How was he mixed up in this, do you know?"

"Well, there I must resort to extrapolation again. I believe that Faversham learned—how, we'll probably never know—that Manolo was a former employee of the ranch who was seriously disaffected with—"

That brought a honk of laughter from Annie. "'Seriously disaffected,' I love it. You mean Pop busted his jaw and fired his ass."

Carl scowled wearily. "Annie . . ."

"One might equally well put it that way," Marmolejo allowed. "In any case, I suspect that those secret discussions that Faversham had with him were with the end in mind of egging him on in his resentment. Was it Manolo's fault that Blaze had found him so attractive? Of course it wasn't. Did he want to get back at Carl for mistreating him so unfairly? Of course he did. Would making off with the ranch payroll assuage to some degree his feelings and even provide a kind of rough justice? Well, it just might."

And so, said Marmolejo, the payroll had been robbed and Manolo had disappeared. When Blaze went missing at the same time, the obvious and inescapable conclusion was that the two of them had run off together with the money. Thirty years later, back came Manolo, having somehow found out that Faversham had been living Tony's life all this time. The attractive possibility of blackmail must have presented itself and it would seem that he had surprised Tony at his repair work; hence—"

"Hence the use of a *desarmador de cruz* as a murder weapon," said Gideon, nodding.

"So," Jamie said slowly and uncertainly as Marmolejo wound down, "this man I've been treating as my brother for thirty years, this man we've been coddling and taking orders from all these years actually murdered my *real* brother . . . and my sister?" He shook his head. Tears gathered suddenly in his eyes. "It's hard to take in, Colonel."

"I understand."

"He killed my mother," Annie said wonderingly, half to herself. "And all this time he's been lording it over us like a . . . like a . . . That miserable, lying, sonofabitch."

Carl, his face unreadable, was too deeply submerged in his own thoughts to reprimand her. Gideon, sitting beside him, was close enough to hear his whispered words.

"She *didn't* leave me."

For a while, Jamie, Annie, and Carl just sat there digesting this latest weird chapter in the Gallagher saga— the Gallagher/Faversham saga—and then Jamie asked, "What will happen to Josefa now? Is she in trouble with the law?"

"For pretending to be your aunt when she wasn't? Frankly, I'm not inclined to pursue it, but of course, if you wish to press charges—"

All three of them responded with demurrals, and Jamie said with a smile, "No way. We're not dumb enough to get on the bad side of our new boss."

"Oh, Josefa's not your new boss," Marmolejo told them. "She doesn't own the hotel."

"But Tony—I mean Faversham—left it to her in his—"

"Ah, Faversham, that's the problem. *Señor* Faversham had no right to leave it to anybody. When your father died he left it to your elder brother Tony, not Faversham. Faversham had no legal title to it, and thus no right to dispose of it."

"So what happens?" Annie asked. "Does his wife, Conchita, get it, along with everything else?"

"Let's hope not," Carl said. "All things considered, I'd a heck of a lot rather work for Josefa."

"Conchita's never going to keep it," Carl said gloomily. "She has no interest in it. She'll just sell it. And then . . . who knows?"

"No," said Marmolejo, who was obviously enjoying himself, "Conchita may well be entitled to the rest of the estate; that remains to be looked into—she was, after all married to Faversham—but the Hacienda? No, under Mexican law it cannot go to Conchita."

"Then who?" Jamie asked worriedly.

"To Tony's next of kin, of course. It was originally left to Tony, but Tony, as we now know, died before the property could be conferred. Thus, his nearest relative is entitled—"

"His nearest relative?" Jamie echoed. "But that's . . . that's . . ."

Marmolejo, laughing, extended his hand. "Congratulations, *patrón*."

"HOME," Julie said with a sigh, as the 747 dipped its wings to allow passengers a better view of Mount Rainier. Seeing the mountain on their right meant that they would be on the ground at Sea-Tac in twenty minutes. "Feel ready to go back to work?"

"Sure," Gideon said. "Looking forward to it."

"Really? You didn't exactly get much of a vacation down there."

"Are you kidding?" He turned to her with a grin. "Julie, if that wasn't the best vacation I've ever had, I don't know what was."

From the Edgar® Award-Winning Author of *Little Tiny Teeth*

AARON ELKINS

UNEASY RELATIONS

Buried ceremoniously, high in a cave on the Rock of Gibraltar, lies the skeleton of a human woman, clutching the skeleton of a part-Neanderthal child, who is quickly dubbed Gibraltar Boy by the world's press. Fascinated, Professor Gideon Oliver jumps at the chance to visit the site. But two deaths, possibly murders, have rocked Gibraltar. As Oliver tries to piece things together, he's about to fall for some deadly tricks. After all, unlike the Gibraltar Boy, he's only human.

penguin.com

Don't miss any of the
Professor Gideon Oliver novels, with
"a likable, down-to-earth, cerebral sleuth"
(*Chicago Tribune*).

From Edgar® Award–winning author
Aaron Elkins

"Aaron Elkins is a gifted storyteller."
—*Midwest Book Review*

"Elkins has established himself
as a master craftsman."
—*Booklist*

SKULL DUGGERY

UNEASY RELATIONS

LITTLE TINY TEETH

UNNATURAL SELECTION

WHERE THERE'S A WILL

GOOD BLOOD

Penguin Group (USA) Online

What will you be reading tomorrow?

Patricia Cornwell, Nora Roberts, Catherine Coulter,
Ken Follett, John Sandford, Clive Cussler,
Tom Clancy, Laurell K. Hamilton, Charlaine Harris,
J. R. Ward, W.E.B. Griffin, William Gibson,
Robin Cook, Brian Jacques, Stephen King,
Dean Koontz, Eric Jerome Dickey, Terry McMillan,
Sue Monk Kidd, Amy Tan, Jayne Ann Krentz,
Daniel Silva, Kate Jacobs...

You'll find them all at
penguin.com

*Read excerpts and newsletters,
find tour schedules and reading group guides,
and enter contests.*

Subscribe to Penguin Group (USA) newsletters
and get an exclusive inside look
at exciting new titles and the authors you love
long before everyone else does.

PENGUIN GROUP (USA)
penguin.com